POINT BLANK

BADLANDS BOOK 6

MORGAN BRICE

eBook ISBN: 978-1-64795-046-0
Print ISBN: 978-1-64795-047-7

Point Blank, Copyright © 2023 by Gail Z. Martin.
Cover by Natania Barron.

Darkwind Press is an imprint of DreamSpinner Communications, LLC

POINT BLANK

BADLANDS BOOK 6

By Morgan Brice

To my family, friends, colleagues, and readers. Thank you for believing.

1

SIMON

"Now I know why people elope." Simon Kincaide studied the email from their caterer with last-minute menu substitutions. His fiancé, Vic D'Amato, split his attention between a how-to video and his image in the living room mirror as he struggled with a bow tie.

"I'm not quite desperate enough to elope, but I finally understand the appeal of clip-on bow ties." Vic sounded resigned and a little chagrined.

"I will tie yours before you commit sacrilege with a clip-on," Simon replied without looking up from where he sat at the table. "How can shrimp be this expensive? We live at the beach!"

Vic dropped the tie on the table and went to stand behind Simon, casually rubbing his shoulders. Simon leaned into the touch, bending his neck to give Vic full access.

"Vendor problems?" Vic kneaded the tight muscles. Simon closed his eyes and let his head fall back against Vic's belly.

"Price changes and shipping delays." Simon sighed. "Supply chain stuff, I guess. And in the grand scheme of things, none of it matters. We're getting married, that's what counts."

"Without shrimp?" Vic feigned horror and then broke out laughing at the annoyed expression Simon gave him.

"I love you enough to marry you without shrimp," Simon confirmed. "But the chocolate fondue is non-negotiable."

Vic dropped onto a chair beside Simon and gave him a peck on the cheek. "Honestly, just do the best you can with the catering and don't stress. My family is likely to show up with a month's worth of frozen pasta dishes and enough cannoli, pizzelles, and Italian wedding cookies to feed an army because, for us, food is love."

Simon gave him a look. "If that's the case, should I be worried you don't cook more often?" Humor softened his question.

"I grill," Vic defended. "And I've got Mom's lasagna and spaghetti sauce recipes down pat; I'm just not particularly awesome at anything else. Which is why I survived for so long on takeout and leftovers."

"You're awesome enough for me." Simon pulled Vic in for a kiss.

"Enough of that, or we won't get anything else done tonight." Vic's expression indicated he wouldn't mind being distracted.

"Rain check. I need to give the caterer a list of acceptable substitutions—type of food and price—tonight, and there's also something here from the photographer to be reviewed and signed." Simon sat back in his chair. "I never knew getting married was so exhausting!"

Vic took Simon's hand and laced their fingers together. "But think how nice it will be to celebrate with our friends, and then we'll be husbands forever."

Simon gave him a tired smile. "I know. These are all 'first-world problems.' I'm just tired from today at the shop, and I was hoping I could come home and crash."

Vic frowned. "Trouble at the store?"

Simon shrugged. "I did a psychic reading that was a little more complicated than usual and a séance that took a lot of energy. Pete made me have a snack and drink water and lie down afterward, but I feel drained. It's normal."

"Still getting used to your 'normal.'" Vic ran a hand through Simon's hair.

Simon was a psychic medium, which meant he had visions and could communicate with ghosts. He'd been a folklore professor at a university in Columbia before a rich donor freaked out about his child being taught about the "occult" and got Simon fired. He had moved to Myrtle Beach for a fresh beginning and started his shop, Grand Strand Ghost Tours.

Vic's initial skepticism hadn't been surprising since he was a homicide detective. It had taken a while for him to accept that Simon's abilities were real. They had met trying to hunt down a supernatural serial killer and fallen in love amid the danger. Now, they often worked cases together if there was a paranormal angle.

"Good for Pete, and kudos to you for listening," Vic said as Simon rested his head on Vic's shoulder. "What was so hard about the séance?"

Simon rolled his shoulders to stretch and twisted his neck from side to side. Vic went back to massaging, and Simon's eyes fluttered shut as he sighed in contentment.

"A woman wanted me to see if I could contact her daughter's spirit—the girl drowned fifty years ago when they were on vacation here, and it took the mother this long to get up the nerve to come to a medium."

"We're in the Bible Belt. People have prejudices against folks with extra abilities," Vic acknowledged. "I can see it taking a while for someone to work through that. What happened?"

Simon reached for his now-cold cup of coffee and downed the rest of it. Sad stories went with talking to ghosts. Regrets, unfinished business, and last messages were part of the service he provided by giving grieving loved ones closure and sending restless spirits on their way. Even though Simon accepted that truth, it never got easier. *And it shouldn't. If I don't feel the connection, it won't work.*

"There used to be a big 1930s hotel called Ocean Paradise up the beach a bit," Simon told him. "Back in the day, it was really luxurious. My client, her husband, and daughter came for vacation back in 1970, and the daughter got caught in a riptide and drowned. The mother has felt guilty all these years because she couldn't swim well enough to rescue the girl, and then she felt guilty for not reaching out to her ghost," Simon told him.

"Could you help?" Vic's hand splayed across Simon's shoulders and rubbed comfortingly up and down his spine. Simon took off his glasses and pulled his long hair into a bun to get it out of Vic's way

"The girl was just waiting to say goodbye," Simon replied. "She moved on, and the mother realized the daughter didn't blame her. It's as much of a win as I get since I can't bring people back."

"Probably a good thing," Vic hurried to assure him. "We've seen the movies where people come back from the dead. It never goes well."

"I know when I schedule one of those sessions that it's going to leave me feeling pensive," Simon admitted. "And then I'm always surprised when it tires me out and kills my mood."

Simon viewed his mediumship as a helping profession, like a therapist or counselor. While he did his best to maintain professional distance, the intimacy of channeling a spirit meant he shared feelings and thoughts with the ghost. That, plus the energy required to use his talent, left him tired and emotionally drained.

"How about if I pick up takeout and you rest until I get back?" Vic suggested. "Then we can tackle the wedding plans together."

Simon smiled and pulled Vic in for another kiss. "You're the best fiancé ever."

Vic's affection glimmered in his dark eyes. His short black hair and olive skin clearly showed his Italian heritage, compared to Simon's shoulder-length, chestnut hair and hazel eyes. Vic stood a couple of inches taller than Simon, with a muscular build, while Simon was lean and slender.

They figured out what to order from their favorite Chinese restaurant, and Vic put on his shoes. He paused. "That hotel you mentioned—I've never heard of it."

"Ocean Paradise went bankrupt and was torn down in the mid-seventies," Simon replied. "I was curious too, so I did a little research. There's another big hotel built on the site now—up the coast from where we are but below North Myrtle. It's a shame—the old hotel really did look fabulous in the photos."

Vic grabbed his jacket. "You can show me pictures when I get back. Go rest," he ordered with mock sternness and headed to get dinner.

Simon knew that protectiveness was Vic's favorite way of showing affection—next to sex. They both did a good job of looking out for each other—Simon had taken a bullet for Vic on their first case, and Vic had returned the favor on another investigation. Fortunately, most of the time, showing the depth of their feelings didn't require bloodshed.

He went into the living room and curled up on the couch, pulling a throw over himself. The blue bungalow was only a block from the beach and within walking distance to police headquarters and Grand Strand Ghost Tours. Simon's aunt had sold it to him when he moved to town, and its quirky character and convenient location proved perfect for him and Vic.

Simon fell asleep almost as soon as he stretched out. He dreamed of the beach and found himself walking along the water's edge, watching the waves.

When he turned inland, he saw the Ocean Paradise hotel as it had been in its glory days, captured in the photos he'd found online. Thirteen majestic red brick stories rose above the ocean, with five-story wings on either side. Lights glowed in the windows, and he heard the faint strains of a swing band carrying on the breeze.

Simon's gaze rose to the top of the tower, and he frowned when he realized that a man stood silhouetted against the sky. Then as Simon watched in horror, the figure leaned forward and let himself fall.

"No!" Simon jerked awake, sitting bolt upright, heart pounding.

Vic hurried in from the kitchen. "Simon? What's wrong?"

The smell of Hunan beef and sesame chicken filled the air. Simon realized he'd slept the whole time Vic was gone.

"Bad dream." Simon rubbed a hand over his face to get rid of that last awful image.

Vic hurried to sit beside him and wrapped an arm around his

shoulder. "Uh-huh. Want to tell me for real this time?" His gentle voice held a thread of steel.

Evading the truth with a homicide detective was a recipe for failure.

Simon took a deep breath, and Vic rubbed circles on the middle of his back.

"I saw that old hotel in my dream," Simon recounted. "I was out for a walk on the beach, and then I watched a man fall off the hotel tower. I couldn't tell if he jumped or was pushed. That's when I woke up."

Vic frowned. "Did you read about a death like that when you looked up the hotel? That sort of thing should have made the news."

Simon shook his head. "I would have remembered. But I think what I saw was real—I just don't know why the vision showed up. Other than the client today, I don't have any ties to the Ocean Paradise. It's not like I even grew up here."

"Maybe your psychic 'antenna' was still receiving signals from the séance earlier, and you got some stray vibes," Vic suggested. "The hotel was around for decades, right? It might have been a showcase in its day, but lots of bad stuff happens at hotels that doesn't always make the papers." He grimaced. "Believe me, I know."

Tourist towns walked a fine line between giving visitors the information needed to stay safe and not wanting to scare them away. The hospitality industry carried a lot of clout in Myrtle Beach, and the hotel and attraction owners weren't shy about throwing their weight around to keep unflattering news quiet. Simon had heard Vic rant more than once about the police being pressured to wrap up an investigation to keep bad publicity at a minimum.

"Maybe," Simon agreed reluctantly. He appreciated Vic's effort to minimize his worry, but Simon's intuition told him that the vision appeared for a reason.

Vic hugged him. "Come on—dinner's getting cold. Let's eat and have a couple of beers, and I'll give you a full back rub. That'll cure the blues."

Simon tried to stay in the moment and keep his thoughts from wandering. He focused on the tastes and textures of the meal, doing his best to banter with Vic as they dug in. Cold beer paired perfectly, and if Simon downed two bottles quicker than usual, Vic didn't call him on it.

He wasn't a lightweight—the beer would take the edge off but not give him more than a buzz. After everything that happened today, Simon just wanted to slough off the tension and erase the feeling that, despite the joy of their wedding plans, a storm loomed on the horizon.

After they cleared the table, Vic and Simon went over the catering changes and the photographer's questions. To Simon's relief, it didn't seem too overwhelming on a second look.

"Thanks for plowing through all this with me." Simon felt chagrined at his earlier near-panic. "The buddy system really reduced the stress."

"I'm happy to 'plow' you anytime." Vic gave an exaggerated leer that made Simon laugh. "I know what I'm like after a bad day—it's okay for you to have those too."

Simon closed his computer and stretched, hearing his back crack as he twisted.

"Let's go in the living room so I can give you that back rub," Vic urged. "Strip down and get comfy. I'll be there in a minute."

Simon ambled into the other room. Vic dimmed the lights, turned on a spa music channel, and lit candles. He dodged into the bedroom and returned wearing only his boxer briefs and carrying a bottle of massage oil and a tube of lube.

"Does this massage have a happy ending?" Simon snarked.

"Of course it does."

Simon spread a blanket on the couch, and lay face down with a pillow under his head. Vic straddled his hips, and Simon could feel his fiancé's semi against the crack of his ass through his boxer briefs.

"Just relax," Vic urged.

Simon heard the *snick* of a cap opening, the rasp of calloused palms sliding together to warm the oil, and then Vic's capable hands warmed his back. He started at Simon's shoulders and neck, fingers and thumbs digging deep enough to loosen tight muscles without bruising.

Broad strokes down either side of his spine made Simon shiver despite the heat. The weight of Vic's body on his hips kept Simon grounded as the firm press of hands worked away the tension.

Vic tugged Simon's underwear down and started working the tightness in his glutes. "It's so easy to hold tension in your hips," Vic said in a low rumble. "Need to take care of that."

"Mmmm." Simon let himself float, not bothered with making words. Aside from feeling Vic's now-hard cock pressing against his thigh, the massage loosened knots Simon didn't know he had.

"Roll over." Vic nudged Simon to move, and he let himself sprawl bonelessly on his back.

Vic continued the massage, working down Simon's arms. Somehow when Simon was turning over, Vic had lost his own underwear and straddled him naked. The friction and close contact had both of them hard and leaking.

Vic slicked up his palm again and wrapped his hand around their cocks. "This okay?"

"Very." Simon was content to let Vic take the lead. He closed his hand around Vic's, fully encasing both their dicks.

"Lie back and let me do all the work." Vic set the pace. He started slow, jacking them as his other hand tweaked Simon's nipples. He traced the dark hair of Simon's treasure trail with one finger, down to the wiry pubes at the base of his cock, and then slid back up to his chest again.

"So good," Simon groaned. Vic's weight on his thighs kept him from moving much as he strained to let his hips buck. Vic moved their hands faster, swiping his thumb over the heads of their cocks, using their pre-come to add to the lube.

He stroked Simon's nipples again, circling them slowly with the pad of his finger, brushing a barely-there touch across the peaks, and as tension built toward orgasm, giving each a firm pinch.

Simon's back arched, and he cried out as his release fountained over their joined hands. Vic followed him seconds later and continued to jack them through the aftershocks.

Vic leaned down to kiss Simon. "Feel better?" He had a naughty glint in his eyes.

"Much better." Simon raised his head to kiss Vic again.

Vic got up and walked to the bathroom to clean up. He returned with a warm, wet cloth to wipe away the evidence of their climax from Simon's belly and thighs. He tossed the cloth back toward the hallway and settled next to Simon.

"Glad I can take your mind off things," he whispered close enough to Simon's ear to make him shiver.

"Oh, you're good at shutting off the 'upstairs' brain, that's for sure." Simon chuckled and turned his head to kiss Vic on the tip of his nose.

Reluctantly, they got up and dressed. Simon threw the blanket in the laundry and settled onto the couch, where Vic joined him a few moments later.

"No more talk about work or weddings," Vic said. "You know what that means."

Simon grinned. "Baking show marathon!"

The next morning at the store, Simon couldn't shake off feeling jittery. He wondered if it was an emotional hangover from the day before or a warning about something to come. The coffee maker beeped, signaling a fresh pot was ready. He poured a cup for himself and one for Pete King and walked out to the front of the shop.

"You doing better, boss?" Pete asked as he got the register ready for the day. Although he'd graduated a few years earlier, he still looked like a college kid on Spring Break with his sandy blond hair and blue eyes. Pete was Simon's assistant manager and a popular ghost tour guide. Over time, he'd also become a good friend and a trusted confidant.

"That remains to be seen." Simon grimaced. "I still feel off. Maybe we'll be busy, and that will bump me out of it."

Pete checked the schedule. "You and I both have tours tonight, so that should help."

While Simon's tours drew on his academic background and were historically accurate, Pete dressed as a pirate and gave a dramatic interaction that drew on local urban legends and tall tales. That gave them tour options to appeal to a range of tastes.

"Plus, we're expecting a new shipment of T-shirts, a box of your books, and more shot glasses," Pete told him.

In addition to ghost tours, psychic readings, and séances, Grand Strand Ghost Tours offered tourist merchandise and the books he had written about the paranormal.

"That selfie corner you put up has been popular." Simon grinned. "People come in after the tour to take photos and always end up buying some souvenirs."

Pete had rearranged to open up a corner of the shop to provide enough room for a photography backdrop and some fun props so people could snap pictures of themselves to remember the experience and share with friends. Simon had been amazed at how popular the free feature had become.

"It's totally 'pictures or it didn't happen,'" Pete agreed. "Plus, all those photos with the shop name on the backdrop are good free advertising."

When Simon came to Myrtle Beach after he had been fired from his teaching position, and his previous relationship had crashed and burned, he thought he might take a month to hide from the world and lick his wounds. His aunt had offered the use of her beach house, and Simon had been grateful for a chance to disappear.

Within a couple of weeks, he had fallen in love with Myrtle Beach. He had spotted the vacant storefront along the boardwalk and originally planned to do tours and readings. Little by little, the store's merchandise expanded to T-shirts, mugs, crystals, and more. Simon discovered he could make a good living doing what he loved, no longer hiding his psychic abilities. His aunt and uncle sold him the bungalow, and Simon found himself successfully relocated.

After that, all he needed was love.

Once Simon and Vic hit it off, Simon decided that all the

previous hardships put him in the right place at the right time for the pieces to fall into place.

"You don't have any readings booked today, but there was a voicemail from a guy named Denton Samuels at the art museum. He thinks they might have a ghost problem." Pete jostled Simon out of his thoughts and slipped him a note with the phone number.

"I'll call him back." Simon headed for his office.

"Don't worry—I've got the store covered."

Simon drummed his fingers as he waited for Denton to pick up the phone. He had worked with the curator before when they had trouble with a haunting due to a love spell gone wrong. The Grand Strand Museum of Art occupied a vintage converted beach cottage at the far end of the Strand. Simon and Vic occasionally attended events there, although it had been a while. For a small museum, it had made a name for itself featuring South Carolina and Lowcountry artists and hosting a continually-changing series of traveling exhibits.

"Simon? Thank goodness. I appreciate you calling me back," Denton replied as soon as Simon said hello. "I think we've got your kind of trouble again."

"Tell me what's happening."

"You're probably the only person who might believe me," Denton said. "Do you know the history of the cottage we're in?"

"I don't think so."

"This was originally a beach house that was part of the Ocean Paradise Hotel," Denton replied, and Simon caught his breath. "The hotel was envisioned as part of a huge complex that included a golf course and a gated community. It was going to be the hottest upscale beach development between New York and Miami. The hotel and golf course were built, but then the stock market crash of 1929 ruined the developer, and the plans never were finished. One of our donors bought this cottage and relocated it for the art museum."

"I hadn't heard that." Simon's thoughts raced. *Another link to the Ocean Paradise. What are the odds?*

"The ninety-fifth anniversary of the hotel's opening is this year, and we've been planning a series of events around that, touching on the local history, famous visitors, and other aspects. For example, the architect for the Ocean Paradise also planned Rockefeller Center. Those details get forgotten, but they're an important part of who we are here in Myrtle Beach," Denton said.

"Our new exhibit is made up of artwork of the hotel as well as original art that hung inside and was auctioned off when the property closed," Denton went on. "It's taken us a while to track the pieces down and work out the details, but we thought it would be a good beginning for the series, to remind people what the hotel was like in her glory days. We decided to do it now, rather than wait five years for the 100th anniversary. Maybe we'll do something else then."

"So the pieces were originally owned by the hotel?" Simon asked.

"Not all of them. We've also gathered a lot of postcards of the very impressive building—along with photographs and paintings that were done of the hotel itself. This first collection includes letters, film clips, and later some home movie 8mm footage from people who vacationed there. We wanted to frame the subject and re-establish the Ocean Paradise as an important piece of Grand Strand history so the exhibits that follow will make sense."

The retrospective sounded interesting, and Simon felt bad for Denton and his team that something was throwing a wrench into the plans. "What's going wrong?"

"Many of the same things as before. At first, I thought we were all just working too hard and overstressed. Little things went missing and turned up in odd places. Pieces would be rearranged when no one was around. But it was too similar to dismiss." Denton's tone had grown anxious.

"Did you feel cold spots? See shadows moving that shouldn't be, or just get creepy vibes?" Simon asked.

"All of that. You believe me, right?"

"Absolutely. It's probably easier if I come over and you can show me what you have. I might pick up on which items are causing the problem," Simon offered.

"Yes, please. Of course I'll pay your consultation fee. Everyone's worked so hard on this—I don't want to see it fall apart."

"Give me fifteen minutes. See you soon." Simon ended the call after Denton's profuse thanks.

"I'm going to the museum—I'm guessing it'll be quiet here, but call if you need me," he told Pete as he headed out.

It didn't take long for Simon to reach the museum. He paused in the parking lot to admire the Victorian former beach cottage. Its link to the area's history—and the doomed Ocean Paradise Hotel—made the museum even more interesting in Simon's estimation.

"Simon—thank you so much for coming on short notice." Denton Samuels was a slender, dapper man in his early sixties. He wore a sport coat over a button-up with pressed slacks. No doubt his ties by friendship and family to many of the area's well-heeled developers eased the process of soliciting donations to the museum and forging connections to artists and contributors.

"Happy to help. Would you mind walking me through where you've had incidents?" Simon didn't feel anything strange outside the building or in the entranceway. That made him suspect that whatever lay behind the spooky occurrences had a connection to one or more haunted objects and not the building itself.

"The exhibit is designed to give visitors a sense of what it was like to stay at the Ocean Paradise Hotel in its heyday," Denton said. "We've been able to acquire some original furnishings on loan, and as you can see in the first room, we've used old photographs of the hotel lobby enlarged to be wall coverings to give the feel of actually being there."

The room did a good impersonation of the old lobby, including faux pillars painted to look like marble. A conversation grouping of vintage chairs and a coffee table added to the feel. Interspersed throughout were glass display cases with yellowed postcards, room keys, monogrammed dining plates, and letters. Mannequins displayed a bellhop's uniform as well as outfits that would have been the height of resort fashion back in 1930.

Simon had dealt with haunted letters before. He moved slowly among the cases and paused by the vintage clothing. None of the items pinged his sixth sense.

They walked past an artist's model of the hotel as it had looked when it opened—and as Simon had seen it in his vision.

"The Ocean Paradise was painted white at first and later sandblasted to show the red brick in the 1960s," Denton said. "Now in this next room, we have the first art groupings. These are statues, knickknacks, and a few garden sculptures. It's remarkable how much was preserved by collectors, who have graciously loaned the pieces to us. The resort made a big impression on the people who worked or vacationed there."

As Simon passed among the glass cases and walked past the sculptures, he concentrated, trying to pick up any hint of ghostly activity.

"What can I do to help you?" Denton asked. "Are there ghosts here?"

"None that have shown themselves so far. Objects can hold strong emotions, which can almost be like a haunting," Simon told him. "I'm not sure yet what we're dealing with."

The repurposed cottage was a fraction of the size of the massive old hotel, but each room did a good job of recreating the opulent atmosphere and evoking a sense of place. Simon couldn't help being drawn in by the nostalgia.

"Perhaps something in our main gallery." Denton led Simon into the large room. Paintings hung on the walls and in display cases. Pottery and blown glass objects were on plinths scattered throughout. One corner showcased broadsides advertising big-name bands, singers, and entertainers who had headlined at the resort through the years.

Simon halted just inside the doorway, sensing the stir of spirits.

"There's something here," Simon said quietly. Denton jumped as if he had been burned.

"Where?"

"I'm not sure yet." Simon didn't move from the doorway. He stretched his senses, eyes closed, listening with his gift.

"There are several ghosts," he said softly. "Varying strengths.

Some are mostly faded. They're more like a memory loop without consciousness. They might cause a cold spot or give someone a thrill if they spot them, but they can't hurt anyone."

"And the others?" Denton asked as if he was afraid to hear the answer.

Simon frowned, concentrating. No ghosts circulated around the entertainment posters, although he sensed a darker energy than he expected, particularly around one poster of two men in tuxedos next to a magician's cabinet. He picked up the image of an older man in front of a painting of a sailing ship. A younger woman stood in front of a portrait of a sea captain with tears streaking down her face. A little girl stared at the painting of a Cocker Spaniel.

"Three ghosts. I don't think they're dangerous—just stuck," Simon told the curator. He remembered his vision and turned to Denton. "Out of curiosity—did anyone ever fall off the high tower at the hotel?"

Denton looked uncomfortable. "Not that I've heard. I wouldn't be surprised if deaths like that happened, but they would have been kept quiet."

The images from his vision still lingered, and Simon felt sure it had a deeper meaning.

"Can you get the ghosts to leave?" Denton asked.

"If they want to." None of the spirits were recent, so if they were going to become vengeful Simon felt certain it would have happened by now. While he didn't doubt that the haunting was inconvenient for the museum, these ghosts weren't likely to hurt anyone.

"Did the owners of the paintings complain about the ghosts?" Simon wanted to make sure he had the full picture before helping the spirits pass over. Certain collectors were drawn to haunted items, although that defied comprehension for Simon.

"They didn't mention anything. If they knew, I would have appreciated a warning," Denton said.

"I can ask the spirits if they would like to move on," Simon told the curator. "They aren't causing harm, so I won't banish them. If they choose to stay, I can give you some sigils and talismans to keep them from showing themselves. And there's always salt."

Denton clearly looked hesitant, but he finally nodded. "You're the professional. I just don't want them scaring off the guests."

"I suspect they're confused and unhappy to be here as well," Simon told him. "Give me a chance to speak with them."

Denton seemed all too happy to retreat, leaving Simon alone with the ghosts. He took a deep breath and gathered his energy.

"Spirits of the Ocean Paradise, hear me. You've stayed beyond your lifetime. If you want to rest, I can help you cross the Veil. If you remain, you need to be unnoticed. If you can't do that, I need to send you on."

The older man and the little girl winked out, moving on. The woman's spirit remained, but as Simon watched, her image grew fainter until she vanished. The room no longer felt cold, and the unnerving vibe faded.

"Thank you for making this one easy," Simon thought to the last ghost. *"Go in peace."*

Denton thanked him profusely when he let him know that he'd finished, so tangibly relieved that Simon struggled not to chuckle. But his humor faded as he walked back to the car.

I had never heard of the Ocean Paradise Hotel, and now it's everywhere. Even the art museum building is a relic. These ghosts were benign, but maybe there are others that aren't. There's got to be a reason why this is all showing up now—and these things never turn out to be fine on their own.

I need to get to the bottom of this fast before anyone gets hurt.

2

SIMON

"I think we've got your kind of problem," Horry County Librarian Laura Conrad told Simon when he met her in the lobby of the library. "I'm finding books on the floor and displays moved around when no one else is here. Cold spots. Footsteps in an empty building. We've got a big event coming up tomorrow, and I'm afraid it's not safe to invite people here."

Laura often asked Simon to give presentations on ghosts. Her short, graying hair was dyed in rainbow hues, and she loved big jewelry and sparkly clothing.

Simon followed her inside. Myrtle Beach's library wasn't huge, but it held a well-stocked variety of books and catered to the tastes of the town's residents. Simon had done a few signings himself here when his ghost books came out.

"When did the problems start?" He looked around, loving the immediate feeling of comfort that came from being surrounded by books. Libraries and bookstores had always been his favorite refuges.

"Yesterday, when we put up the signs about the upcoming events," Laura told him. "At first, I thought it was my imagination. Then the other librarians mentioned having similar things happen when no one else was around. I wondered if we might have someone who wanted to sabotage the events because they didn't like a book or an author, but I checked the security footage and no one showed up."

"Are any of the books about the supernatural?" Simon hadn't told Laura that before his signings he always did a cleansing and a banishing and put protective hex bags at strategic places in the building. He would remove them afterward, not expecting that the library would need continued warding. Now, he regretted not leaving the protections in place.

"No. That's part of what makes it so weird," Laura replied. "We have two signings we're promoting right now. The one this weekend is a local history book, and the other is a romance set in Myrtle Beach by an author who grew up here."

She led Simon to a display case. Inside was a poster for *Paradise Lost—the Rise and Fall of the Ocean Paradise Hotel* by Jeremy Long, as well as a hardback copy. A second poster featured *Warm Summer Sand: A Grand Strand Romance* by Elle Cullen, with a sample paperback.

"The Ocean Paradise Hotel seems to be coming up a lot lately," Simon told her. "How much do you know about it?"

Laura smiled. "It was before my time, but I had an aunt who used to tell stories about the fancy parties and the celebrities who vacationed there. Quite the place, before it went downhill. Although I guess there were rumors that it wasn't always a paradise."

"What have you heard?" Simon picked up a nearby copy of the book and thumbed through it. A center section of black and white photos showed the hotel through the years, from its heyday to implosion.

"The same sort of gossip you hear about all the hotels. Famous people having affairs, marital spats that get out of hand, drunk college kids making bad choices…that sort of thing."

"Did any of the Ocean Paradise rumors suggest something supernatural to blame?" Simon asked.

"I haven't had a chance to read the book, but you can ask the author—he just dropped by to get a look at the location for tomorrow's event. I figured you'd want to chat." Laura led the way to the library's special event room. A man with short brown hair turned.

"Mr. Long—I'd like you to meet Dr. Kincaide," Laura introduced. "He's one of our local author experts, and he's curious about your books."

Jeremy Long looked familiar, and Simon realized he had seen the other man on a television show about "lost" vacation attractions.

"I'm Simon." He extended his hand. "I've seen your show."

"Jeremy." The other man gave a firm shake. "I've read your books. You're a psychic, right?"

To Simon's surprise, Jeremy's tone didn't hold an edge of mocking. "Yes, and a medium. I run Grand Strand Ghost Tours."

"I'll let you two chat. Just call if you need me," Laura said and ducked out.

"She told you that things have been strange here since I arrived?" Jeremy asked.

Simon nodded. "Have you seen anything odd yourself?"

Jeremy grimaced. "I feel watched, but there's no one here. The hair on the back of my neck rises like there's an electrical charge. Twice I thought I saw someone moving in the stacks, but when I went to look, there was no one."

"Can you show me where? I'll be glad to check it out," Simon offered.

Jeremy motioned for him to follow. They left the event room and retraced Jeremy's steps from the poster in the front lobby to the glass case with a display of books including his, and into the rows of shelves where he thought he had seen movement.

"I'm not picking up anything now, but I don't doubt that you felt something." Simon wondered why a ghost would make the effort to haunt a book signing and be upset enough to cause havoc.

"How did you pick the Ocean Paradise to write about?" Simon asked. "And did you dish any dirt about the dead?" They walked together to the special events room, which was located in a back corner.

Jeremy leaned against a nearby armchair. "I got into writing about vacation spots that don't exist anymore because when I was a kid we went to some cool parks and hotels that eventually closed and were torn down. I love my memories of those places, and I don't want their history to be forgotten. With the television show, we've gone beyond my personal memories, and I started to look into other destinations you can't visit anymore. The Ocean Paradise showed up in a lot of suggestions when I asked viewers to recommend places to write about."

"Every vacation spot has its tragic stories." Simon chose his words carefully. "What do you make of the stories associated with the Ocean Paradise?"

"The thing I love about writing about places like the Ocean Paradise is that they grow their own legends as time passes." Jeremy backed up to half-sit on the table. "As people share memories, anything odd or unusual gets inflated, and the legend grows."

"So what do you make of the hotel's decline—the stock market crash and the owner's financial troubles? I'm curious."

"Finances weren't the hotel's only bad luck. There's a rumor that one of the owner's wives made a deal with the Devil to save the hotel," Jeremy replied. "If so, she got a bad bargain. The rumor claims she ended up cursed, and she's the reason so many people who were associated with the hotel came to a tragic end."

"They did?" Simon asked, raising an eyebrow.

Jeremy nodded. "More than usual for that sort of place, at least in my opinion."

"And did you tell those stories in the book?"

Jeremy chuckled. "I didn't mention anyone by name in a context like that. I vetted everything that I could. But I don't want to risk getting sued by a survivor or relative. This wasn't a tell-all kind of book, so there was a lot of stuff I unearthed in the research that I didn't put into the manuscript. The book was honestly more of a 'love letter' to a place in its heyday, so I wrote about the celebrities who vacationed there and the famous entertainers who performed."

Simon felt a shift in the temperature. A blur of movement made him turn his head, but he saw nothing. Energy gathered—angry and unsettled. "I just felt something—did you?"

Jeremy nodded and looked scared. Simon passed him a small

bag of salt and an iron washer. "Hold these. They'll help keep a ghost away from you." He looked around the room, trying to figure out a reason for the ghost to show up, but given the timing he felt certain it had to do with Jeremy's book.

"Did you bring anything from the actual hotel with you? Memorabilia? Heirlooms?" Simon asked.

Either Jeremy picked up on the energy as well or he read the urgency in Simon's voice.

"I have a couple of things in my messenger bag for 'show and tell' during my presentation."

No one else was in the room, so the footsteps and the sounds of pages rustling had to be a ghost attached to something Jeremy had brought with him.

"Show me."

Jeremy grabbed his briefcase from another table and opened it. "I have pieces of monogrammed silverware that I picked up at auction. Some menus and photographs of the hotel in its heyday, as well as postcards and key fobs. I've had all those for a while, and nothing weird ever happened."

"Any new pieces?" Simon sensed that the spirit had drawn closer.

"I keep an eye out on eBay and local estate sales," Jeremy said. "The wedding picture is new—I picked it up on my way into town for the signing. It has a story—apparently the ceremony was held at the Ocean Paradise and there was a big reception. Then the bride —Christiana Irving Crosby—went for a walk on the beach and drowned."

A chill scurried down Simon's back.

The temperature dropped, and Simon felt a wave of deep unease. A book on one of the tables wobbled, rose into the air, and flew at Jeremy's head like a pitched baseball.

"Get down," Simon yelled and threw a handful of salt into the air as Jeremy ducked just in time.

"What the hell?" Jeremy yelped as another book zinged past his head and slammed into the floor.

"Get under the table," Simon ordered. Jeremy crawled as fast as he could as books tumbled from stacks and sailed through the air.

"Hold onto the salt. And keep your head down." Simon dodged for the open messenger bag and plucked out the faded wedding photo. He dropped enough handfuls of salt around his feet to keep the ghost at bay while he tried to un-haunt the library.

"Show yourself!" Simon opened his senses, hoping for a glimpse of the poltergeist even if it couldn't—or wouldn't—appear. He felt the apparition's anger, and beneath that despair and desperation.

A stack of books crashed to the floor. Jeremy cowered under the table, pale and wide-eyed with fear.

Simon eyed a metal waste can against the wall. He gripped the lighter in his pocket and held the photo in his other hand. In three steps he was across the room, and before the ghost could react, he flicked the lighter and set fire to the faded photograph over the trash can. Flames consumed the photo, ashes falling into the nearly empty bin.

"Restless spirit, leave this place and let go of your anger. So mote it be." Simon sensed the ghost's presence vanish, but he had the distinct impression that she chose to leave instead of being driven away by his words.

When the last of the ash dropped away, the chill in the air lifted. Simon grabbed a bottle of water from his bag and doused the smoldering ashes in the trash can.

"Is she gone?" Jeremy whispered from where he huddled beneath the table.

"Yes." Simon searched with his senses, but the ghost's presence was beyond his reach. "That was an unusually strong spirit. It's not gone from this realm. I didn't expect it to resist being sent on."

Jeremy crawled out from beneath the table, looking badly shaken. "Are you okay?"

Simon nodded as the fatigue set in. "All in a day's work."

"Thank you. I thought she wanted to kill me."

Simon helped pick up the books scattered across the room. While most were undamaged, some had torn pages or dented covers. "Did the person who sold you the photo say anything about it being haunted?"

Jeremy shook his head. "No. Either he hid that information, or she didn't bother him."

Simon frowned, thinking. "Do you mention Christiana in your book?"

"No. I didn't get the photo until today and thought it might make the whole thing more real to people if they could see memorabilia from the old hotel."

"It's possible that the ghost didn't manifest for the photo's previous owner if he didn't have a connection to the Ocean Paradise." Simon stacked the books on a nearby table to be reshelved. "Some people collect vintage photography like art. The person who sold you the photo might have gotten a bad feeling about it, but my bet is that the ghost never bothered anyone—until the hotel turned into a hot topic."

"Is everything all right in here?" Laura peered into the room.

"We're okay now. You missed all the excitement," Simon told her with a wan smile. Her gaze flickered between Jeremy's shell-shocked expression and the pile of books.

"I have coffee and cookies in the break room when you're ready." Laura looked almost as spooked as Jeremy and beat a quick retreat.

"How...did you do that?" Jeremy asked.

"I'm a medium. I have a connection to the spirits. They can speak to me and through me, and they hear what I say. Usually, I can give them a nudge toward the afterlife. Sometimes, it's more of a shove. What's odd is that this ghost didn't move on—she just left."

"Wow." Jeremy looked a little dazed. "You're the real deal."

Simon didn't take offense. He'd gotten that reaction more times than he could count. "Yeah. It comes in handy sometimes. I'm guessing that was the ghost I sensed watching us earlier."

They headed toward the break room, looking for caffeine and sugar after the attack. "I didn't think any of the ghosts would be angry at me," Jeremy said. "I didn't put any of the really bad stuff in my book."

Simon's head snapped up. "What 'really bad' stuff?"

Jeremy looked uncomfortable. "I probably shouldn't have said anything."

Simon managed what he hoped was a comforting smile. "I promise I won't put anything you tell me on the internet, but it might come in handy setting some ghosts to rest. Please, tell me what you found."

Jeremy squirmed, then settled into his chair. "Something I love about researching history is finding out that people throughout the ages are pretty much the same. The classes you took in high school leave out the messy and unflattering parts, but real history is full of squabbles and duels and affairs and all sorts of dirty deeds."

"Sad but true," Simon agreed.

"I wasn't trying to write an exposé of the Ocean Paradise. Mostly the opposite—remembering its heyday and its golden age," Jeremy said. "But when you start digging, you get the bad with the good."

He fidgeted again and ate a shortbread cookie from the plate on the counter. "Because the Ocean Paradise catered to famous and wealthy guests, there were plenty of affairs, jilted mistresses, drunken indiscretions, that sort of thing," Jeremy went on. "I didn't write about the worst parts, rumors that some of the people in charge at the hotel took advantage of some of the staff. Mostly, I talked about the people who seemed bigger than life.

"Like Timothy Sheldon," Jeremy added. "He was a hot shot stage magician back in the sixties who headlined at the Paradise. Sheldon made a lot of enemies, and some people were jealous of his success. Apparently he broke a lot of hearts. Sheldon's rivalry with one particular magician was legendary—and people said the other magician could use *real* magic."

Simon raised an eyebrow. "What do you mean, 'real' magic?"

"Serious hocus-pocus. Not illusions."

"Do you remember that magician's name?"

"Nathan Irving." Jeremy looked around, jumpy as if they might be overheard. "He never got as famous as Sheldon, or got as many girls, so of course he hated Sheldon's guts."

"Figures," Simon agreed.

"But people I talked to and some articles I found made a case for him being able to perform feats without tricks and illusions."

"So why wasn't he more famous?"

"He was sort of a toad," Jeremy admitted. "Not handsome, not a showman. Bad temper. In fact, there were some people around him who died under odd circumstances, and the gossip was that he caused it, even though the cops didn't believe in magic. People said Irving was a witch."

"Were there names associated with those rumors?" Simon asked.

Jeremy looked up. "You actually believe that?"

Simon shrugged. "I'm a psychic medium. I know for sure that some of the 'woo-woo' is real."

Jeremy took a deep breath. "You promise you won't put this stuff on some ghost-hunting internet site? I left that part out of the book because I wanted to focus on the positive memories."

"I promise."

"Okay. I don't remember off-hand, but when I go home I can check my notes, and if you give me your number, I can text you."

"Did anyone say the same about Timothy Sheldon or other magicians at that time, that they had 'real magic'?" Simon asked. He passed over a card with his cell number on it.

"It's funny—there was a rumor right about the time Sheldon's career really took off that he'd sold his soul or done some sort of Voodoo ritual because he had tricks even other professionals couldn't figure out," Jeremy said. "Strange stuff happened. People swore he used *real* magic to do it."

"And Irving? What happened to him?"

"He was sort of a flash in the pan, as my grandma used to say. Made a big splash for a while but never had his breakout moment to take him to a major stage. He faded as Sheldon's career took off. I didn't pay attention once he quit being featured at the Ocean Paradise since the hotel was my focus. Guess he just faded away."

Simon frowned. "The bride in that photo's middle—probably original—last name was Irving. Do you know if there was any relation to the magician?"

Jeremy shook his head. "I don't know. Didn't think to look, honestly."

"This might sound crazy," Simon told him, "but since a ghost showed up here because of your book, I'd like you to take some precautions when you go home." He smiled, trying to set Jeremy at ease. "At best, they keep the spooks away. At worst, they give you peace of mind even if they don't work."

Jeremy nodded. "Okay. I'm game. What do I need to do?"

"Ghosts don't like salt or iron," Simon explained. "Get a big container of salt and put down an unbroken line across windows, doors, and vents. Don't let it get smudged. That will keep out a lot of bad things. In case a ghost gets through, hit it with something made of iron—like a fireplace poker."

"That works?"

"Most of the time. If you have a problem, call me." Simon paused. "I also think you should postpone the signing. Since the ghost didn't move on, she could come back, and people could get hurt if she acts up again."

Jeremy nodded. "I wondered about that. Do you think Laura will mind?"

"I'm sure she'd be glad to find you a new date. That way I can look into the ghost and make sure it doesn't return. Then you can reschedule and not worry."

"If my writing the book about the hotel stirred up a ghost, you ought to talk to the guy who did the documentary," Jeremy said.

Simon looked up sharply, even as he groaned inside. *Another connection to the same hotel?* "Documentary?"

Jeremy's hands shook as he grabbed three more shortbread cookies and poured himself a cup of coffee. Simon took a couple of cookies and made a coffee with creamer before settling into a chair at the table across from the author.

"Gideon Kent is a local filmmaker who has been working on a documentary about the Ocean Paradise for a couple of years for the Myrtle Beach PBS station," Jeremy told him. He ate the cookies quickly and gulped down the coffee, perhaps hoping to steady his nerves.

"When I was researching the book, the PBS station gave me his name. They thought it might be good publicity for both of us if we could release the book and the documentary close together. It's the fiftieth anniversary of imploding the hotel."

Shit. No wonder the ghosts are restless. Two projects stirring up memories. An anniversary. The museum exhibit. That's a perfect storm for a spookapalooza.

"Has the documentary been released yet?"

Jeremy shook his head. "No. But we did our best to coordinate, so it should be airing next week. I haven't talked to Gideon in the past couple of days, but that was the plan." He paused. "Gideon's a bit odd, but he's a good historian and an excellent documentarian."

"I think all the recent interest in the old hotel has stirred up energies—and ghosts—that had gone dormant." *And magic.* "There might be other restless spirits. I'd like to talk to Gideon and make sure he stays safe. Would you be willing to connect us?"

Jeremy grabbed a few more cookies, then nodded. "Sure. Yeah. That would be a good idea. He's a nice guy—real history buff. I'm not sure he ran across any of the scandals in his research like I did —or at least he never mentioned them. Maybe the ghosts won't be ticked off at him. Give me your number and I'll text you his. I'll let him know to expect a call."

A minute later, Simon's phone pinged with a text message. "Thank you. And I want to buy a copy of your book. With everything that's gone on, I want to know everything I can about the Ocean Paradise."

Later, Simon walked toward the information desk. Laura looked up with a worried expression, then sighed in relief. "Everything okay?"

"I'm glad you called me," Simon told her. "It was a poltergeist problem. The ghost is gone for now, but I wasn't able to banish it, so it might be back. I'd advise rescheduling the signing. And I'm afraid there's a mess in the trash can."

She made a dismissive gesture. "Better than anyone getting hurt. Is Mr. Long willing to reschedule?"

"Yes, although he's disappointed about having to postpone. Did he tell you about the documentary?"

Laura nodded. "Yes. I've reached out to the producer and he's going to do a screening of it here at the library after it airs on the public station —although now I'll wait on that until you say it's okay. I think it'll be a good tie in. You know we love anything we can get on local history."

"I believe the ghost was linked to Jeremy's old photo, but just in case I'll stop back with more protective anti-ghost charms," Simon promised her. "I can put them in discreet places where no one will see, but they'll keep unwanted visitors from showing up."

Laura gave him a warm smile. "Thank you, Simon. And don't think I've forgotten that you said you'd have a new book out soon. Whenever you're ready, we'd love to have you back for an event."

Simon grinned. "Definitely! Let me get through the wedding first. You're coming to the ceremony, right?"

"Wouldn't miss it for the world. I'm so happy for you two. Can't wait to see you tie the knot!"

By the time Simon finished at the library, he had a text from Jeremy with Gideon Kent's phone number, address, and a warning.

Jeremy Long: *Approach gently—he's a little squirrelly although he knows his stuff.*

The caution gave Simon pause, and made him wonder what lay behind the comment. He went out to his car and called the number. It rang until it went to voicemail.

"I'm calling for Gideon Kent. Jeremy Long gave me your number. I'm Simon Kincaide, and I'm a local author with an interest in the Ocean Paradise documentary. Please give me a call."

Simon sat back, wondering what new light Kent might shed on the old hotel. He wasn't sure how long it would take for the film-maker to get his message, so he was surprised when a video call requested his attention right away.

"Simon Kincaide? I'm Gideon Kent." The man in the video looked to be in his forties, graying at the temples of his thinning dark hair. He appeared haggard and sallow, something Simon couldn't blame completely on bad lighting.

"Thanks for calling me back. Jeremy told me about your documentary. I'm working on a project of my own about the Ocean Paradise, and I'd love to talk with you about your film—maybe get together."

"I don't go out," Gideon said. "And if you know what's good for you, you'll forget you ever heard about the Ocean Paradise."

"Jeremy told me that the two of you coordinated a bit on your projects." Simon hoped the conversation didn't end before it had barely begun. He figured he'd wait to mention the poltergeist.

"There's a reason that hotel has a bad reputation, even after all this time. Everything about it is haunted—maybe cursed. People connected to the Paradise die. Find another project—anything else," Gideon begged him. "I wish I had."

At first, Simon thought Gideon might be playing up the drama for publicity's sake. But as he watched and listened, he became convinced that the man's terror was real. *He's genuinely scared shitless about something.*

"Does the name Timothy Sheldon mean anything to you?" Simon asked.

Gideon startled. "The stage magician from back in the Ocean Paradise's glory days? I saw in the paper that he just died—and the article said there were 'questionable circumstances.'"

So guess who's probably going to get called in to investigate? This can't be all coincidental, but what's behind all this sudden interest in the old hotel?

"I'm an author—but I'm also a psychic medium, and I work with the Myrtle Beach police department on deaths like Mr. Sheldon's that might have a supernatural element," Simon replied. "My curiosity about the hotel isn't completely academic."

Gideon gave a bleak laugh. "You're too late. Sheldon isn't the only one to die from the curse. I'm marked. I should have warned Jeremy. He's got to be marked too. That's why you should stop poking around now, before it's too late."

"Curse?"

"People died in strange ways who had a connection to the Ocean Paradise. You don't want to be one of them."

"I can't give up until I get answers," Simon returned. "Could I stop by and ask you some questions?"

Gideon licked his lips, a nervous gesture. "It's too dangerous."

"Has something happened to make you feel like you're in danger? Was it connected to the documentary?" Simon felt bad for the filmmaker.

Gideon looked defeated. "I started seeing shapes in the shadows. Then things in the house would suddenly get moved around—even though I live by myself," he admitted.

"It really spooked me, so I called a priest, and he came out and did a blessing. I hung up crucifixes and garlic, put down salt around the doors and windows, and burned sage. It worked—at first," Gideon continued.

"At first?"

Gideon nodded and cast a nervous glance over his shoulder, as if afraid speaking about the haunting would make it return. "Whatever it was went into my yard instead. I saw shadows at the windows and heard scratching along the side of the house where there aren't any trees. I heard a man mumbling, but when I turned on all the lights, no one was there."

He licked his lips nervously. "I swear that something is watching me, trying to get inside. Then a few days ago, a really creepy shadow chased me. I got into the house, and it pounded on the doors and windows. Now I'm scared to go out or have anyone come here. I don't usually have company except for the food delivery drivers, and I'd keep them away if I could figure out how to survive without them."

"How are you protecting yourself?" Simon grew more concerned as Gideon told his story.

"I ordered a bunch of stuff online and decked out my lawn and porch with bottle trees, witch balls, wind chimes, and a light-up plastic Virgin Mary," Gideon admitted. "That's stopped the scary stuff in the yard—for now. When I go out at noon to get the mail and pick up deliveries, I carry a bunch of amulets and charms I ordered. No one comes in, and I don't go past my gate. I'm afraid the ghost is going to get me, like he got the others."

"The others?"

"The other people connected to the hotel who died in strange ways. Either ghosts got them or maybe a witch."

"A witch like Nathan Irving?" Simon guessed.

Gideon nodded. "Irving was scary. People back in the day said he was a witch, and I think they were right. Sheldon wasn't an angel himself. People who crossed either Irving or Sheldon ended up destroyed or dead. The Ocean Paradise seemed to attract doomed people. I know that sounds weird, but I believe it. And now I'm one of them."

"Jeremy mentioned some people close to Sheldon and Irving had very bad luck," Simon replied. "If you can share any of the names of those folks, I'd sure appreciate it."

"What can you do about it?

"I can find a way to make the dangerous ghosts move on. Sometimes closure is the next best thing to justice." Simon jotted down the people Gideon mentioned to cross-reference with Jeremy's research. He didn't need to be psychic to suspect that the lists would match.

"The documentary and book are already finished. What does the ghost gain from going after you now?" Simon mentally catalogued the way he might be able to dispel the spirit and keep both Gideon and Jeremy safe until the mystery surrounding the old hotel was solved.

"I don't know," Gideon admitted. "But it's like something that was sleeping woke up and wants blood. I wish I'd never heard of the Ocean Paradise."

"You didn't cause this," Simon assured him. "Neither did Jeremy."

"How do you fight a ghost? Or a curse? Are you a witch?"

Simon shook his head. "No. But I can talk to spirits, and we have some friends whose abilities could come in handy. Sit tight and stay in your safe place for now. We're going to get this settled soon."

"I hope you know what you're doing," Gideon told him. "And I hope I live long enough to see you make good on that promise."

The video call ended, and Simon realized he'd been sitting in the library parking lot all this time. He pulled out his phone and sent a text to Vic.

Simon: *Any chance we're going to get pulled in to the Timothy Sheldon death? It sounds like our kind of thing. I just tripped over some information that might apply.*

Vic: *I just heard about Sheldon today. I imagine I'll find out more soon. Fill me in tonight when I get home. Love you—stay safe.*

Simon: *Love you too. Be careful.*

Simon sat with the phone in his lap for a few minutes after ending the call, going back over what Jeremy and Gideon had told him and the other strange connections to a long-gone old hotel.

Everything keeps coming back to the Ocean Paradise. Why there? Why now? And why do I keep getting a feeling that there's a storm coming our way?

3

VIC

"Get in. We caught a new case," Ross Hamilton said when Vic opened the passenger side car door. "Brought you coffee. The file's on your seat—I can fill you in while I drive."

Vic slid into the front seat and took the takeout cup from its holder. "Thanks for the caffeine. I only had time for one back at the house."

"Trouble sleeping?" Ross raised an eyebrow.

Vic shrugged. "Not really. There's just a lot going on, and that's on top of all the normal shit."

"Wedding stuff?" Ross prompted.

"Yeah. Simon's handling most of it —but when he's stressed out, it stresses me." Vic paused to sip his coffee, savoring the taste and the burn.

"Problems?"

Vic considered himself lucky to have such a great work partner. He gave Ross a quick recap. "I wish we could just show up and have everything be perfect, without having to do all the detail stuff."

"Dream on." Ross snickered as Vic closed his eyes and leaned back against the headrest. "Sheila could probably organize an entire military operation with two hours' notice and the contents of her purse, but a simple beach wedding put even her scarily-awesome skills to the test. I'm convinced that every planning phase hits a point where there are only three options—murder, calling it off, or living happily ever after."

"I definitely prefer option number three." Vic drank more of his coffee without opening his eyes. "And honestly, I know our friends and my family would be fine if we said our vows standing in the backyard and served cookies and chicken nuggets."

"Well, we'd still support you, but there'd be some grousing about the refreshments, especially from *your* family," Ross joked.

"Yeah, I told Simon that it's not a real wedding if we don't have shrimp."

"Damn right. You don't mess with tradition."

Vic finished his coffee and reluctantly sat straight, looked around, and then opened the file folder and paged through it. "Simon would have taken the catering problems in stride if he hadn't had a bad day in the shop." He glanced at Ross, who had grown up in the area. "Did you ever hear of a place called the Ocean Paradise Hotel?"

Ross gave him a strange look. "Why are you asking? Timothy Sheldon—our new case—was a bigshot entertainer there."

Vic felt the hair on the back of his neck rise. "Simon did a séance for someone whose daughter drowned on the beach there back in the seventies. The new art exhibit about the Ocean Paradise needed him to send away ghosts. Then he ran into an author and a filmmaker who did projects about the hotel and seem to be stalked by a dangerous spirit. It really threw his mood off."

Ross nodded in sympathy. "And if your partner ain't happy, ain't nobody happy."

"That's the truth," Vic agreed.

"I've heard of the hotel. I think my aunt worked there when she was in high school, and I've heard my mom talk about going to parties. The hotel's been gone a long time. But it's funny that you ask…the victim definitely had strong ties to Ocean Paradise back in the day," Ross said.

"Tell me what you know, and I'll give you more scoop from

POINT BLANK | 35

Simon." Vic returned his attention to the file. "Fill me in. The caffeine hasn't hit the bloodstream yet."

"The victim's name is Timothy Sheldon, age eighty-six. He was a retired career stage magician. Guy used to work up and down the East Coast at all the swanky hotels. A regular David Copperfield—only not as famous. Never played Vegas."

"Guessing it wasn't natural causes despite his age. Murdered, right? Since we're on the job."

"Yeah—but it's weird. Sheldon collected magical props. All sorts of stuff—vanishing cabinets, card tricks, costumes, saw-em-in-two-boxes. The house is full of it, according to the notes."

"Did he get sawn in two? Disappeared into his cabinet? The file doesn't say."

"Choked on a deck of cards," Ross said. "Cause of death—suffocation from an obstructed airway."

Vic turned to him, incredulous. "How?"

"That's what they pay us the big bucks to find out, remember?" Ross joked.

"Any chance he did it himself?"

"Unlikely, since he was handcuffed to a chair at the time."

"Kinky."

"Yeah, but they were supposed to be trick cuffs, ones he'd gotten out of hundreds of times. Except they were stuck," Ross said.

Vic continued to study the file. "House was locked from the inside, no evidence of breaking and entering, no security camera footage to show an intruder," he noted aloud. "Could be suicide."

"You'd think. But riddle me this—how does a guy who's cuffed to a chair choke himself swallowing a deck of cards?"

"If he did manage to do it, did he leave a note? Was there a reason? Terminal cancer? Bankruptcy? Divorce?"

Ross shook his head. "None of the above. He was in as good health as a man his age could expect. He was a lifelong bachelor, active in clubs and professional societies. Bit of a player, even at his age."

"String of wronged girlfriends?"

"Yes, actually…and we have a list of people to talk to. But he dated women near his own age. I'd be more inclined to think they'd poison him instead of taking such a…physical approach."

"Arsenic and old playing cards?" Vic snarked. Dark humor helped them deal with the worst parts of their job.

"It doesn't sound right for a broken heart murder," Ross mused. "But it definitely seems like a personal vendetta."

"And since the room was locked from the inside, unless we find a way someone got in and out, then odds are good we need to bring Simon into this because we're dealing with something supernatural." Vic closed the folder. A sour feeling curdled in the pit of his stomach. "We've only got a week and a half before the wedding. I was hoping nothing would come up to involve Simon. He's got enough on his plate with the plans. It would be nice if he wasn't completely stressed out by the time we get to the ceremony."

"Yeah, but think how awesome it'll be to work off all that stress on the honeymoon." Ross gave an exaggerated waggle of his eyebrows.

"I didn't really think we'd need help with the honeymoon part." Vic rolled his eyes.

"If it's any consolation, Sheila and I were a strung-out mess by the time we got to the ceremony. It felt like everything that could go wrong did go wrong. We made it to the altar on time, got through the vows without passing out or throwing up, and I don't remember anything about the actual reception." Ross laughed.

"We missed the plane to our honeymoon, spent our wedding night in the airport, caught a red eye, and once we got to the hotel, we were so exhausted we slept the entire first day," Ross added. "But something must have gone right because it's been ten years, and we're still going strong."

Vic grinned. "I'm going to pretend I didn't hear all the problems and focus on the happy ending."

"Denial is a perfectly adequate coping mechanism." Ross slapped him on the shoulder. "And you know if you need me, I've got your back."

"That's why you're my best man."

Ross pulled up to a nondescript house in an older neighborhood. Crime scene tape blocked the door.

"Don't let the boring suburban ranch fool you. Apparently the inside is pure Criss Angel," Ross said. "Really freaked the guys out who were first on the scene."

Ross had the key. He put on gloves and booties and flicked on the light, revealing more magical equipment than Vic had ever imagined.

"Wow. This looks like something out of a movie." Vic couldn't help feeling a little star-struck at all the props. He was quick to don gloves and booties and turn on his body cam.

"Pretty sure some of this came off movie sets," Ross said as they entered a living room too cluttered to leave space for anything except an armchair and side table.

"The guy was a hoarder—of magic stuff. Looks like he filled just about every square inch," Vic said when they edged from the living room through the hallway to an equally crowded dining area. Even the kitchen was packed with boxes and crates.

"There are three bedrooms in the back, no attic, no crawlspace," Ross reported. "I looked up the house online from an old real estate listing."

"Efficient of you."

"I can't figure out whether he was keeping mementos of his faded glory or if there was a reason he picked these pieces, maybe to keep them out of other hands," Ross said. They wandered down the hallway to see through the rest of the small house—a bathroom and three bedrooms.

"You think he might have been trying to do real magic?"

"Before I got partnered with you, that wouldn't have made sense," Ross admitted. "But yeah, that did occur to me."

"Simon will be able to sense if anything has magic," Vic said. "But from the dust, it looks like most of this stuff has been here a while."

In the middle bedroom, which doubled as an office, old theater posters papered the walls, announcing the appearances of Sheldon the Magnificent along with drawings or photos of a handsome man in a tuxedo with a magician's cape. In most of the posters, Sheldon was alone or featured with a pretty stage assistant, although one or two of the pictures showed a second older man with him.

Sheldon looked the part of a casino magician—debonair and arrogant. Vic suspected that he attracted more than his share of lovers, although it didn't seem to have given him any comfort at the end of his life.

"You said he played the Ocean Paradise?" Vic carefully looked into steamer trunks and wardrobes but avoided containers decorated with runes or sigils.

"That was one of his first headliner gigs," Ross replied. "Before that, he worked his way up at smaller venues, private events, and television variety shows. Getting a regular spot on the Paradise's calendar was making the big time. The hotel got A-list singers and bands who also played New York and Miami. He would have made important contacts, gotten publicity, and earned good money."

"You've done some digging." Vic saw a garishly painted box he recognized as being the sort to make a scantily clad assistant "vanish." Top hats, capes, and a rack of tuxedos vied for space with straitjackets, shackles, and feathered boas.

There are fetish clubs that would probably pay a good price for most of this stuff. Not to mention other magicians—or museums. It's strange and creepy but probably valuable.

"I keep thinking this should all be in a museum somewhere." Ross sounded a little wistful as he caught up to Vic. "Those posters of famous stage performers from the past are like a who's who of magicians. But none of it explains the man's death."

"Where was the body?"

"In the kitchen," Ross replied.

"Doors locked from the inside, and no indication that anything was stolen?" Vic slowly turned to take in the details of the crowded room. Simon maintained that the intuition on which Vic had built his career might be his own version of a minor psychic gift. Vic wasn't sure he believed that, but just in case there might be any truth to it, he did his best to open his senses and pick up new impressions.

"You see how thick the dust is," Ross replied. "It would be pretty obvious if something was missing."

The door to the bedroom at the far end of the hall was locked, and Vic felt a deep, visceral aversion to seeing what was inside. "I've got a bad feeling about that room," Vic told Ross, knowing his partner would take him seriously. "Let's leave that one for Simon."

Last on the hallway was the master bedroom, also crammed full of stuff, although it held a bed, chest of drawers, nightstand, and dresser, as well as a closet. Memorabilia filled every flat surface.

Vic tried to tune in to what his emotions told him as well as his detective-trained observation. He'd always trusted his gut, but before Simon called him out on his methods, he had never thought it was any different than having a talent for music or art.

The longer they were in the house, the more uncomfortable Vic became on a deep level. He was new at paying attention to these feelings, and he wasn't entirely comfortable with the vulnerability that came with them. But Simon's example had shown him the value, so he kept trying.

"We definitely need Simon in on this." Vic sorted through his impressions, trying to put them into words. "I've got the feeling that some of these things might be dangerous in the wrong hands. I'm not the guy to ask about ghosts, but since these props belonged to talented, driven, ambitious, and probably narcissistic performers, it's not impossible that energy—or ghosts—came along for the ride."

"That might determine recommendations on how the items should be handled, but it doesn't explain how Sheldon died," Ross pointed out.

"Did he have next of kin?"

Ross shook his head. "Not according to the report. What happens to his stuff isn't usually anything we'd care about unless it's evidence in a crime."

"It might be nice to prevent the pieces from being part of future crimes," Vic muttered, but he knew Ross was right. "Simon has contacts. If the lot comes up for auction, he'll know how to make sure the bad stuff goes home with people who can handle it."

"And the murder?"

"I can't prove it, but I think there's something supernatural involved—whether it's a ghost or a curse." Vic carefully chose his words since "gut feeling" only went so far in policing. "And I don't think Sheldon killed himself. I'm going out on a limb here, but I can't shake the idea that this is somehow tied into the Ocean Paradise hotel—or to people Sheldon knew or things that happened when he played the venue."

"Guessing we're not putting that into our report until we can back it up?" Ross replied, and Vic knew he was lucky to find a partner who accepted the paranormal part of life.

"Captain Hargrove gives us a lot of rope, but I'd rather not push my luck. Simon should be able to validate those hunches, and if he finds spirits, maybe he can get answers."

They walked into the kitchen where Sheldon's body had been found. The chair lay on its side, but the cuffs had been taken for evidence.

"How did anyone find him if there wasn't a spouse or family?" Vic thought it sad that for all his one-time fame, Sheldon had died alone and unmourned.

"Someone called the cops reporting screaming and strange lights in the house," Ross said.

"You've seen the whole place now," Ross added, walking ahead of Vic toward the front door, which opened into the living room. "Let's see when we can get permission to bring Simon in."

Vic felt the temperature drop and caught motion out of the corner of his eye. He turned and thought he saw a flash of gray in a large mirror. For just a second, he saw the insubstantial form of a woman in the revealing costume of a magician's assistant, complete with the headband sporting a large plume.

"Get out!"

The voice reverberated in Vic's mind, nearly distracting him from the large armoire that suddenly toppled toward him.

"Vic!" Ross shouted, too far away to help.

Vic threw himself out of the way, diving and rolling to come up in a crouch, ready for the next attack. The big armoire landed with a thud and a crack, sending up a cloud of dust that left both men choking for air.

"What the hell happened?" Ross walked over to help Vic to his feet. Vic stared at the toppled wardrobe like it might bite.

"I saw a woman's ghost. She looked like someone who might have worked with Sheldon on one of his shows. She screamed at me to get out and then apparently decided to flatten me," Vic recapped.

"Why you? I don't know whether to be put out that she ignored me or happy she picked you,"

"No idea." Vic walked back for a look at the large cabinet. "She pushed this at me, and I figured it would have landed front-down. But it's door-up now, so the back of it was turned *toward* the room before. Was the ghost trying to hurt me, or are we supposed to see something inside?"

Vic carefully opened the cabinet. Dozens of boxes lay askew, contents spilling out. Vic pulled one toward him and found hand-written letters and photographs of women, mostly headshots.

Ross looked up from his box. "More of the same. Do you think Sheldon was blackmailing the women? Or was he just a tomcat who kept mementos of his conquests?"

"Hard to say." Vic checked the other boxes and found still more photos and letters. "You said he was a player—he could have had a woman in every town and groupies on the road. If the posters are accurate, the guy was good looking in his prime, and he probably had a lot of charisma. Maybe it boosted his ego to get letters and photos from them, string them along. Hell, he could have kept a harem going for years."

"The photos look posed, not like a Peeping Tom would take, so that means the women had the pictures taken and sent them along with the love notes. There's nothing indecent about them. None of these are recent—hell, they go back decades. So why would a ghost get angry now?"

Vic frowned, thinking. "Maybe she changed her mind, or they had a falling out, or she married someone else and didn't want the affair to be known. We'll get an idea real quick about whether

Sheldon was blackmailing anyone when we look at his bank records. And maybe he just didn't want to give up his 'trophies,' but the ghost woman didn't want them falling into other hands now that he's dead."

"Since all this stuff will probably be made public, that's a fair concern," Ross agreed. "Sheldon was a minor celebrity and well-known in the area. A sale will draw magic collectors, regional historians, curiosity seekers, and nostalgia hounds. Old love letters could probably fetch a good price."

"I wonder if there are more recent letters and photos around here. And many of the women from Sheldon's past might still be alive, even if they're up in years. They probably don't want their hearts spilled open to the world. It's not just embarrassing; it could cause problems with family and friends," Vic said.

"Why not just tie Sheldon up and take the letters? Why kill him, and use such an awful method? And how could the murderer have gotten out of a locked room without a trace?" Ross looked around the crowded room like the ghost might show up and explain.

"The ghost looked like she'd been his assistant in one of those flashy outfits—but since those costumes don't change much, I've got no clue about when she might have worked with him. Maybe Sheldon had a dark side. I doubt he made it clear to his girlfriends that they were part of a herd. It doesn't take much to suspect that fact didn't go down well when they found out."

"Probably not." Sarcasm was thick in Ross's voice. "But why wait until now to kill him for it? And is the ghost the killer, or just a spirit tied to the letters?"

"Good questions—and no answers." Vic put the box of letters back. "Let's get a warrant to take the boxes back to the station and go through them. We might narrow the list of suspects, and it'll keep the letters from accidentally disappearing."

"If we can get Hargrove to clear Simon on the case, we can pick up the letters when we bring him back. He'd probably like to get a read on the place with it in as close-to-original condition as possible." Ross stood by the front door. "Go on out. I'll lock up."

They stripped off the gloves and booties and returned to Ross's car. "We can stop and see if our suits are in at the tailor on the way back to the office," Ross suggested.

"That works. One more thing knocked off the to-do list," Vic agreed.

As they drove, Vic turned the events at the magician's house and the comments by neighbors they had interviewed over in his mind. He hadn't been surprised that Sheldon kept to himself. *I wonder if I'd recognize the ghost from one of the pictures. Or from promotional shots—Sheldon certainly would have kept any "beauty shots" of his act. Maybe I'm wrong in assuming that all the assistants were dressed alike. What happens after we I.D. her? Can't arrest a ghost.*

"We're here." Ross parked behind the menswear shop. "Let go of the case for a few minutes and worry about wedding stuff for a while instead."

They walked in together, and Vic scanned the shop for the man who had taken their measurements a week before.

"Have you been helped?" A portly, middle-aged man in a suit looked at them intently as if measuring them in his mind.

"We were in a week ago, and Curtis helped us order suits," Vic spoke up. "My wedding's in a week."

The man's expression grew pinched as if he'd tasted a lemon. "Curtis isn't with us anymore," he told them. "I'm Floyd. Your names, please? Let me go in the back and see if your suits are here. Please—have a seat."

Vic hoped that the negative vibes he picked up from Floyd were just in his imagination, but he had a bad feeling about the fitting. Curtis had been an upbeat younger man with a British accent who had joked, teased, and harmlessly flirted his way through their first appointment.

Floyd came back with two suits on hangers. Vic's eyes narrowed, getting the impression that something had gone very wrong.

"I'm afraid there's been a problem." Floyd looked horrified but gave them the news point-blank. "Curtis was not precise with his measuring. In particular, he had a habit of trying to convert measurements from metric in his head instead of using a calculator or just measuring in inches. His math was often…incorrect."

Floyd handed them their suits, and without having to try his on, Vic knew it was hopelessly ill-fitting. The pants were too short, and the jacket too small across the shoulders. From Ross's expression, Vic knew his friend's luck was no better.

"I'm getting married in a little over a week." Vic did his best to stay calm. "Ross is my best man. We need suits. What's possible?"

"I'm afraid we have to start over. I'll take your measurements myself right now, and since this was our mistake, I'll see if our tailors can bump you both to the front of the line given the circumstances," Floyd offered.

Getting measured all over again was the last thing Vic wanted to do after a busy day, but he didn't see any way around it. Ross nodded, looking equally unenthusiastic.

Then again, Floyd stepped right up with a way to make good, and we didn't have to fight for it, so it could be worse. This might work out. If not, I guess I'm renting a tux.

Floyd led them into the fitting room and left to get his equipment.

"Is Simon going to have the same problem?" Ross asked.

Vic shook his head. "Simon already owns plenty of suits. Between his parents' lifestyle and events at the university, he had lots of chances to wear them. He talked me into buying one because he says he wants to go on cruises."

Ross chuckled. "Yeah, that was Sheila's reason too. I pointed out that nowadays you don't have to dress up for dinner if you don't want to on ships, and she said dressing up is half the fun." He shook his head with a fond expression. "I know when I've already lost the argument."

Vic texted Simon to let him know he'd be later than usual.

Simon: *Don't sweat it. I'll make baked spaghetti. See you when you get here.*

The heart-eyes emoji in Simon's response made Vic laugh despite the circumstances.

"Hey, none of those eggplants. This is a respectable establishment," Ross fake-admonished.

"No vegetables were harmed in the texting of that message,"

Vic said. To his relief, Floyd's experience showed in how quickly he completed the new fitting.

"Give me a call tomorrow after lunch, and I should be able to tell you when they'll be ready," Floyd told them. "And again, we apologize for the inconvenience."

They thanked Floyd and walked back to the car. Vic's phone buzzed as they pulled away from the curb. He expected it to be Simon, but he frowned when "Beach House" came up on his screen.

"Mr. D'Amato? I'm calling about the beach houses you've reserved. There's been a water main break, and due to flooding, they won't be ready by your reservation dates. We will be glad to assist you in finding suitable replacements at as similar pricing as possible."

Vic closed his eyes, took a deep breath, and counted backward from ten as he tried to keep his temper. "I'm bringing my family in for my wedding. We need two large houses for the week. I don't remember seeing a lot of alternatives. Please—I really need you to come through for me on this."

"We will do our best, Mr. D'Amato," the man replied in a calm voice. Vic would have felt better if the man sounded concerned.

"I need a workable alternative. It's too large a group for a hotel, and they need kitchen access," Vic told him.

"We'll do the best we can," the man repeated, which did not fill Vic with confidence.

"Call me when you've got options." Vic ended the call and sighed. He felt a headache coming on, and his stomach had soured.

"It's off-season," Ross consoled. "That should mean more alternatives than in the middle of summer."

"I know we'll figure out something, but it's one more added stress. I want to be able to enjoy my wedding instead of being a hot mess." Vic leaned back against the seat, eyes closed.

"I think the only people who aren't stressed-out wrecks on their wedding day probably eloped to the Elvis chapel in Vegas while they were drunk."

"You're probably right about that," Vic mumbled. "But I'm a Springsteen man at heart, not much of an Elvis fan."

"Heresy!" Ross teased. "Seriously—my sister-in-law is a real estate agent. She knows all the property management groups. I'll give her a call and see if she can shake something loose. There are usually properties that aren't publicly listed but could be available if the circumstances are right."

"Still has to be affordable." Vic felt overwhelmed. "I guess we could take over the RV rentals at the campground—"

"It's not going to come to that, and no one's going to be sleeping on the beach, either," Ross told him. "Let me work my angle on this, and try not to give yourself hives over it."

"I don't have hives. But I might want to throw up a little."

"Perfectly understandable," Ross replied. "Let's hit Hargrove up to get permission to take Simon into the crime scene and get those boxes of letters, get phone records to see who Sheldon was talking to. I bet both the suits and the house rental will be fixed by the end of the day tomorrow."

Vic sat up and rubbed his temples, trying to chase away the dull throb. "Thanks. I really appreciate the help."

"That's what friends are for."

They spent the next several hours at the station, setting up what they needed for the next day. Hargrove stopped in their doorway.

"Simon's approved, and you've got a warrant to bring the boxes back to the station. Go home, start fresh tomorrow," he told them. He looked to Vic. "You can bring Simon up to speed tonight, and both you and Ross can research Timothy Sheldon online from home as easily as you can from here. Come in early. Beats spinning your wheels."

Neither man needed more prompting. Vic's stomach growled, dissatisfied with crackers from the vending machine. They packed up and headed for Ross's car.

The smell of garlic and marinara greeted Vic when he opened the door, followed seconds later by Simon in a "Kiss the Cook" T-shirt.

"Bad day?" Simon asked. "You're late, even for you."

"Too much going on. Kinda like what you had yesterday," Vic admitted. Simon pulled him in for a quick kiss.

"Go get cleaned up. Everything's ready. It's not fancy, but it'll hit the spot—and I used some of your mom's sauce that was in the freezer."

"I thought it smelled like her recipe."

"Go." Simon sent him toward the bathroom with a slap on the ass.

By the time Vic returned, the table was set with salad, bread, heaping plates of baked spaghetti, and glasses of wine.

"That looks wonderful. Will you marry me?" Vic sank into his chair.

"I already said 'yes,' but I'll be glad to say it again. No matter what went wrong, it'll look better on a full stomach."

Vic dug into the spaghetti, letting comfort food work its magic. His headache faded, and the tightness in his gut went away as he ate. Simon refilled his wine glass, and regaled Vic with the latest gossip among the boardwalk shop owners, funny things he saw on the beach earlier in the day, and some clueless tourist comments that were funny enough to break through Vic's mood and earn a laugh.

"Thank you," Vic said when he finally pushed back from the table. "You knew exactly what I needed."

"I'm glad it hit the spot." Simon gathered the dishes, and Vic put the leftovers in the fridge. Simon opened a second bottle of wine and carried it into the living room with their glasses.

"You're holding your shoulders funny, like they hurt. Did something happen?"

Vic plopped on the couch and winced. "I landed hard trying to get out of the way of an armoire a ghost threw at me."

Simon raised an eyebrow. "I'm going to get you an ice pack, and then how about you explain that a little more?" He handed Vic his wine glass, went to the kitchen for the ice, and came back, giving Vic his full attention.

Vic caught Simon up on the new case and described the magician's house in detail. Simon's expression shifted from interest to analysis when Vic mentioned the sigil boxes, and his jaw set when

Vic got to the part about the ghost's attack. The problem with the suits and the issue with the rental house made Simon reach out and take Vic's hand.

"I'm glad you got Hargrove to call me in on this one," Simon said when Vic finished. "Odds are pretty good that the magician had some dark objects in that collection—whether he knew it or not. Plus, that ghost is dangerous. I don't know whether it's the same one from the library or that's been terrorizing Gideon, but I need to do a true banishment so the ghost—or ghosts—can't hurt anyone else. You were lucky."

"I know it could have been worse. It just hasn't been my best day," Vic confided, but he smiled as he clasped Simon's hand. "Until now."

"If the ghost who attacked you is the one who killed the magician, I might be able to get her to confess," Simon replied. "It wouldn't be admissible, but you can't take a ghost to court anyhow, and at least you wouldn't have to look for the killer."

"What about the other stuff? I could end up in a bad prom tux for our wedding, and we can't fit my extended family in the bungalow even if we put a tent in the backyard." Vic knew he was exaggerating, but the pile-up at the end of the day had felt overwhelming.

"I don't care what you wear when we get married as long as we're together," Simon assured him. "We can both wear Hawaiian shirts. That's the least important part of the day. And you'll be glad to know I worked everything out with the caterer—there will be shrimp."

"Ross was worried."

"I'm sure he was." Simon leaned in to kiss Vic, and his lips tasted of garlic and shiraz.

4

SIMON

Vic was quiet the next morning. They'd received authorization to bring Simon in as a consultant. Simon had called Pete to ask him to handle the shop and was driving Vic to the magician's house, where they'd meet up with Ross.

"Cat got your tongue?" Simon teased as he drove.

Vic shrugged, then winced from the bruises he'd gotten the previous day. "I only got a couple of hours sleep, and that hurts worse than it did when I was younger. Ross was up too. We were texting while we searched everything we could find online about Sheldon and the Ocean Paradise Hotel."

"I know. I heard the keys clicking when I woke up and you were gone."

"Sorry," Vic said. "I didn't mean to wake you."

"It goes with a fresh murder and the whole cop thing," Simon replied. "Find anything?"

"A lot of information—not sure if it's going to shake out to be clues yet or not." Vic sighed.

"Sheldon's house gave me the creeps—and I don't even have your abilities. I was hoping we could coast this last week before the wedding without any chance of either of us getting hurt. Guess that was too much to ask for."

"I imagine that would be easy for plenty of people in other professions. But I talk to dead people and you're a cop."

"And we're good at what we do, and our jobs are important," Vic replied. "I know that. I'd just like to be unimportant for the next couple of weeks."

"Maybe we'll get to the bottom of this murder and things will be quiet for a while. Hey, we can hope, right?"

Vic directed Simon to Sheldon's house. Ross was waiting in his car outside.

"Don't be surprised if you get the third degree from the neighbors who weren't around when we did interviews yesterday," Ross said when he joined them on the sidewalk. "Four retirees stopped to ask me why I was 'loitering.' On the plus side, once they found out I was a cop, they were happy to talk about the 'weird' magician and his 'creepy' house."

"Oh yeah?" Vic asked as Simon stood a few feet away, trying to tune into the house with his psychic abilities while still listening to the others talk.

"Nothing concrete—just neighborhood gossip," Ross replied. "Sheldon didn't socialize. When he was still performing he'd be gone for long periods of time, but since he retired he barely left the house. Lights were on at odd hours, and he didn't bother to get to know the neighbors even though most folks on this street have lived here forever."

"Guess it wasn't a surprise that someone reported the screams to the police, if they've got a real Neighborhood Watch thing going," Vic remarked. "Sounds like they keep a close eye on things."

"I got names and phone numbers in case we have questions. I think this is the most excitement to happen here in a long while."

"Picking up anything?" Vic moved to stand beside Simon as he tried to get a read on the house. Most of the time, Simon didn't have trouble sensing ghosts or psychic energy. Light magic bubbled like champagne, while dark power felt like blood. He picked up traces of both, but heavily muted.

"Yeah—but it's strange. Maybe I'll have a better idea of what we're dealing with when we get inside," Simon replied.

He had insisted that they carry protections in the magician's house. Simon, Vic, and Ross all had amulets that deflected offensive magic—powerful enough to have saved their lives more than once. He'd gotten Vic and Ross to keep bags of salt in the pockets of their jackets and to carry iron weapons—a length of rebar, a wrench, or a crowbar—as well as their guns. Bullets wouldn't stop ghosts—but iron and salt were formidable protection.

Simon wore a silver bracelet inscribed with protective runes and had an agate whorl in his pocket to help him focus and amplify his abilities. He also had salt and an iron dagger. But unlike Vic and Ross, Simon needed to access the spirits instead of locking himself away behind a barrier. That meant leaving himself vulnerable enough to make contact, which required a calculated risk.

That was the part Vic complained about the most.

"Picking up any interesting juju?" Vic asked as the three of them put on gloves and booties.

"There are multiple ghosts, and both light and dark energies," Simon told them. "I also think that Sheldon knew he had objects with real magic—maybe even cursed—and took precautions. There are wardings on the house, and I suspect we'll find more spell work inside."

"Do you think he was a witch?" As Ross had grown accustomed to Simon's abilities, his initial reserve had given way to curiosity.

"Whether or not he was trained, I'm almost positive he at least dabbled. That can be more dangerous," Simon replied.

"You ready?" Vic met his gaze, taking his cue from Simon.

"Yeah. Just stick close and don't touch anything," Simon warned.

Ross unlocked the door and turned on the lights. Simon followed and paused just over the threshold with Vic behind him.

"What?" Vic asked.

"Everything feels different inside than it did outside," Simon replied. "I'm going to bet that Sheldon had some sort of perimeter set up around the foundation with salt and iron. All the energies are much stronger in here."

"So the question is—did he want to *keep* something out, or make sure something didn't *get* out?" Vic mused.

Simon moved into the small entranceway and had to step around the downed armoire. "Maybe a little of both. There are people—and creatures—who could be drawn to a concentration of powerful objects like dogs to the smell of food."

"Well, that's not creepy at all," Ross muttered and fingered the amulet in his pocket.

Simon saw the overturned armoire and shivered, realizing how badly Vic might have been hurt if he'd caught its full weight. "Where did you see the ghost?"

Vic eyed the wardrobe like it was a snake, and pointed to the mirror where the ghost had appeared. "Here. I was jittery the whole time we were going through the house, so I won't be surprised if you find more spooks."

"Did you have the feeling we were being watched?" Ross spoke up. "Because I did. Told myself it was my imagination."

"It wasn't." Simon examined the mirror closely without touching it, and gave the armoire a good look as well. He turned from side to side, taking in the magician's hoarded treasures. "I'd like to walk through before I reach out to the ghosts. That should give me an idea of what we're dealing with."

Ross dug in his pocket. "Here. Take these. We don't have warning stickers for 'cursed' and 'haunted' things, but if you put a biohazard label on or near something, no one is going to touch it."

"Did you have any luck figuring out who inherits this mess?" Vic asked Ross.

"No. I've got the guys at the station chasing down Sheldon's information. We know that he didn't marry and there are no children—at least none he acknowledged. Who knows if anyone can find a will under all this stuff," Ross replied.

"Once the obituary hits the news, I imagine claims will come out of the woodwork," Vic said. "Especially since Sheldon was a local celebrity."

Simon wasn't paying full attention to Vic and Ross—other voices caught his notice, and he stepped toward them, focused but not yet trancing.

"Simon? Don't go wandering off." Vic hurried to catch up.

"This place is a psychic stew." Simon walked through the living and dining rooms and into the kitchen where he studied the place where Sheldon had died. "No surprise that this room has bad vibes. There are several ghosts here. Some are active spirits, and others are repeaters—ones who are just memory loops with no personality. I'm also picking up on pieces with very dark energy that are spread through the house—and I wonder if Sheldon separated them on purpose. Those are cursed, possessed, or used blood magic. Nasty stuff."

"I'm still getting used to the idea that 'Sheldon the Magnificent' did real magic," Ross said.

"A little power and no training can create big problems." Simon's attention was divided between the conversation and the disturbing sensations.

"If I had to guess, I'd say that Sheldon was a collector who stumbled into the magic by accident," Simon continued. "He probably bought pieces he wanted to use in shows or vintage items that caught his eye. Maybe he wanted to preserve stage magic history. He might have gotten his first bad piece by accident, or maybe he knew it was off and thought he could protect people."

"Are we talking 'normal bad luck' dark energy or 'mushroom cloud' level bad?" Vic asked.

"Somewhere in between. I don't think we're likely to find something that could cause a magical Chernobyl, but it would be better if the tainted pieces don't get loose out in the world."

"Can Cassidy help? She's coming into town for the wedding. She handles this kind of thing all the time," Vic suggested.

Simon's cousin, Cassidy Kincaide, ran an antique shop in Charleston that also had a mission to get cursed and haunted items out of the wrong hands. She was a psychometric, able to read the history and magic of objects by touching them, a different kind of gift than Simon's visions and mediumship.

"Yeah, I was going to see if she could get Teag to ha—*research* public records to help figure out if there's a will or heirs." Simon had nearly said "hack," something he didn't mention in front of his cop partner for plausible deniability's sake. Cassidy's best friend Teag was one of the best hackers Simon had ever seen—aided by magic.

"If heirs or a will aren't found, the property eventually passes to the state and will likely go to auction," Ross pointed out. "That's probably not a good thing."

Simon shook his head. "No. Not good at all. But Cassidy's got a crew of friends with connections. I'm betting one of them could make arrangements to buy the place 'as is' and deal with it one piece at a time."

They walked from room to room; Simon tried to scan the piles and stacks with his eyes and his psychic gifts. Thankfully, most were inert—just plain stuff. He ignored his curiosity at the stage props and magic equipment, feeling like they'd gotten a backstage pass.

They passed a vanishing cabinet, and he felt the temperature dip. Simon didn't get too close, but he caught the fleeting image of a middle-aged man in a cutaway tux beside the box, giving off very angry vibes.

"Be at peace," Simon murmured, not a full banishing but a request for the ghost to stand down. To his relief, the ghost did not attack, although he watched them with a baleful glare.

"You should find out if Sheldon partnered with other magicians over the years, and what happened to the relationships. I just saw a ghost by that cabinet." Simon was grateful for his protective amulets and having backup because being this attuned to his gift left him vulnerable.

"Think Sheldon stiffed a sidekick or two?" Ross asked.

"Is that guy the ghost you saw?" Vic pointed to one of the posters that showed Sheldon with another man, both of them wearing tuxes.

"Yeah, that's him. We need to figure out who he was. Did we get permission to take the boxes of letters?"

"They have to be checked in as evidence, but we can go through them at the station," Vic replied.

Simon nodded. "There are women's ghosts—several. They're... sad, angry, possessive. I don't think he killed them, but either he or they couldn't let go."

"He had quite a reputation with the ladies," Ross said. "I'm surprised he lived to a ripe old age."

Something felt off to Simon. While many of the pieces around him were old and most of the spirits were not recently dead, he had the impression their power surge was new.

"I think something dialed up the magic recently," Simon told them. "I can't imagine that someone with even latent abilities could have lived in this house, let alone been a recluse. I'd guess that before then, the precautions he took worked to contain the bad mojo. Then the 'power surge' effectively shorted out his protections and made it open season."

Simon thought the only reason they hadn't been susceptible to the darker magics or besieged by restless and pissed off ghosts were the charms they wore and the weapons they carried. The spirits and the tide of magic held back—for now. He wasn't sure how much longer those protective measures would last.

As he retraced his steps through the house, Simon used the warning stickers Ross provided, marking sullied objects without touching them.

Simon glimpsed other spirits—mostly women, some dressed like performers and others in clothing from a range of decades. All were young, pretty, and tied to this place long after they should have gone to their rest. They crowded the hallway, reluctantly letting them pass.

He started with the office. "There's so much going on psychically in this house it's hard to tune into just one location," Simon told them. "I can tell there must be pieces with strong energy here, but it feels like having a dozen radios turned up to top volume all at once. Sifting through the noise is going to take time."

Next he walked around the crowded master bedroom. "I get the feeling that Sheldon was terrified of something. I'm betting he rarely left the house at the end. But was he a prisoner or a jailer?"

"Whoa." Simon stopped when they came to the bedroom with the locked door. A wave of malicious energy rocked him back on his heels, and he threw his arms out to the side to keep Ross and Vic back.

"Can you feel it?" he whispered, all his senses on high alert. It seemed impossible that his companions could have gone near that room without noticing the malevolent vibes.

"I don't like being near it," Ross admitted. "The first cops on the scene said they couldn't get it open, pick the lock, or break it down. No luck trying to jimmy the window from outside, either."

"There's some sort of spell working. I'm going to guess a containment spell to keep something in or keep everyone out," Simon whispered as if that would keep spirits from overhearing. "There's a ghost—an older man, salt-and-pepper hair, distinguished-looking but kind of...smarmy. It's more like he's imprisoned, not that he's haunting the room on his own."

"The other magician whose ghost you saw?" Vic asked.

Simon shook his head. "No, this isn't Sheldon either. No idea who the guy is."

"Can you sense Sheldon's ghost?" Ross looked worried.

"No. But that's not surprising. He just died. It can take spirits a little while to figure out they're dead and then get the hang of being seen or interacting with objects," Simon told them. "I wouldn't be surprised if Sheldon turns up. He doesn't seem like the type to just go into the light."

"Why—" Vic began when the hallway suddenly got cold enough to see their breath. Something in the locked room started pounding on the door.

"Let's go to the kitchen. I need room." Simon led the way, and the others followed.

"Cover me." Simon hurriedly removed items from the bag he had brought with him. He laid down a cloth marked with a warded circle and runes, a way to have the magical space he needed without

POINT BLANK | 57

marking the floor. Simon lit four candles at the quarters, set down salt around the outside, and stepped into the circle.

"Make a salt circle around yourself and don't step out of it or break it." Simon handed Vic a bag from his pocket. Vic and Ross knew the drill, having helped Simon face down dangerous ghosts before.

"Whatever's in there wants out real bad." Ross raised his crow-bar, although his voice sounded uncertain.

Simon felt the press of spirits around them, some curious, others frustrated, and a few faded enough to barely remember themselves. The entity in the other room had quieted. Simon's hand shook as he lit the candles, but then he stood and began the banishing ritual.

"Spirits, listen to me. If you choose to move on, I can help you. If you stay behind, you may not hurt the living. Angry ghosts— show yourselves and speak your grievance."

The air shimmered, and Simon saw a shadowy form of a young woman in a red body suit with a plume headband.

"That's her," Vic whispered.

"Why are you still here?" Simon asked.

"Tim promised we'd be together. He said he'd marry me when we finished the tour. Then I told him I was pregnant, and he said I couldn't tour like that. He cut me out of the act and ran off with my replacement."

"What is your name?"

"Sylvia."

"Sylvia…you deserved better. How did you die?"

"In a car wreck, along with my baby, just a month after Tim and I broke up."

Traumatic death, the loss of a child, and a faithless lover—all classic reasons for a vengeful spirit.

"Did you kill Sheldon?"

"No. I still loved the bastard."

"Did you see who did kill him?"

"It was the witch."

Simon frowned. "You mean the ghost in the bedroom?"

Sylvia shook her head. *"No. Tim trapped B's ghost in the bedroom. But he also bound a witch and stole his magic. When the witch died, Tim enslaved his spirit."*

"So what the audiences saw was real magic?" Simon guessed. "And the witch's ghost got away?"

"Broke loose. He wanted revenge—returned and killed Tim. I hid until it was over."

"Where is the witch's ghost?"

Sylvia's image flickered like a bad television signal. Simon realized she had already spent a lot of energy talking to him, although she didn't make herself heard to Vic and Ross. *"I don't know. He's dangerous. So is B's ghost. That's why we stay—to keep B trapped. Don't let him out,"* she warned just before she wavered and vanished.

"Simon? Are you okay?" Vic sounded worried.

Simon came back to himself and nodded. "Yeah. Could you see her? Was that the ghost you saw before the wardrobe fell?"

Vic nodded. "That's her—the ghost I saw yesterday. At least she didn't throw furniture this time."

"Her name is Sylvia, one of Sheldon's lovers. Apparently Sheldon trapped the ghost of someone named 'B' in the back bedroom. But he also stole a witch's magic and that ghost killed Sheldon and is out for blood," Simon recapped. "Gideon and Jeremy thought that Nathan Irving was a witch, so that's my top suspect."

"What about the other ghosts?" Vic asked.

"Some are the women's spirits who are B's jailers, and then there's the ghost of Sheldon's old partner who's hanging around. No sign of Sheldon yet, and the witch's ghost is gone—for now."

"Crowded place. All those ghosts are going to make it hard to get fingerprints," Ross deadpanned.

"So there's a killer ghost on the loose?" Vic swore under his breath. "How do we catch it?"

"We'll figure something out," Simon replied. "We need to take the letters and leave. This house is getting to me. But first—I've got a question." He blew out the candles, gathered the ritual materials, and nodded to let Vic and Ross know they could break their salt circles.

Simon walked to stand in front of the locked door. "Why did Sheldon trap you?"

The ghost threw itself against the invisible barrier that kept it in the room. *"He was an arrogant bastard."*

"What did you do to make him lock you up?"

"Figure it out for yourself."

Simon staggered and felt a nosebleed start.

"That's it. Pack up. You're bleeding. We're going—now," Vic ordered. His stern expression made it clear he had made up his mind. Simon nodded, drained from encountering the ghosts.

"Here." Vic handed Simon a tissue and gave him an assessing once-over. "You okay?"

"Yeah, just took a lot out of me."

"Okay, we're going to get you to the car. I've got snack bars and energy drinks," Vic said, taking charge. "You can wait there while Ross and I go back in for the letters."

"The ghosts—"

"Putting in an appearance wears them out too—right? So they should be weak until they charge up. And we'll take the salt and iron with us, so we'll be protected," Vic assured him as he walked Simon to the car.

Simon didn't like having Vic and Ross go back into the house without him, but he wasn't sure he could be much help right now. Simon got into the car while Vic dug out a sports drink and food. Simon didn't feel like eating, but he knew the aftereffects would be worse if he didn't.

"Don't go near the room with the trapped spirit. We already know that one of Sheldon's binding spells failed—let's not make it two," Simon cautioned.

"We'll be right back." Vic turned back to the house, and Simon sagged in the passenger seat, tilting his head up and pinching the bridge of his nose to stanch the blood. He nibbled the snack and washed it down, hoping eating would make him feel better.

Sheldon clearly knew that some of the objects he collected were either haunted or cursed. Did he gather the pieces to exploit them? This whole thing reeks of dark magic. But who is 'B,' and why did Sheldon hold his ghost prisoner?

Worse—what do we do about it? I'm not sure I can banish the trapped ghost by myself, and we can't let him get loose.

Vic and Ross took several trips to carry out the boxes of letters. Afterward, Vic slid into the driver's seat.

"I sent the boxes in Ross's car covered with your salt blanket to dampen the spirits. He'll get them checked in at headquarters, and once you catch your breath, we can go through them." He paused. "Feeling any better?"

"Some. Putting distance between me and the house will help— along with some Advil. I've got a killer headache."

"Ross said he'd get a start on the boxes tonight. He'll feed me names, and I'll see what I can turn up on the internet about them from home. That way you can recuperate, and we can dive back in tomorrow," Vic said.

Simon glared at him. "Don't stay up all night, or I'll be the only one standing tomorrow. We have an eyewitness testimony swearing that the killer is a ghost. He's not a flight risk. You can get more than two hours of sleep."

"The ghost could kill again," Vic pointed out. "We might not be able to arrest him or put him in jail, but we can keep him from murdering more people."

"And our odds of doing that are better if you're actually awake and functioning instead of propped up on caffeine and macho work-til-you-drop bullshit," Simon returned. "Hargrove's going to officially call this a suicide because he can't call it murder-by-ghost. So there's enough breathing room to do this right."

Vic was silent for a moment, and Simon knew his partner needed time to process.

"Thanks for what you did in there," Vic said finally. "Captain Hargrove is going to gnash his teeth over us tracking a ghost as the killer—again."

"He should be getting used to it." Simon kept his voice quieter than usual to soothe his aching head.

"Do you think that the witch's ghost was just out to get Sheldon, or is he a general threat?" Vic asked.

"When a spirit gets strong and angry enough to do murder—

especially that kind of a death—it's a danger to everyone, like a rabid animal," Simon answered. "We're going to have to find him and stop him."

It didn't take long to get back to the blue bungalow. Vic went ahead to unlock the door, then came back to walk Simon from the car, despite Simon's protests.

"I can tell you're hurting," Vic said. "Lie down on the couch. I'll bring you the ibuprofen, a sandwich, and some water."

"Are you sure you don't need to go back to the office?"

"I told you, Ross and I have a system. I can do exactly what I'd be doing at the office right here online until you're settled," Vic told him. "Once you're okay, I can go back in. After all, you got hurt in the line of duty."

"I'd better if we want to try to tie this up before the wedding." Simon didn't voice his concern that the vengeful spirit could turn the tables and come after them if it realized they were pursuing it.

Vic brought him food and ran some searches on his computer until Simon's pills kicked in, and he seemed convinced that Simon would be safe alone. "You okay for me to go to the office to get through the boxes faster? I can still do the follow-up here on the internet."

Simon waved in his general direction. "Go. You can fill me in when you get home."

Vic headed out, closing the door with a quiet *snick* behind him. Simon sank into the couch, breathing deeply until the pain eased.

He slept and finally woke two hours later feeling much better. When he sat up and nothing hurt, Simon realized he was hungry again. Since his headache was gone and it was only midafternoon, Simon decided to go for a walk and get something to eat while he tried to clear his mind over what had happened at the magician's house.

For Myrtle Beach, the temperature was brisk. The wind always blew this close to the ocean, making it feel colder and rustling Simon's long hair. Habit took him to Le Mizzenmast— called Le Miz by its customers—which was not packed at this time of day.

"Simon! It's about time you showed up. I'll make you a Dread Pirate Roberts," Tracey Cullen called out from behind the counter.

Tracey owned the shop, Simon's favorite place for coffee on the Grand Strand. The building had once been a pirate attraction that had gone bankrupt. The previous owners had taken all of the valuable exhibits but left the décor. Tracey couldn't afford to change it when she started the coffee shop, so she made it the theme and named all of the drinks after swashbuckling lore.

Simon headed for the counter as Tracey made the specialty coffee. He picked out a chopped salad with plenty of protein—egg, steak, and nuts—from the cooler case and paid the bill. "Do you have time to chat?"

Tracey glanced around the shop. Only a few people were sitting at tables, and they were deeply involved with their computers.

"Sure. Samir can cover the register if anyone comes in." Tracey glanced at the barista, who responded with a smile and a nod. She poured herself a cup of regular coffee and led them to a quiet table in the corner where she could see if they got a sudden surge of customers.

"So, what brings you here in the middle of the afternoon?" The tips of Tracey's long braids were blue and white in honor of Simon and Vic's upcoming wedding. She was Simon's best friend and had agreed to stand for him at the ceremony.

Simon glanced around, assuring himself that no one was close enough to hear their conversation.

"I think I'm being haunted by an old hotel."

Tracey raised an eyebrow. "Want to explain that—after you eat your salad? No offense, but you look like something the cat dragged in right now."

Simon wolfed down his food, surprised that he was still hungry and taking it as a good sign. Tracey filled him in on local gossip as he ate.

"So here's what's going on," he told her when he finished. Simon filled Tracey in on the "coincidences" connected to the Ocean Paradise Hotel. "Now we're dealing with the murder of a magician who used to be the headliner there. Even the ghosts are linked to the hotel. I don't know whose spirit is trapped, but he's big trouble—and the ghost that actually killed the magician is still on the loose."

Simon ran a hand through his hair. "I've got a lot of puzzle pieces but no idea what the picture looks like that I'm trying to put together."

Tracey had listened quietly, with clear expressions of surprise and concern. "The hotel was torn down fifty years ago. Why is it causing problems now? What made it switch on?"

Simon sipped his drink for a moment, savoring the rich warmth. "There's an exhibit at the art museum that brings together photos and paintings from the hotel as well as furnishings. Plus, a new book and documentary. I think all of that gave energy to the memories."

"Are those things enough to do that?"

Simon shrugged. "I'm guessing…maybe. Then there was the woman who asked me to do a séance—her daughter drowned at the Ocean Paradise. The magician who was killed did shows there. The showgirl ghost worked for the magician. The witch might have been a rival magician. And whatever that evil spirit is who's trapped, I'm betting there's also a connection."

"How do you deal with a haunted hotel that no longer exists?"

Simon had always appreciated that Tracey accepted his psychic abilities without issue. She had been one of the first people he met when he moved to Myrtle Beach, depressed over losing his academic career and boyfriend. Tracey had encouraged his idea for Grand Strand Ghost Tours, helped him make local connections, and introduced him to people who had become some of his closest friends.

"I don't know," Simon admitted. "But we've got to solve this before the wedding. I'm afraid that if we don't, it'll put everyone in danger."

Tracey leaned back in her chair, one finger toying with the rim of her coffee cup. "If something stirred up old energy, then maybe it's because things from the past were never laid to rest. If you can find the connection and settle it, then things might go back to normal."

"I like that theory, but I'm still a little fuzzy on the details," Simon confessed. "I'm dreading going through those letters, but I'm hoping we'll find some clues."

"Did you ever work at a hotel?" Tracey asked.

Simon shook his head. "No. Although I waited my share of tables while I was in grad school."

"I worked my way through a lot of the hotels up and down the Strand from the time I was in high school. Sometimes I was wait staff, sometimes kitchen help. I had aunts who worked housekeeping. I heard all the gossip—and saw plenty myself. Lots of bad stuff happens in even the nicest hotels."

Simon considered what she said for a moment. "What are you thinking?"

"People have affairs, commit murder—or suicide, they run con games and scams based out of the hotel rooms. Managers take advantage of their workers; powerful people misuse weaker ones," Tracey said. "There's a lot of room for grievances and grudges— some for a very good cause."

She finished her coffee and set the cup aside. "The entertainers were a whole 'nother thing. They were always sabotaging each other, jockeying for better placements or more pay, and they didn't care who got hurt. It wasn't a business for nice guys. So what the ghost told you about the magician betraying his partner—it probably wasn't the first time or the last."

"You're making me pretty glad I stuck with waiting tables."

"I imagine you saw some of the same. It happens everywhere— kitchens, offices, hotel rooms," Tracey replied. "Hotels just have so many people working in different roles, and a turnover in staff, that there's way more drama."

Simon shifted in his chair, thinking hard. "Sheldon was king of the hill for a while—until he wasn't. So he had the chance to do a lot of damage—and probably survived a lot of bad things on the way up the ladder. Lots of reasons to hold grudges and cause them. I don't know if he's the reason for the disturbance, but I think he's key to figuring it out."

He fell silent, thinking as he sipped his coffee. Much as Simon knew they needed to unravel the connection between Sheldon and the ghosts and the old hotel, he still worried that something would go wrong and affect the wedding.

"Hey." Tracey reached out to take his hand. "Quit catastrophizing. I know that look in your eyes. You've jumped from A to C to Z and decided that the world is going to end. It won't—because you and Vic aren't going to let that happen."

"I'm glad you have faith in us. I do too—honest. Everything is such a tangle right now with the wedding, even without a murder case that is unconventional."

"What kind of tangle?" Tracey leaned in, concerned.

"There were catering issues, problems with the suits for Vic and Ross, and then an issue with the beach houses we rented for his family. So far, everything's worked out okay or looks like it will, but there isn't much time left, and chasing down fixes makes everything more stressful."

Simon felt like he was whining, but he knew Tracey would understand. He didn't like to let on to Vic just how much the snafus had bothered him because he didn't want Vic to be even more upset. Tracey was safe and neutral…and a good listener.

"Wedding jitters are totally normal," she assured him.

"I don't have 'wedding jitters.'"

"You sure? It's not the same as cold feet. My sister was a wreck the week before her wedding…the whole month, to be honest."

"Really?" Simon had attended the weddings of friends and colleagues but hadn't been in the wedding parties. He'd never gotten the behind-the-scenes view, just the polished ceremony and reception.

"Oh, my God," Tracey replied. "My mom was threatening to spike my sister's coffee to get her to calm down. She had us all on edge. Same sort of hassles—the dress didn't fit right, people in the wedding party had travel problems, the flower girl got sick…it was a bunch of small stuff all at once when everyone was already stressed. I thought we'd all be washing down anxiety meds with vodka before we ever got to the ceremony."

"I've got to say…it's crossed my mind. Just kidding," Simon hurried to assure her.

"You wouldn't be human if you didn't think like that." Tracey smiled. "Just understand when Vic is probably doing the same thing."

"He comes from a big family. Lots of High Mass weddings. He's used to this sort of thing. Compared to that, we're low drama."

Tracey shrugged. "Maybe. But he hasn't been at the center of it before. It's different when it's you—or so I've been told."

"Is that why you and Shayna haven't tied the knot yet?" Simon teased.

Tracey blushed. "No…we just haven't gotten to that point yet."

"Want to make it a double wedding?" Simon couldn't help joking.

"And steal your thunder? No way! You and Vic get to be the stars." She squeezed his hand. "You know you two are so cute together."

"Don't let Vic hear you say that," he mock-warned. "He's allergic to cute."

Tracey made a face. "Spare me the macho bullshit. You are so. Stinking. Cute."

"If you say so."

"I do…and I'm queen of the world," Tracey said with a grand gesture. "Okay, queen of this coffee shop."

"Thank you." Simon felt much lighter than when he had arrived.

"Any time. That's what besties are for."

Simon promised to call her with any wedding news and headed home. He took the longer route, enjoying the sunshine despite the chill, knowing that Vic wouldn't be back for quite a while.

I need to get my nerve up to go through those letters. It won't be that bad… we've faced worse. They're just letters and photos…some of them from a long time ago. And they might be important to the case.

We'll figure out which ghosts are stuck and which ones are angry, and I'll deal with them. I'm a medium. That's what I do.

Tracey's right. It will all be okay. Just jitters. I know Vic is the right guy for me. I love him, and I can't wait to be husbands.

We're lucky to get married. Our community fought hard for the right. All these distractions don't matter. I need to focus on the important stuff.

Simon had just entered the kitchen when his phone rang, interrupting his thoughts.

He took one glance at the number and stopped in his tracks. *Mom.*

Simon's hand shook. He waited for the call to go to voicemail before he pressed play.

"Sebastian, dear. It's been too long since we've talked. Your father's gotten a promotion, Jacen is Chair of the department now…there's more. Call me." Gloria Kincaide sounded as imperious as always and used Simon's hated first name instead of the middle name he preferred.

Simon took a few deep breaths to calm himself. After the upset his mother had caused months ago by trying to force Simon to return to the university and reconcile with Jacen, his former boyfriend, he'd made it clear that he no longer wanted anything to do with her. To his surprise, Gloria had not tried to contact him.

She knows. Somehow, she knows about the wedding.

Simon had no intention of inviting his parents to the wedding. He'd sworn his aunt to secrecy and knew she shared his views about Gloria's habit of manipulating people like chess pieces.

He dropped onto one of the kitchen chairs, shaking. The phone clattered to the table.

Goddamn it! How can she still do this to me? I'm thirty-four years old. I'm not a child. She's got no fucking right to bother me when I told her to stay away.

I should have blocked her number. I still can.

The only reason Simon hadn't was in case something happened to his father. Their relationship had always been complicated, but not nearly as fraught or controlling as with Simon's mother.

I guess cutting all ties is harder than it sounds, even when it's deserved.

"Simon?"

He startled, not having heard Vic come in. "I didn't expect you back yet."

Vic waved him off. "Ross and I got through nearly all the boxes. He's going to finish up and text/email me what he finds. I'll do the online thing again. Hargrove was fine with it. He knows we're all much safer when you get to recover."

Simon nodded, still upset by the call, staring at his phone like it would bite.

"Sweetheart, what's wrong?" Vic knelt beside his chair and took both of Simon's hands in his. "Tell me."

"Mom called. She hasn't tried to contact me in months, and now she called out of the blue—Vic, somehow she knows about the wedding."

Vic reached up to touch Simon's cheek. "Maybe not. And even if she does, we didn't invite her."

Simon gave a bleak laugh. "My mother the narcissist always finds a way to make everything about her. I wouldn't put it past her to show up with Jacen and make a scene."

"Your father wouldn't stop her?"

Simon shook his head. "He's never been able to stand up to her. I think he was afraid if she stopped trying to run my life, she'd turn her focus on him."

"You do remember that between my family and our friends from headquarters, the wedding is going to be lousy with cops," Vic pointed out. "Bad place to disturb the peace."

Simon leaned forward, head in his hands. "Yes, we could stop her. It's not like I think she's going to show up and shoot anyone. But the disturbance is the whole point—to ruin the day and leave her mark on it. She can't stop us from getting married. She's just pissed I didn't marry the guy she picked for me."

"The asshole," Vic growled.

"That's as good a name as any." Simon felt a panic attack coming on. He hadn't had one in a long time, not since the aftermath of the last time his mother interfered, trying to break up his relationship with Vic.

Gloria preferred Jacen because he came from a well-off family, had tenure teaching at the university—and most of all, because he flattered her and let her push him around.

"How do you want to handle it?" Vic asked in a gentle voice.

Simon raised his head and gave him a wobbly smile. "I'd like to ignore it. But if she did somehow find out about the wedding, she could still show up and make a mess. I'm going to have to man up and deal with it. Except…I'm not sure how."

"You have faced down vengeful ghosts, monsters, and demons. I believe in you. You can handle Gloria."

"You'd think, huh?"

"We could get a restraining order."

"She'd ignore it. Arresting her would be the drama she wants."

"We're inviting Cassidy's friend, the vampire, to the wedding. Maybe he…"

Simon glared at him. "No."

"Anyone you can send to haunt her?"

"She's oblivious to things like that. She barely notices living people unless she wants something from them."

"Okay…what does your mother like even more than ruining your life?"

"Being the center of attention," Simon replied. "She'd pass up the wedding if she won the lottery, or the Nobel Prize, or was named Patron of the Year."

"I imagine something could be arranged…" Vic mused.

Simon looked up sharply. "What are you thinking?"

"Captain Hargrove knows a lot of people in Columbia. He's worked with a lot of charities. Your mother likes to make big donations, right?"

Simon nodded.

"Maybe the chief can call in some favors."

"I'm glad you're honest, because you're devious."

"They say that there's a certain type of person who either becomes a cop or a criminal," Vic replied. "Good thing I have you to keep me on the straight and narrow."

Simon couldn't resist a smirk. "I'm not sure about 'straight.'"

Vic grinned. "That's my boy."

5

VIC

"Timothy Sheldon was a real love-em-and-leave-em sort of guy." Ross leaned back in his chair.

"The short way to say that is 'asshole,'" Vic replied. He, Ross, and Simon had the boxes of letters spread out on a large table in the police department conference room.

"He must have had incredible charisma. That's probably part of how he was so good on stage," Simon suggested. "But when he used it one-on-one, it became a weapon."

Ross and Vic had made a couple of passes through the letters the night before, making notes and searching for the writers online, even if the only reference was an obituary. They gave Simon the key points, and then dove in once more, trying to look at the correspondence from yet a different angle in search of clues.

Today they sorted through the letters by date mailed and then grouped them by girlfriend. While many of the envelopes held snapshots, none were risqué.

"So the guy was a total heartbreaker but not a creeper." Vic stared at the piles of yellowed envelopes. "He took advantage of them, but nothing in the letters suggests he bilked them out of money or was a bigamist or assaulted anyone."

"He led them on, abused their trust, and then either he broke it off, or they found out he was cheating," Simon put in. "Not exactly a victimless crime…but hardly illegal. From what you found online, it sounds like most of them dusted themselves off, found someone else, and lived a long and reasonably happy life."

"Except for Sylvia," Ross pointed out. They had found letters from the former stage assistant and identified them by her photo, which matched her apparition. "Sheldon didn't directly cause her death, but his actions created the circumstances that led to her accident."

"That wouldn't have held up in court," Vic replied.

"No, but it's the chain of events that's probably led more than one jilted lover to commit murder." Simon set the letter he'd been reading aside. "Sylvia was angry at Sheldon, but she didn't kill him," he mused. "Although I suspect she and the other ghosts made his life miserable. Now that they've had a chance for their story to be heard, and assuming we can keep the letters from going public, the ghosts might fade or move on of their own accord."

"That doesn't explain the scary thing trapped in that bedroom." Ross shuddered.

"Since the Ocean Paradise keeps popping up, let's take another look at the women who were involved with Sheldon when he played there." Simon toyed with an envelope as he thought aloud. "Maybe there'll be something in their letters that stands out."

They dug into the piles once again, narrowing the range.

Simon looked up after they had read for a while. "There's a letter from Valerie who says that B had been bothering her since Sheldon went on the road. That seems to be a theme through her letters. I interpret that to mean B was hitting on her when Sheldon wasn't around to stake his claim. So who is B? A full name would be good."

"The letters I have are from Amy," Ross said. "Same sort of thing. B harassed her, but no one would listen or do anything, and she said that only Sheldon had the clout to make him stop."

"I'm not sure whether Lacey was before or after the ones you've read, but very similar story." Vic put down the envelopes. "My guess

POINT BLANK | 73

is that B was someone senior enough to have protection. He harassed and probably assaulted female employees and entertainers with impunity. That sort of scumbag knows how to stay under the radar and cover his ass."

"We have the date range of the letters to narrow the search." Simon got up and paced, swinging his arms to loosen tight muscles after sitting for hours. "There are two ways to find him—comb through employment records—assuming those still exist after all this time. Or hunt down other women who worked at the Ocean Paradise during those years. I'd bet anything that they'd know who B is."

"Well, that's the next step then," Vic said. "If the ghosts wanted us to read the letters, then maybe finding B is still important to figuring out how Sheldon died."

"Once we know who the angry ghost locked in the bedroom is, can you send him packing?" Ross turned to look at Simon.

"I should be able to—with a banishment or an exorcism. Sylvia's ghost said a witch killed Sheldon. The bedroom ghost couldn't have been the killer because it's locked up. The other spirit, who I think was an old magician partner, wasn't very strong. He glared at me, but left when I told him to go. And the women who are haunting the house—they're guarding the trapped ghost, but we can't rule them out as Sheldon's killer just yet."

"I'd like to know more about the witch," Vic said. "Sheldon enslaved a spirit and made it serve him. So did it kill Sheldon when it escaped?"

"Odds are good that Nathan Irving was the witch, at least from what Gideon and Jeremy uncovered in their research. But it isn't a certainty." Simon toyed with a pencil as they talked. "I'm worried about what happens when—not if—Sheldon's ghost turns up."

"Speaking of which…while you're here, how about you take a look at the cards Sheldon choked on," Ross suggested. "Not exactly pleasant, but you're likely to pick up something about them beyond what our crime scene folks saw."

"Sure." Simon looked nauseous at the thought. "Just remember

—I'm a psychic, not a psychometric. So I'm not going to read anything by touching them, although I might get a vision later."

Vic and Ross accompanied Simon down to the evidence room. The cards were in a plastic bag, mangled and warped.

"They look like a custom deck." Simon pointed to the ornate art on the backs. "Let's suppose that Gideon and Jeremy are right and Irving really was a witch. Maybe Irving had commissioned a special deck of cards, something he could have used in a ritual to enhance his abilities. I'm betting they would have been very personal to him —and that would have given the cards power. Sheldon might have stolen them and used the cards against Irving to siphon magic."

Ross snapped photos of the cards' art on both sides, and the officer returned the bag to the evidence locker.

"So where is Sheldon's ghost in all of this?" Vic asked as they went back to the workroom. "Why isn't he haunting the house along with everyone else? Where do ghosts go when they're not…ghosting?"

"Like I mentioned before, sometimes it takes a spirit a little while to get its bearings after death," Simon told them. "Apparently dying is disorienting. I know you're in a hurry to solve this, but ghosts don't usually show up immediately. Sheldon might be collecting his wits, so to speak, after being murdered. More like gathering energy. And since new ghosts aren't usually as powerful as older haunts, he might be staying out of the way of the other spirits —especially if one of those spirits is Irving."

"You think they're all in the house together?" Ross asked.

Simon frowned. "Here's my theory. If Gideon and Jeremy are right, Irving is our best candidate for being a true witch. He was always competing with Sheldon and probably resented that Sheldon was more famous even though he lacked real magic. We can see if anything in their research for the book and the documentary bears this out, but Irving might have used his magic to harm people he didn't like. At some point, Sheldon found a way to steal Irving's magic and use it. Later, he might have killed Irving and enslaved his ghost to help in the show."

Vic nodded. "Then Irving's ghost broke loose from Sheldon's

control and maybe had something to do with the other people your sources say came to a bad end." Vic theorized. "He also found a way to get past the protections Sheldon set on the house and returned to kill him."

"What about the ghost behind the locked door?" Ross asked.

Simon shrugged. "No idea. But I'm sure he's related somehow to the Ocean Paradise."

"Won't poking around in the house bring Irving's ghost back?" Ross looked worried.

"I think Irving's spirit might have been the one who has been harassing Gideon and Jeremy," Simon speculated. "He got out after Sheldon died, and he might be dealing with loose ends. But I don't think he can move on—and we can't let him stick around."

"Can you banish that many spirits?" Vic asked, worried.

"Looks like I'm going to have to. But I think we can get help from Gabriella and Miss Eppie. This is starting to feel like *Murder on the Orient Express*. Lots of suspects and everyone's got a motive." Simon sighed, looking at the stacks of letters.

"Except I'm not getting the impression that the murder was a group project," Ross pointed out. "And the most likely ghost to have done it is in the wind."

"It would be good to get rid of Irving's ghost before Sheldon's returns," Simon replied. "If the two of them go at it in spirit form, it could be…epic."

It took less time than they expected to come up with a list of women in the area who had worked for the Ocean Paradise at the right time. Simon returned to the shop while Vic and Ross went to see if the old hotel's former employees could shed light on who Sheldon might have hated enough to trap his ghost and become his jailer.

"It's been a long time. I was just a waitress. I'm not sure what good it does to talk about it," Margaret Kennison said as she sat on the front porch with Vic and Ross. "Most of the people from back then are dead."

"New evidence has surfaced in a related case. I'm sorry to bring up bad memories, but anything you recall could help," Ross said. "Especially about people Timothy Sheldon didn't get on with. There are some...peculiarities...around his death."

Margaret gave an unladylike snort. "People Tim didn't get on with? We could be here all day and not get through the list. Tim had terrific charisma when he turned it on, but he could be a real jerk when he didn't bother being charming."

"Anything you could tell us might help," Vic coaxed. "Did he part ways badly with a former magic partner? Have a falling-out with his manager?"

Margaret thought for a moment. "Sheldon treated the staff and crew well. He didn't get on well with other magicians or some of the people in management, from what I saw and heard."

"Do you remember any names? Does Nathan Irving ring a bell?" Vic asked.

"The witch? That's what everyone said about him back in the day. I didn't believe it at first, but later on, I wondered," she said. "He and Sheldon had a terrible rivalry, according to the gossip."

"Anyone else come to mind?" Ross probed.

Margaret tucked a lock of gray hair behind one ear. At seventy-something she had a lean energy that made Vic guess she had been utterly vivacious as a young woman. "Billy Bowden. He was a pig," she said finally, with a set of her jaw as if to dare them to say otherwise. "Always hitting on all the women. Sheldon had his faults, but when he was around, Bowden kept his hands to himself."

"I don't recognize that name," Vic said. "Who was he?"

"Bowden was the events manager at the Ocean Paradise back in the day," she answered. "He didn't run the hotel, but he held sway over the entertainers, and because he booked and managed the special events, he also had a lot of influence over the food service side of things."

"Did people call him B?" Vic asked.

Margaret chuckled. "Not to his face. And that didn't stand for his name—it stood for 'bastard' or 'SOB,' Because he was all that and more." Her voice held contempt and cold anger.

POINT BLANK | 77

"What do you remember? He might have been involved in some crimes that have recently come to light," Ross said.

She gave a harsh laugh. "Oh, B was 'involved in some crimes'— that's for sure. Never punished for any of them, in this life at least. He was abusive to the staff—screamed, swore, and threw tantrums if everything wasn't just to his liking. Had big burly male chefs on the verge of tears or homicide, more than once."

"You said he harassed women?" Ross ventured.

Margaret turned a cold eye on him. "What do you think? He tried to seduce everything in a skirt that caught his eye, and if he couldn't get them willingly, he threatened their jobs or caught them alone in a hallway. B always got what he wanted," she added bitterly.

Margaret sat back and shook her head. "Timothy Sheldon was a tomcat for sure, but he didn't have to threaten or assault anyone. That man could charm the birds from the trees. All he had to do was turn his charisma on most of the women—and some of the men—and they'd give him anything he wanted."

"Most of them? What about the hold-outs?"

"Some of us had partners, and we didn't play those games," Margaret said. "Not that we didn't see the appeal—we just knew nothing would come of it, and it wasn't worth the grief. But that was the difference between Sheldon and Bowden—Sheldon knew there were more fish in the sea and moved on. Bowden took rejection as an affront to be conquered." Her expression twisted in disgust.

"Sheldon and Bowden must have had to work together, with Sheldon headlining so often at the Ocean Paradise," Vic prompted

"By the time I worked there, Sheldon was taking his act up and down the coast. But he always came back to the Ocean Paradise twice a year for an extended engagement. So I wasn't around when he was on his way up and played there for years at a time. But I heard the stories."

"Do you remember the names of any of the women who were romantically involved with Sheldon?" Ross asked. "If you wouldn't mind sharing them with us."

The day was pleasant, and Margaret had settled them on the

porch with a pitcher of iced tea. She sat on the swing while they turned rockers to face her.

Margaret chewed her lip as if deciding what to say. "What the hell. I don't know if the women will want to talk to you, but that's up to them." She thought for a moment and then gave five names that Vic wrote down.

"Did Bowden and Sheldon fight over a woman?" Ross asked.

"Bowden was jealous of Sheldon. That was plain as day to everyone. He hated how easily Sheldon got women. Sheldon was handsome and debonair. He knew how to make a girl feel like a princess, and he rarely had one-night stands. Serial monogamy, I think they call it now."

She took a sip of her tea. "Bowden, on the other hand, was smart, but he wasn't good looking, and he had the charm of a rabid dog. He was extremely driven, and a chronic liar. There was nothing attractive about the man—although he could organize and put on a good show."

"Why didn't Bowden just fire Sheldon?" Ross asked.

"The way we heard it, he couldn't," Margaret said. "Because the owner of the hotel liked Sheldon, and his act brought in a lot of money. I don't know if it's true, but rumor had it that Bowden fired him once, and the owner rehired Sheldon and called Bowden on the carpet."

"I don't imagine that improved their relationship," Vic deadpanned.

Margaret snorted. "Ya think? But Bowden was sneaky. So he just undermined Sheldon any way he could. Short staffing on nights he played, so guest service was bad, and the restaurant was slow. Poor stage lighting and incompetent stagehands until Sheldon got to the point where he wrote it into his contract that he picked the crews. It was all stuff that the owner didn't notice and could be passed off as bad luck, but Sheldon and Bowden both knew it was war."

"Did Bowden ever threaten Sheldon?" Ross asked.

Margaret looked like she was picking her words carefully. "I'm positive Bowden took financial advantage of performers because I overheard some of them talking in the bar more than once. He took bribes to book acts, blackmailed them if anyone in their band got out of line, held it over their heads if he had to bail them out of any trouble. There was talk that he had some connection to the Atlantic City Mob. I don't know if he spread that around to make people afraid of him, but I don't think he would have had any qualms about working with that sort if they'd have had him."

"Did he try any of those things with Sheldon?" Vic found himself pulled into the story.

She frowned. "I doubt it. Sheldon would have gone straight to the owner, and while Bowden was good at managing events, he could have been replaced in a heartbeat compared to Sheldon."

"I'm guessing that it couldn't go on like that forever without coming to a head," Vic said.

Margaret nodded. "Oh, they were heading for a showdown for sure. Thing is, once Sheldon went on the road after he got famous enough to tour, we heard rumors that maybe some of his magic wasn't an act. Like 'sold his soul to the Devil' kind of things."

"Like what people had said about Nathan Irving?" Ross asked.

"Irving hated Sheldon. Irving wasn't flashy enough to compete, even though people said he might have been a better magician," Margaret recalled. "And I don't know the details, but I think Irving and Sheldon did fight over a woman at one point. I never heard a name. Then there was the wedding. Irving's daughter and Sheldon's nephew. Only a tragedy happened, and that turned a rivalry into a blood feud."

"The rumors about Sheldon selling his soul or having real magic. Did people believe it?" Vic knew that while there could be truth to such things, most folks considered them legends.

"Stage people are superstitious. I heard the gossip because I worked the dinner theater nights. Sometimes Sheldon played to the auditorium, but other nights he'd do a more intimate show for high ticket folks in a smaller room at the hotel. The audience loved him. I've got to say—some of his effects were awfully hard to explain."

Vic and Ross exchanged a look. *That's because Sheldon really might have been using stolen magic to enhance his show.*

"Did Bowden believe Sheldon was doing 'real' magic?" Ross asked.

"I thought Bowden always underestimated Sheldon. I mean, I was just a waitress watching everything from the edge of the room, but Sheldon had talent, and he was a very good performer. Bowden was always putting him down to anyone who would listen. And when the stories about actual magic started going around, Bowden lost his mind over it," Margaret recalled.

"What happened?" Vic couldn't help feeling like he was caught up in a soap opera.

"I didn't see it happen, but we all heard about it. One night a spotlight started to fall. It would have killed anyone underneath it. And everyone swore that Sheldon put out his hand and yelled something and the spotlight hovered in midair and lowered gradually to the stage." She smiled at their reaction.

"No wires?" Ross asked.

She shook her head. "No, and I got that account firsthand. Everyone was talking about it. The audience loved it—thought it was part of the show. It wasn't—and the stage crew was going bananas because they thought it was sabotage."

Margaret finished her glass of tea. "Afterward, I heard that Sheldon and Bowden got in a huge fight. Sheldon accused Bowden of rigging the light to fall, Bowden denied it but used a lot of ugly words, and Sheldon said he'd make sure Bowden got fired and never worked again."

"And did he get fired?" Ross looked as caught up in the story as Vic was.

"Worse—or better, depending on your point of view," Margaret shared with a cat-that-ate-the-canary expression. "Bowden got so angry he had a heart attack in his office. Probably wasn't really that strange—he was middle-aged, heavy-set, and always angry about everything. But…"

Vic raised an eyebrow. "But?"

"Bowden had this fancy watch. Super-expensive—he always wore it, and he made sure he pulled his sleeve up so everyone saw it. Gold and diamonds and some big brand name. It disappeared. His body was in a locked room, and when they came to take him away, the watch was gone."

"Did they find it? Was anyone convicted of stealing it?" Ross asked.

"Oh, plenty of accusations flew around, but I never heard that anyone was charged or that they ever found the watch," Margaret replied.

If Bowden cared a lot about that watch, I bet Simon would say it was the kind of thing that a witch might use to trap his spirit. Is Bowden the ghost in the bedroom? Why would Sheldon keep him prisoner? We need to look again in Sheldon's house and see if we can find the watch.

Vic and Ross had finished their tea, and Vic set his glass aside. "You've been very generous with your time. Thank you for sharing your stories. I'm sorry to bring up bad memories."

Margaret stood to walk them to the steps. "You know, it wasn't as bad as I expected, because that son of a bitch Bowden didn't win. After he died, the new events manager was a big improvement, and he was there until the hotel closed. All the people Bowden hurt didn't exactly get justice, but they got to see his downfall, which was all the justice we were ever going to get."

Ross and Vic thanked her again and drove away. They were quiet for a few minutes, and then Vic glanced at his partner. "Some story, huh?"

"Sounds like Sheldon wasn't an angel, but he used his clout to protect women from Bowden."

"If he stole magic from Irving, did he use that to kill Bowden? Because what Margaret said about Bowden's death sounds mighty suspicious," Ross replied.

Vic nodded. "Yeah, I thought so too. But if the trapped ghost is Bowden—and how do you trap a ghost; I thought they could float through walls—why did Sheldon keep him locked up in the spare room? On one hand, it's rough justice, and it's petty vengeance. But did Sheldon think Bowden as a spirit might do more harm if he was loose than he did as a living person?"

"You and Simon know more about the woo-woo stuff than I do, but Bowden sounds like a real piece of work," Ross replied. "Irving was a real peach too. But what did Sheldon plan to do with the ghosts—or did he figure once he died, it was someone else's problem?"

"I think Simon would have zeroed in on Bowden's watch. He always says ghosts who don't move on often have an object that anchors them here. If Sheldon had the watch, that might be the key to getting rid of Bowden's ghost," Vic said. "I'm honestly surprised nobody offed Bowden sooner."

"No kidding."

They spent the rest of the morning interviewing other former workers at the Ocean Paradise. They all recounted stories similar to what Margaret had told them, adding details and other incidents. Nothing undercut her recollections, and everyone agreed that Bowden was a dangerous asshole, Irving was a jealous loser, and Sheldon was a philanderer.

"I never should have said anything about having a wedding coming up," Vic lamented as they left the last interviewee's house. "How come everyone thinks it's a great idea to share wedding disaster stories? Like I didn't have enough to worry about."

Ross chuckled. "We heard some doozies, didn't we?"

People in the food, beverage, and events staff would have been the ones with the closest acquaintance to both Sheldon and Bowden, so they also were the employees who worked the weddings that had been held at the Ocean Paradise.

That meant they regaled Vic and Ross with tales of jilted brides, drunk grooms, unfaithful members of the wedding party, vindictive exes, and petulant parents, as well as food poisonings and a few disasters Vic thought might have been curses in action.

"By the way—how are the wedding plans going?" Ross asked.

"I need to check in with the tailor on our suits," Vic said. "And I'm supposed to call the rental company this afternoon to go over the beach houses they have available for the family. We might have to get two houses near each other, but I'm afraid the aunts will have a fit if we do that. I'm hoping it all works out."

He tried and failed to stifle a yawn. "And I could do with more sleep, but that's not happening until we close the case."

"How's Simon holding up?"

Vic sighed. "He's worried that his mom will somehow find out—or has found out—and will make a scene. Unfortunately, I don't think that fear is completely unfounded."

"There are government events that don't have as much police presence as your wedding is going to have. Do you think it's really a risk?"

Vic turned to look out the passenger window. "Simon's right that her goal wouldn't be stopping the wedding. It would be ruining the day for him, putting her mark on it, spoiling the memory, and making herself the center of attention."

"That sucks. Could you ask Miss Eppie to put a root on Simon's mom?"

Miss Eppie—Ephigenia Walker—had a local reputation as a powerful Hoodoo practitioner. She had helped them out on more than one occasion when they had needed allies to go up against a supernatural enemy.

"I could, and I'm sure she has the ability to do that, but she doesn't do curses," Vic replied. "That's why she's one of the good guys."

"Bummer."

"On the 'bright' side, since Gloria doesn't believe that Simon's abilities are real, she's unlikely to try to put a curse on *us*." Vic had been turning the problem over in his mind all morning. He hated seeing how distressed Simon had been and wished he could come up with a simple solution.

"I guess that's something," Ross said. "Be grateful for small favors."

Just as they parked at the police department, Vic's phone rang. "It's my mom," he told Ross. "I'll catch up to you."

Vic walked over to a picnic table in the shade at the side of the parking lot. "Hey, Mom, what's up?"

"I'm sorry to call while you're at work," Bernadette D'Amato said, "but Aunt Sophie has been asking whether you've found a new beach house yet. I told her I'd ask to keep her from calling you directly, but I figured if you had, you'd have told me already."

"I'm working on it." Vic sighed. "I'm sorry it's gotten so complicated."

"No reason for you to be apologizing, honey. You got the rug pulled out from under you. I wish you'd let us help."

"It's easier if I handle it because I can go see the properties. Not all beach houses are created equal. I don't want to book you in some place that has great photos online and is a trash heap in person."

"Much appreciated, but I believe we could handle that if it happened," she assured him. "How's everything else? You sound a little off."

"You know how it goes," Vic admitted. "I was hoping we'd have a quiet week, and we got sucked into a case. I'm doing my best to get it resolved before the wedding."

"A regular case or one that needs Simon's abilities?"

His parents were still getting used to the idea of Simon's psychic gifts being real. But they were doing their best to accept that truth and had already proven their fondness for Vic's fiancé.

"We've already pulled Simon in to consult. It's messy. But we got a couple of breaks today, so that's a good thing."

"You know the wedding doesn't have to be perfect, right? We aren't coming to have you put on a show to entertain us. And no matter what happens, it won't be as bad as when your cousin Christopher's plus-one turned out to be allergic to incense and threw up all over Great-grandma Isabella during Mass."

"That was pretty hard to forget," Vic agreed, chuckling despite himself.

"And the wedding still went on," Bernadette—Bernie for short —said. "So relax. It will all work out. Everyone's rooting for you. Uncle Peter says he's glad it'll be a shorter service because that means we get to eat sooner. By the way, you are still having shrimp, right?"

"Definitely having shrimp," Vic assured her. "And…thanks for being you. I see what Simon has to deal with, and I feel lucky."

"We're all insane, but in a good way," his mother agreed with a laugh. "Now go catch all the bad guys so you and Simon can relax on your honeymoon."

"Love you," Vic said.

"Love you and Simon. Now go kick ass."

He smiled as he ended the call and walked to the office. Ross was back in the conference room, going through the boxes of letters from Sheldon's house.

"Any new insights after today?" Vic settled at the table with a fresh cup of coffee.

"I'm thinking that Bowden got what was coming to him."

Vic ignored the bitter taste of the coffee and enjoyed the warmth as he took a swallow. "Interesting that both Sheldon and Bowden were locked-room murders. I wonder if the same was true of Irving's death. If Sheldon stole magic from Irving, wanna bet he caused Bowden's mysterious heart failure? And maybe Irving's death as well?"

"Hard to prove, but likely," Ross agreed. "I'll see what I can find about Irving. If Sheldon could do enough real magic to stop one of the stage lights from falling, I'd be willing to bet he could mess with someone's heart. I might have a lead on one of Sheldon's partners. I found some old articles online and a few photos."

Ross sat back with a pleased smile at his discovery. "Sheldon originally worked with an older magician who taught him the ropes. Charles Magnuson, aka 'Magnus the Amazing.' He was the ghost Simon said was in the poster. From what I pieced together, once Sheldon got established, he ditched Charlie and went solo. Magnuson died of lung cancer, nearly penniless, a few years later."

"That's a dick move. So Sheldon seems to have double-crossed one of his early partners and might have stolen Irving's magic. Are there more people he might have killed? And are they all ghosts?" Vic mused.

"I guess Magnuson's ghost came back to haunt their old stage equipment. Simon didn't think he was dangerous. Maybe he just figured he'd hang around and be an annoyance for the rest of Sheldon's life," Vic added.

"Things are definitely more interesting now that we're on 'paranormal patrol,'" Ross agreed.

Vic looked up. "Do you regret it? Getting partnered up with

me? You were willing to take a chance on me when I moved down from Pittsburgh. My record didn't look good the way they wrote up the supernatural situation that happened up there, and I was still denying that woo-woo was real. Now it seems like we're always hip-deep in crazy shit."

Ross pushed back in his chair and crossed his arms. "Are you kidding? You and Simon are the best partners I've ever had. And after years of chasing lowlife perps for drug violence, you've definitely introduced me to a better grade of murderer."

Vic couldn't help being amused. "There is such a thing?"

Ross rolled his eyes. "You know what I mean. The cases are a lot more interesting since we paired up."

"And we've almost died several times," Vic added.

"Goes with the badge." Ross shrugged. "The point is, I'm happy with how things are. And I got two new best friends out of the deal —plus a window into a whole new creepy-ass world I never knew existed. So what got your knickers in a twist? Bad news from your mom?"

Vic shook his head. "No—not at all. She's chill with everything. I just want all the drama to be over and be married."

"Don't you know that the drama just starts when you get married?" Ross said with a laugh. "I thought we might want to go through the letters again now that we've got a little different perspective on both Sheldon and Bowden. And we need to get back into that house to look for Bowden's watch."

They worked in silence for the next hour, reviewing the letters. Finally, Vic looked up as he replaced the last envelope.

"The letters from the women who worked at the Ocean Paradise are different from the letters the other women sent—at least the ones in my batch," Vic said. "They aren't happy with Sheldon for going away, but it's less because he broke off their relationships and more about leaving them without someone to stand up to Bowden."

Ross nodded. "I'd say the same. Sheldon was a Romeo, but his relationships were consensual; the personal drama seems less important. Bowden was the abuser. All their comments about B are pretty damning."

Vic glanced at a wooden box they had gathered from the armoire. When they opened it and saw the inside marked with sigils and odd item it held, they put it aside for Simon and surrounded the box in a salt circle.

"I want Simon to take a look at that runed box," Vic said. "The cards inside look singed, and covered with some sort of dust. If it's true that Sheldon stole magic, I'm wondering if he used that box to work a spell."

"A love potion?" Ross asked.

Vic shook his head. "He didn't need that. My bet is some sort of protection spell, maybe to keep them safe from B when Sheldon was out of town. Simon or Gabriella might be able to say for sure."

He leaned back in his chair and stretched. "I think we're dealing with three main ghosts. Bowden—who we think is locked in the bedroom. The killer witch—probably Irving, especially if Sheldon stole magic from him, and the most likely suspect for Sheldon's killer. And Sheldon, assuming he comes back as a ghost. The other spirits seem to just be bystanders."

"While we were out, I asked Jackie to see if she could do a public records search on the women who wrote the letters during the Ocean Paradise years to see if she turned up anything you didn't find online," Ross replied. "I gave her the names Margaret told us. I figured they might know more since they were involved with Sheldon—maybe they saw or overheard something useful."

"Did she find anything?"

"Yep. There was a lot of overlap—big surprise. Some are dead, others moved away, and some disappeared. That's understandable if there were marriages and divorces or if they used a stage name when they worked with Sheldon."

"It's been fifty years," Vic said. "Not surprising."

"But we found three who are alive and living near here. It's still early—want to see if they'll talk to us?"

Privately, Vic didn't expect to make much headway. He couldn't imagine dredging up old memories of long-ago flames, even if it was the cops asking to help solve a crime.

The first name on the list wasn't home. A neighbor told them she was on an extended vacation. The second woman slammed the door in their faces as soon as they mentioned Sheldon's name, with a few choice curse words to go with it.

"Third time's a charm," Vic muttered as they approached the apartment of the last woman on their list.

A look of alarm crossed Olivia Charles's face when she opened her door to see two men with badges in her hallway.

"You want to talk about who?"

"Timothy Sheldon. You worked a magic act with him at the Ocean Paradise hotel," Vic reminded her.

"Now that's a name I haven't heard in a long time," Olivia replied with a wistful expression. "How about we go to the lounge if you want to talk."

They sat on the teal vinyl-covered chairs in the apartment lobby. The nearby soda machine rattled and buzzed.

"Now, why on earth do the police want to know about Tim after all this time? Didn't I see that he passed on recently?" Olivia's dark hair was up in a knot, a style that flattered her high cheekbones. She had a dancer's figure, even now, and carried herself with the poise of a performer.

"There are some details we're trying to make sense of," Vic told her. "We found the letters you wrote to him."

Olivia's cheeks colored, and her smile turned knowing and sad. "Oh, my. I wondered if he still had them. I'm not surprised—Tim kept souvenirs. I never made the mistake of thinking he was going to be a keeper—but he sure was a fun diversion for a while."

"So you didn't hate him?" Ross prodded.

"I wasn't happy when we broke up. But deep down, I knew Tim wasn't the marrying type. Things were good while we were together. When his contract at the Paradise ended, he moved on."

"You helped in his act?" Ross confirmed.

She laughed. "Believe it or not, I was one of those fancy stage assistants in the skimpy outfits. It was fun and paid good money— and got me out of my little podunk town, all the way to the metropolis of Myrtle Beach."

"Was there a magician that Sheldon saw as a rival—or who

disliked him? Someone who was very talented but not as famous?" Vic asked.

"Or another magician he worked with early in his career and cut out of the act later on?" Ross added.

Olivia thought for a moment. "There were rumors that Tim had a habit of stealing illusions from other magicians. Those tricks they do are closely guarded secrets, and coming up with unique ones is how they make a name for themselves. I don't know whether the stories were true. Tim had a lot of talent. Other performers could have been jealous, or he could have figured the tricks out for himself without 'stealing' anything."

"What about rivals?" Vic prompted.

"There was a guy who did a magic act at some of the other hotels on the Strand when Sheldon was headlining at the Ocean Paradise," Olivia replied. "I don't remember his name. Irving, maybe. I never saw him perform, but I heard he put on a very good show. Good enough that the reviewers couldn't figure out how he did some of the effects."

She leaned in. "The gossip was that he was a witch, doing real magic. He never denied it, and seemed to like having people specu-late. But true or not, he lacked Sheldon's stage presence. That's as much a part of a magician's act as his actual effects. The really great magicians have star power charisma. This other guy wasn't the sort anyone would look at twice."

"Did Sheldon ever go see his show?" Ross asked.

"If he did, he wouldn't have told me. Sheldon had a big ego— he would have thought it made him look weak to check out someone who wasn't even a real competitor. Now that I look back on it, I suspect he would have gone—in disguise—just to see for himself," she added.

"Did Sheldon change his show around that time? Mix in any new tricks?" Vic fished.

Olivia paused. "After all this time, things run together. Toward the end of when I worked with him at the Paradise, he did add one or two new things. They weren't effects I helped with, but I saw them from the wings. I remember thinking they were pretty impressive—I knew a lot about how things worked, and I couldn't figure out how he did them."

"Did the audience like the new tricks?" Ross pressed.

Olivia threw back her head and laughed, and Vic could see a shadow of the younger woman she had been. "The audience loved Sheldon. They lapped up anything he gave them, especially when he broke out a new trick in the act. And for all the shade he got for sleeping around, I've always wondered if he didn't have a girl in every town to give him a reason to turn down the groupies, because they got pushy."

"Sheldon wasn't a forever kind of guy, but he never took advantage of me, never promised me things he didn't mean, never harmed me. If I got a little too attached, that was my fault," Olivia said with a level gaze. "He protected me from much worse. As for the other magician…I never heard what happened to him. Maybe he gave up the gig, but he never played the Ocean Paradise while I was around."

They thanked Olivia and left a business card in case she remembered anything else.

"What now?" Ross asked in the car.

"Let's go see what we can turn up on other magicians who played the Grand Strand," Vic suggested. "They might have had more reason than Sheldon's jilted girlfriends to want him dead. Irving's my prime suspect, but we need to rule out any flesh-and-blood perps."

They stopped for a sandwich on the way back. Vic got a Reuben, and Ross got a Philly cheesesteak, and they ate outside at a table. Vic's mood lifted by the time they headed back to the office.

Vic searched the internet while Ross gave the letters another once-over, this time looking for the witch magician.

"I might have something," Vic said after a while. "Apparently, magicians have a professional association. I did some digging and found their archive. Timothy Sheldon was in it. Nathan Irving was a member from 1968 to 1973 and then isn't mentioned again."

"So maybe he stopped performing—the question is, why?" Ross

replied. "Did Sheldon really steal his magic? He wasn't mentioned in the letters, so Irving must not have been a threat to the ladies."

Vic brought up new search results and whistled in surprise. "Had to go back a few pages, but I found an article in the archives of the *Myrtle Beach Sun*. 'Local performer Nathan Irving reported missing.' It goes on to say his manager alerted the cops when he didn't do his show. There's no follow-up article that I see saying he was ever found."

"Do you have a picture?" Ross brought his chair around to look over Vic's shoulder.

Vic typed in a couple of prompts. His first attempts struck out, but finally a few grainy photos turned up. "I can see where Irving would have needed amazing charm to compete with a guy like Sheldon."

Nathan Irving's looks were unremarkable, certainly not movie-star handsome like Sheldon. His short, squat body and ill-fitting tux made him look more like a bodyguard or bouncer than a show headliner.

"If you're incredibly talented and charismatic, people forget to care about your looks," Ross noted. "But if you're not, you'd better be handsome and suave."

Vic got up to pace. "I'm going to spin out a theory here—I need you to poke holes in it."

Ross grinned. "I've got no problem doing that."

"What if Irving was getting buzz about his act despite not being as debonair as Sheldon?" Vic theorized. "Irving's act razzle-dazzled because he was doing real magic. And suppose that Irving resented coming in second to a guy who was a sleight-of-hand showman."

"Sounds possible," Ross said.

"Sheldon's always watching his back, checking out the competition. He's climbed the ladder, and he knows how fast someone can get knocked back down. Irving is good enough to worry Sheldon. Even worse, Sheldon can't figure out how to steal Irving's tricks like he's done to other rivals."

"And when he realized that the trick couldn't possibly have been an illusion, Sheldon decided he needed to steal Irving's magic," Ross finished.

Vic sat back down and crossed his arms. "If any of that checks out, it gives us motive and opportunity—but what's the means? How the hell do you 'steal' someone's magic?"

6

SIMON

"Do you remember the Ocean Paradise Hotel?" Simon asked.

Gabriella Hernandez eyed Simon across the table in the back room of her botanica. Her talent as a *bruja* had saved their asses more than once. Simon counted her as a true friend and looked to her for guidance on magical topics like a trusted aunt.

"Of course I do."

Simon gave her a recap of the case. Gabriella frowned as he told the tale until she looked thunderous. "You've certainly stepped in it, haven't you? That's some bad shit going on."

"Was there ever a dark witch linked to the hotel?" Simon asked.

Gabriella leaned back in her chair. She'd made cups of espresso for both of them, and she sipped hers for a moment before speaking.

"Just one. Nathan Irving only performed there a few times, but when his daughter drowned at the Ocean Paradise after her wedding, that was a strong connection. Irving was never really part of the magical community," she recalled finally. "He was one of those sorts who takes but never gives back. We were wary of him. He was a stage magician as well as being a fairly strong witch. The others in the Craft thought he wanted to exploit magic for personal gain and that he might bring unwanted attention to the rest of us."

"Could he have learned magic on his own?" Simon asked.

Gabriella's expression suggested that question gave her heartburn. "There are always people who think they can cobble together a few spells from what they find in books. They don't care about the danger—to themselves and others. It doesn't occur to them that study and discipline are part of being able to wield the magic and control it. Things usually go bad."

"I'm guessing Irving wanted to use what he learned in his stage show. Maybe things like levitation, making something appear and disappear—"

"Those sound simple, but to control the power properly takes practice and understanding," Gabriella replied. "Untrained magic can go wrong in many ways. The witch can drain themselves dangerously because they haven't grounded their energy right. Depending on the spell, they can open themselves to possession by dark entities. Or they can damage their minds—become unstable."

"What do you mean?" Simon set his cup aside and leaned forward.

"I've seen improperly trained witches become jealous—even paranoid—about their power, always afraid someone is looking to take it from them. They start to see everyone as an enemy and a rival. I suspect Irving already had that mindset before he ever dabbled in magic—and maybe he had reason to be suspicious—but the energies didn't help when they weren't properly channeled. People can burn themselves out—or cause their own death, or that of others."

"If Irving was driven to succeed at any cost, he probably didn't worry about the long-term effects," Simon mused.

"I was not an elder in the Craft back then, so I don't know for certain why he wasn't welcomed into our circle, but I would guess that the coven leaders recognized his recklessness and selfishness and kept him away for everyone's safety. Magic can be taught. After a certain point, character can't."

"Sheldon wasn't a natural witch," Simon replied. "If he coveted Irving's magic, could he have taken it?"

"Yes, it's possible to 'steal' someone's power. Though that requires dark magic, and there are always repercussions." Gabriella frowned. "If Irving had been properly trained, it would have required a witch of exceptional strength to take his power. If Irving was self-taught and poorly disciplined, it's possible Sheldon came upon a binding spell that gradually siphoned off Irving's magic and possibly even his life force."

She muttered in Spanish. "That is very, very bad. It is theft, violation, and murder all in one. Taking a witch's power by force would make Irving even more unstable if he survived. There are dark spells that can steal magic without killing, and others that kill as part of taking the magic. If Sheldon succeeded, then he must have had some latent power of his own, just as wild and untrained as Irving's, but stronger."

"What would that situation ultimately do to Irving and Sheldon?"

Gabriella's hand went to the amulet on a chain around her neck, and she made a sign of warding. "If it went on long enough, Irving would sicken, go into a coma, and eventually die. Sheldon would gradually lose the stolen magic after Irving's death until it failed completely."

"And then?" Simon found himself holding his breath.

"Irving would either cross over to the afterlife or become a vengeful spirit," Gabriella replied. "Sheldon might take on the characteristics that Irving acquired from illicit magic—suspicion, paranoia, instability. Magic always has a price."

"What if Sheldon bound Irving's ghost to keep hold of the stolen magic?" Simon voiced the question he'd been thinking about all morning. "Would that work?"

"That would be extremely dangerous. That's not trapping a spirit to keep it from causing harm. It's more like enslaving the soul to leech off its power. It would make the repercussions even worse. Such a binding wouldn't last forever. Eventually, the person who stole the magic would die or grow too weak to maintain the spell, and the magic would revert to the original owner, so there would be a vengeful—possibly insane—ghost who retains his magic. Be careful, Simon. Don't try to face off with the ghost alone—you'll need reinforcements."

"Will you help?"

Gabriella snorted. "Of course, child! I didn't teach you magic just to see some spirit lay you out. You know Miss Eppie will lend a hand as well. We need to wrap this up. You've got a wedding soon, and you don't need a ghost causing you problems."

Ephigenia Walker—Miss Eppie to just about everyone—was a powerful local root woman and Hoodoo practitioner. She and Gabriella were like second mothers to Simon, his treasured mentors.

"Thank you." Simon felt his throat tighten. "That's the best wedding present I could imagine. As soon as I know more, I'll fill you and Miss Eppie in on the details."

Gabriella gave a curt nod. "Be sure you do. I'm going to make some protective charms for your wedding—you never know what clings to people who come in from elsewhere. We want all the light and positive energy we can gather for your special day. Now get going. And don't wait too long to find out those particulars."

Simon thanked Gabriella and left her shop feeling lighter than when he had entered. He stopped at Le Miz and picked up lattes for himself and Pete, staying long enough to fill Tracey in on wedding updates before he headed for the shop.

"Glad you're back—it's been busier than usual." Pete accepted the coffee gratefully. "Word must have gotten around that you're taking time off. Your psychic readings and séances are booked solid, and so are your last two tours before the wedding. I updated your calendar."

Simon spent the next few hours handling the front desk while Pete restocked merchandise. They took turns eating sandwiches in the break room for lunch, and Simon breathed a sigh of relief when the rush slowed to a trickle late in the afternoon.

He headed to the office to answer the emails and text messages that had come in while he'd been up front. The caterer had a few questions and wanted to confirm some last-minute minor substitutions, but Simon felt relief that the changes were not something guests would notice.

Simon's phone rang, and he checked the ID. "Hi, Cassidy! What's up?"

"Everything's fine. Just checking in on you. Wedding jitters yet?"

Simon smiled. "Not about the wedding itself. The preparations are going to drive me nuts."

"I'm probably not the only one telling you that nothing matters except ending up married," Cassidy said.

"I'm trying to listen," Simon confessed. "But I want it to go right and be memorable for all the right reasons."

"Relax. Everything will be okay," Cassidy assured him.

"I hope so." Simon nudged the door closed. "We had a case land in our laps, and we need to finish it before the wedding. No pressure, right?"

"Since you've been pulled in, I'm guessing it's not a regular murder."

"Lucky guess." Simon gave her a quick overview. Cassidy and her friends helped keep the world safe from supernatural threats. He knew she would understand.

"You've got Gabriella and Miss Eppie, so you have magic back-up," Cassidy assessed. "Irving's ghost might be pissed, but he isn't undead. A banishment should work—and while he isn't a demon, an exorcism could pry him loose if he's stubborn."

"That's the plan," Simon admitted. "Nothing I haven't done before."

"I wish I could send Archibald Donnelly up for reinforcements, but he and Sorren are taking care of Alliance business in Antwerp. They'll be back a day before the wedding. In the meantime, I can look into how to secure any dangerous items."

"Hopefully, I won't need to bring in the big guns," Simon replied with a dry chuckle. Donnelly was a powerful necromancer, and Sorren was a nearly six-hundred-year-old vampire. Both were good friends and trusted allies—and were invited to the wedding. "But I'm probably going to need your help handling some of the objects in the house. There are definitely things with bad mojo."

"Just give me the details when you're ready."

"Hey—does your dad ever talk to my dad?" Simon's father was the brother of Cassidy's father, and while the two hadn't been close for a long time, Simon was still trying to prove his theory that his mother knew about the wedding.

"Not that I've heard," Cassidy replied, not shying away from the hard truth. "Why?"

"She called—out of the blue. I haven't talked to her since she tried to hook me back up with Jacen. She hasn't seemed to miss me, and then a week before the wedding, she decides to catch up?" Simon shook his head, even though Cassidy couldn't see him. "I'm afraid she's planning something."

"You'll have dozens of cops, a vampire, a necromancer, and the most powerful witches in the Lowcountry at your wedding," Cassidy reminded him. "That's a lot of firepower against Aunt Gloria."

"Don't underestimate her," Simon grumbled. "We might have a slight advantage...but I wouldn't say it's guaranteed."

"If I can help with the case, I can be there in under two hours."

Simon appreciated Cassidy's offer and the concern he heard in her tone. "Thanks. And if I need backup, I'll call. But I should be able to handle the ghosts—we just need to track down a few details."

"You know where to find me. I'll see you at the wedding—if not sooner."

Simon ended the call, feeling a little better. He turned back to his computer as a stabbing pain in his temples brought a vision. He pressed his hands to the sides of his head as he slipped out of the chair and sank to his knees.

Simon saw Sheldon kneeling in a cramped room illuminated by a ring of candles. Desperation shone in the man's eyes, and his hand shook as he lit the final wick. All around him were the trappings of magic, and from the bones, feathers, and blood, he knew that the power being called upon was dark.

"I summon the energies of creation and destruction." Sheldon peeled off something from what he held in his hand, dropping it into a burning brazier. A green flame flared.

"I call upon the currents of magic to do as I bid." He tossed something else into the fire, and Simon realized it was a playing card.

"I require the powers above and below to heed my words." Another card went into the flames.

"Bind to me the power I seek. Take it from the unworthy and fill me with true magic that does as I direct. Draw from me the power needed to bring my desire into reality. As I will it, so must it be. As I seek, so shall I find. Let it be so."

Green fire leapt high into the air. Sheldon fell back a step, but his expression remained resolute. What remained of a deck of cards fell from his hand as the fire turned to tendrils that reached for him, winding around him and capturing him in their folds. He screamed, but the fire didn't burn him. For a second, his eyes blazed the same verdant shade before the fire released him, dropping back into the brazier and extinguishing itself.

Simon gasped as the vision departed. He shook, and his mouth felt parched.

I saw Sheldon making his bargain, working the magic to steal Irving's magic. And the cards…were they special to Irving for some reason and that's why Sheldon used them to do the spell? They looked like the deck from the evidence locker. That might explain why Irving's revenant choked him with them.

Was there anything that would help us stop his ghost from killing again? Maybe Sheldon kept the rest of the deck as insurance. If we find it, can it help us stop Irving?

Simon knew that any other thoughts would have to wait until his head stopped pounding. He dug out one of the candy bars he kept in his desk drawer and a bottle of sports drink from the bag next to his chair. Since there was no telling when a vision would take him, Simon had learned to keep what he needed close at hand so he could revive himself.

He leaned against the desk as he finished the candy and guzzled the drink, closing his eyes and waiting for the shakes to quit.

First I see a long-ago murder or suicide at the Ocean Paradise. Now, I get a glimpse of how Sheldon stole Irving's magic. But both Sheldon and Irving are dead. Irving's magic should have returned to him when he murdered Sheldon, so what does the vision mean?

"Hey, Simon—" Pete stopped when he didn't see Simon at his desk. "Are you okay?"

"I will be," Simon replied. "Give me a couple of minutes."

Pete walked around the desk and reached to give Simon a hand. "C'mon. Let's get you to the couch."

"I ate and drank." Simon accepted the help to stand. "I just need the headache to quit pounding."

"Vision?"

"Yeah. Not exactly random…but not real clear, either."

"Want me to call Vic?"

Simon started to nod and thought better of it. "No. I'll be fine. Just close the door and give me a few minutes to rest."

"I'll handle the wild mob," Pete joked. "Holler if you need anything."

Simon lay back as best his tall frame could fit on the small couch. He closed his eyes and took deep breaths until the pain eased.

It's the cards. Irving didn't use a full deck to kill Sheldon. If the cards were special enough to Irving that they were what Sheldon used to steal his magic and enslave him, then where are the rest of them?

He woke with a start. The headache had faded, but the memory of the vision remained clear. Simon pushed himself up to sit and tensed, expecting the pain to return. When it didn't, he went back to the desk and sat at the computer.

"Everything seems to come back to the Ocean Paradise, and it all has links back to Timothy Sheldon. Could there be a connection between what I saw now and the last time?" he muttered.

An internet search found articles about star-crossed newlyweds who died at the Ocean Paradise. Simon noted their names and ages and then went looking for anything he could find about the pair.

"Christiana Irving Crosby." He found her name far more important now than when he'd first glimpsed the doomed couple. "That's the woman in the picture Jeremy brought to his signing. Nathan Irving's daughter."

"Darian Crosby," he murmured, turning his attention to the

unlucky groom. Digging through the articles after the tragedy, his eyes widened when he found the connection.

"Timothy Sheldon's sister married a Crosby. Darian was his nephew. The wedding would have blended the two rival families. Was it all a terrible accident, or did Sheldon and Irving interfere?"

Intrigued, Simon settled in to dig for more information. Between the sensational deaths and the high-profile families of the newlyweds, he found considerable newspaper coverage.

Pete stuck his head in after a while. "Find anything interesting?" He brought in a fresh cup of coffee, which Simon accepted with gratitude.

"I think that the man I saw jump or fall from the tower in my other vision ties into our case more than I expected," Simon told him. Pete stayed in the office doorway so he could hear if anyone came into the store.

"The articles said Sheldon and Irving—the two rival magicians —the father of the bride and uncle of the groom—had a heated argument during the reception. No one seems to know what the fight was about, but it disrupted the party and caused a scene."

"That sucks," Pete commiserated.

"Irving's daughter—the bride—was so angry she went for a walk on the beach. It doesn't say why the groom didn't go with her. Maybe she slipped out by herself," Simon continued. "When she didn't come back, they went to look for her. They found her body a few days later—drowned. She must have gone for a walk in the surf and gotten pulled into an undertow."

Simon took a sip of his coffee. "The groom blamed both men because their fight triggered the situation. He publicly denounced them and wished for them to lose what they loved most. Then he threw himself off the tower at the hotel. Sheldon and Irving had been fairly civil about their rivalry before the fight and the deaths, but after that, they were ruthless competitors."

Pete looked thoughtful. "I get that the groom was grieving. But doesn't it seem odd for him to jump off the tower after several days had gone by? I mean, it wasn't a heat of the moment, temporary insanity sort of thing."

Simon looked up. "Yeah, I thought that was odd, but grieving people do strange things."

"What if someone wanted to even the losses?" Pete suggested. "Irving's daughter died in a terrible accident. But Sheldon's nephew was still alive. Could Irving have used magic to cause the groom to jump off the tower?"

Simon's thoughts reeled at the possibility. "Good question. Or was it real grief but Sheldon couldn't accept that the young man made that choice on his own and blamed Irving for controlling him?"

Either way, it created a blood feud between two professional rivals. They could never fix what went wrong, so the only way it could end was with one of the magicians' deaths.

We've got method, motive, and opportunity. But can we stop the ghosts before they ruin another wedding—ours?

7

VIC

"How can finding a couple of rental beach houses be as nerve-wracking as actually house hunting?" Vic asked when he got home that evening.

Simon took the cornbread out of the oven and ladled chili into bowls as Vic set the table.

"It's the last-minute thing that's causing the real problem," Simon diagnosed. "You thought you had it all set up, and then the water main broke, and now you're scrambling, and even though it's not peak season, the weather is nice enough that places aren't empty."

Vic pulled two beers from the fridge and settled into his chair. "I know. And my family will work with whatever I can find, but I'd like them to be happy about it. Otherwise, they'll still be telling stories thirty years from now."

Simon leaned over to kiss him on the cheek before sitting. "I'm looking forward to telling wedding stories with you thirty years from now."

"Sap."

"Always." Simon grinned. "Have you found anything that's at least close?"

"Yeah. I'm going to look at a couple of houses first thing in the morning. They might do." Vic frowned. "I know I'm overthinking this."

Simon shrugged. "Maybe. Maybe not. You want your family to be comfortable, and you know what kinds of things are important to them—a kitchen, and having both halves of the group close to each other, plus enough room for everyone. That's not unreasonable."

"I feel like I'm asking for the moon. Ross's sister-in-law found a couple of prospects that don't get widely listed. They're the ones I'm going to see. Keep your fingers crossed."

"Any luck with the suits?" Simon broke off a piece of cornbread and spread it with butter.

"They didn't get in until late today, and their tailor called off sick, so Ross and I are going tomorrow over lunch."

Simon reached for Vic's hand. "I know that right now all the details seem important. I felt the same way when I had my melt-down over the caterer. But you were right—all that matters at the end of the day is that we're married."

Vic squeezed Simon's hand. "It's so much easier to be the one saying that instead of the one in a dither," he admitted. "I can be a rock when you're stressed. Hell, I've been trained to think clearly when I'm being shot at. This feels different. I don't know how some people plan weddings for a living."

Simon snickered. "It's not their own wedding, so the stakes are different."

"You're probably right."

Vic had promised himself an hour off to enjoy dinner and Simon's company. He'd gotten back from the office late and planned to be up most of the night again chasing down names and details online.

They took bowls of dulce de leche ice cream into the living room to eat while they watched television, finishing the last episode of a sci-fi show. Vic appreciated that they didn't have to have a constant conversation to feel connected and close.

He and Simon sat pressed together from knee to hip, not worried about personal space. Having grown up with so many siblings and cousins, Vic was used to having people in close contact, but for years he had rebelled when he left home by wanting to keep from being crowded.

With Simon, Vic didn't mind. That had been one more realization that assured him Simon was the right one for him.

Vic's attention wandered. Simon had called him about the vision that afternoon and his theory about the rivalry at the heart of the Sheldon/Irving feud, and Vic's mind couldn't leave the case alone.

"Do you want me to pause the show?" Simon asked.

Vic felt grateful that Simon didn't seem to take his lapse personally. They could both be a dog with a bone when it came to figuring out the details of a case. "I'm sorry. I was trying hard not to think about work, and then something popped into my head, and now I can't let go of it."

Simon stopped the episode and turned in his seat so he faced Vic. "Tell me. Maybe your brain is trying to point out something important."

"You're the absolute best," Vic said, relieved.

Simon grinned. "I can be bribed with blow jobs."

"Not exactly a hardship."

"Oh, I promise to be plenty *hard.*"

Vic felt his tension dissipate. "Okay—here's the thing that keeps going around in my head. What if Sheldon, Bowden, and Irving weren't the only weird deaths connected to the Ocean Paradise?"

He shifted positions. "My working theory is that Bowden is the ghost stuck in the bedroom and that Irving was the witch who somehow got free and killed Sheldon and is loose out there somewhere. The man's ghost you saw was Magnuson, one of Sheldon's old partners he screwed over. Maybe the guy was annoyed enough to haunt Sheldon but not pissed enough to kill him. Which is plenty strange already. But I think there might have been other deaths that had supernatural causes that were swept under the rug."

Simon nodded. "If there was a paranormal cause, I can see authorities covering it up and going with the simple answer. No one would question that, and the cops wouldn't have known where to start to rule out magic or ghosts."

"Ross and I have a list of people whose deaths during the Sheldon/Irving period seemed strange. It might be nothing. But once Irving and Sheldon got a taste for murder, maybe they got rid of other 'obstacles' before their big showdown with each other."

"Gideon—the filmmaker—was convinced that Irving and Sheldon eliminated people who got in their way. Jeremy said there was bad stuff he uncovered but didn't put in his book. So your theory is possible," Simon replied.

Vic passed Simon the list of names he pulled from his messenger bag. Each had a short description of the circumstances around the suspicious deaths and the date.

"This is…not good," Simon murmured as he scanned the names.

"A list of murder victims usually isn't," Vic replied.

Simon took a deep breath and pushed the list away. "The earlier deaths tended to be locked room situations and sudden deaths with no previous medical indicators. Heart failure, aneurysms, asphyxiation with no blockage. But the later deaths were suicides. Overdoses, jumpers, alcohol poisoning—or self-inflicted wounds. That's an important difference."

Vic needed to ask and didn't want to know. "What are you thinking?"

"I think that the locked room people could have been killed by Irving before Sheldon stole his magic or by Sheldon afterward. But the 'suicides' are more recent—four right before Sheldon was murdered," Simon replied. "I think it's possible that after Irving's ghost escaped from Sheldon, he possessed the victims, forcing the suicides, then circled back and killed Sheldon."

"Shit. More reasons for bad dreams," Vic muttered.

"Welcome to my world." Simon fiddled with a pencil. "If I'm right, Irving's ghost is even more dangerous than we first thought. He'd have to be very strong to manage possession. We need to make sure that anyone who goes near that house is warded up the wazoo."

"If Irving could possess people and make them kill themselves, why didn't he kill Sheldon like that?" Vic asked.

"My bet? Because Irving was a sadistic mofo who wanted Sheldon to suffer and be humiliated. He hated Sheldon most of all. The others were just on his bucket list. But those were relatively easy deaths. Sheldon's wasn't. And if the cards were what Sheldon used to bind Irving's ghost, then using them to kill him would have felt like poetic justice."

"I'm never going to watch a magic act again," Vic vowed. "Was Sheldon's death a cause or an effect? Had Irving's spirit been looking for a chance to get free and kill Sheldon and just happened to find the chance right now—or did other events 'juice up' his ghost to give him the power to finally escape and then murder a guy he'd wanted to kill for a long time?"

"I know working out the details on the Sheldon murder goes with the case, and we need to get rid of Irving's ghost even if there isn't someone who can be arrested for the killing," Simon replied. "But we also need to remove the bedroom ghost—who I'm sure is Bowden—without letting him hurt anyone. We can't let the house go for auction with him trapped in there."

"Aren't you just a ray of sunshine," Vic mumbled, but without heat.

"I need to tell you more about the visions I've had," Simon confessed. "I didn't think of this earlier because I didn't see how they were connected. Now, I'm positive that they are—especially after I talked with Gabriella."

Vic listened intently as Simon recounted the vision of the man on the hotel tower and of Sheldon burning the cards. He explained the family ties between the doomed couple. "Curse magic requires something personal from the victim. Some spells want hair or a piece of clothing, and others need an object with a deep emotional connection. In my vision, Irving had a set of playing cards that were special to him, and Sheldon used them in a spell to steal Irving's magic."

"Wow. Hanging out with you really has taught me a lot about woo-woo. That's the theory I pitched to Ross earlier today. I feel like we're starting to find the right pieces. Now we just have to put the puzzle together."

Simon took a pull from his beer. Vic watched the long line of Simon's throat and the sensuous bob of his Adam's apple as he swallowed. He set his beer aside and slipped off the couch to his knees, then shimmied to the side until he knelt between Simon's legs.

"What are you doing?" Simon asked in a fond tone.

Vic hummed as if he wasn't paying attention while he opened Simon's belt and unzipped his fly. "Bribing you." He stroked his hands up Simon's thighs.

"Oh, really? And what do you need to bribe me to do?" Simon played along.

"Trade favors."

"You know that really doesn't require either a bribe or a favor," Simon told him in a deep rumble. "I'm always hard for you."

"You certainly are." Vic showed his appreciation by mouthing his way up the denim inseam. He jerked on the hem of Simon's jeans, and Simon lifted so Vic could pull his pants and briefs down to free his hard, wet cock.

Vic wasn't in the mood for any more cheesy teasing, no matter how much fun it was at other times. They were both on edge, and Vic needed the validation of touch as much as he wanted the release of orgasm.

He took Simon down to the root in one move, getting a startled but happy yelp from his partner. Sometimes they took their time with lovemaking, spending an evening edging each other and going multiple rounds until they were sated.

Tonight, Vic knew they both needed it fast, dirty, and a little rough. He licked and sucked, running his tongue up the vein and then swirling around the head and through the slit, wet and sloppy and enthusiastic. One hand fondled Simon's balls and taint, sliding a finger back to toy with his hole while the other slipped up his chest to tweak his nipples, then reached into his own pants to free his dick because he knew he wouldn't last long.

Simon tangled his hand in Vic's hair, not holding him in place but making it clear how much he was enjoying the ride. Vic could tell his partner fought to keep from bucking his hips and pushing his cock deeper into Vic's mouth.

Vic gave Simon what he knew he wanted, deep-throating him. He swallowed twice, throat tight around the thick cock, and Simon came, tightening one fist on the couch cushion and tugging at Vic's hair. Vic felt his own climax build and release, streaming over his fist as he licked Simon clean.

He pulled off Simon's prick and wiped his hand on his T-shirt. Simon sprawled against the back of the couch, loose-limbed and blissfully fucked out.

"God, Vic. That was…so good." Simon opened his eyes. "Let's rearrange so I can do you."

Vic laughed. "Too late. I came almost at the same time. Raincheck on that, though. I knew I wouldn't last."

Vic got up and went to the bathroom, bringing back a warm wet cloth to wipe away any stray spunk. He pulled up Simon's briefs and jeans, fastened his own pants, and plopped down next to Simon on the couch.

"Feel better?" He half-sat, half-laid against Simon.

"Definitely. I will never object to you changing the subject like that," Simon assured him.

They watched the rest of their show snuggled in an endorphin haze. When the episode ended, Vic carried the empty bottles to the kitchen and closed up while Simon turned down the covers and brushed his teeth.

"Coming?" Simon patted the mattress beside him.

"We just did," Vic snarked, and Simon rolled his eyes. "I'll be along in a bit. I have some ideas I want to chase online and I'm still too fidgety to sleep. But you've had a rough time with those visions. No more thinking tonight," Vic joked.

"You sucked my brain out through my dick. I don't think you need to worry about that." Simon carded his fingers through Vic's dark hair.

"Good. Tomorrow is one week 'til the wedding—and I want to clear the decks so that's all we have to think about."

Simon leaned in to kiss him. "All I want to think about is you. Sweet dreams."

Vic picked up coffee for Ross and himself at Le Miz before heading into the office. He walked instead of riding his Hayabusa, enjoying the beautiful day. His thoughts wouldn't stay focused, jumping from one topic to another, from weddings to rental houses to murder. The coffee probably wouldn't help his concentration or make up for yet another night with very little sleep, but he figured it might make his jumpiness more coordinated.

"You're officially my favorite partner." Ross received the cup of coffee like a sacrament.

"I'm your only partner," Vic bantered.

"Then it's a good thing you're my favorite, isn't it?" Ross took a sip and made a noise of pure contentment.

"Dude, no one but Sheila wants to hear you sound like that."

"Killjoy. A cup of coffee like this deserves appreciation."

"Looks like you got an early start." Vic turned on his computer and sipped his coffee while he waited for it to boot up. We were both up late."

"I couldn't stop thinking about the list of names and suspicious deaths that might be related. I think Simon was right—and there are more than we originally thought. I didn't sleep thinking about the possible connections."

"And what have you found?"

Ross turned his computer around to share the screen with Vic. "Patterns. Not the sort cops usually pick up on. I confirmed that several were with the Ocean Paradise and had questionable circumstances around their deaths. All of them were in positions where they might have interacted with Sheldon, Bowden, or Irving."

"Locked rooms?"

"Some. For others, the details around their deaths didn't add up. But since they didn't point to foul play and the individuals weren't famous, no one looked too closely," Ross replied.

"Typical." Much as Vic wanted to believe that every situation that warranted investigation got its due, he knew that when cops were overworked and cases didn't pose a threat they were wrapped up quickly and quietly—sometimes incomplete.

"A few stayed open as cold cases, but by now, they're practically frozen," Ross added.

"Did all this give you any new insights into our main problem—finding Irving's spirit? If he was truly bound all those years to Sheldon, then he wasn't the one killing people."

"Yes, and no," Ross replied. "Several of the deaths happened during Sheldon's heyday, after the point we think he stole Irving's magic."

"Sheldon hit it big for a while. He had stolen magic; he was touring up and down the coast, and life was good. Do you think the magic went to his head, and he started knocking off people who slighted him back in the day?"

"Maybe. But for as much of an asshole as Sheldon was, he also had a savior complex," Ross pointed out. "He protected his girl-friends—and others—from Bowden as much as he could. So was he righting old wrongs? He might have finally seen a way to pay back people from the Ocean Paradise who deserved it."

"He was a cocky bastard, so either explanation is possible," Vic said. "Even if we could prove it—or got his ghost to confess—we can hardly update the cold case files with 'death by magician.' Maybe we just have to be satisfied with knowing the truth ourselves."

"Or maybe his hold over Irving's magic started to weaken. In the end, he was their jailer—Irving and Bowden. Locked away in his house with their trapped ghosts, no longer performing—and despite what the fame cost him, he's just a footnote to the history of magic, not one of the greats."

"Interesting—but not as much of a surprise as you think." Vic laid out Simon's theory about the unlucky wedding of the rival magicians' families and the role the bride and groom's deaths played in making the bad blood between the two even worse.

"Wow—one big dysfunctional family," Ross said when Vic

finished. "I'm surprised Irving was married." He drank the last of his coffee and tossed the cup in a bin.

"Divorced," Vic replied. "I get the impression the marriage was brief and tumultuous."

"Are the bride and groom still stuck here as ghosts?" Ross asked. "Lousy way to spend the afterlife. And if they are, can Simon free them?"

"The hotel where they died is long gone, so there's nowhere for them to haunt. And even if they got stuck, they might leave on their own once we get to the bottom of the whole Sheldon/Irving/Bowden mess." Vic drank the last of his coffee. "We still have to safely release the bedroom ghost, make sure Sheldon's spirit doesn't come back swinging—since he wasn't the forgiving type—and prevent Irving's spirit from going after any other old enemies."

"All that in a week—preferably sooner," Ross said. "If we can pull that off, you and I—and Simon—will have singlehandedly cleared a lot of Myrtle Beach's cold cases for the past few decades."

"Too bad no one will ever know."

"We will," Ross replied.

"We need to go back to Sheldon's house. We've got to look for Bowden's watch and the rest of Irving's playing cards." Vic was sure Ross could read his reluctance. "He didn't use a full deck to kill Sheldon, and Simon said Sheldon only used a few cards to do his spell, so the rest must be somewhere in the house."

"The watch might not be too hard, but a deck of cards in a magician's house? Sheldon was a pack rat—he's probably got hundreds of decks."

"We just need to find the ones that match the deck he choked to death on. I'm betting that the watch and the cards are the keys to getting rid of the bad spirits," Vic replied. "Simon's working on the magic we're going to need."

"When do you want to go?"

"No time like the present, but we need Simon. I'll give him a call."

"I'll get the Van Helsing bag and the house key."

When Vic and Simon became official work partners, Vic created a go-bag with Simon's help for supernatural crime scenes. The kit included a lead box to store items with bad energy, iron tongs to handle questionable pieces, salt, iron filings, holy water, amulets, a piece of cloth woven with protective magic, iron knives, steel machetes, a couple of wooden stakes, and a few silver bullets.

Ross called it the "Van Helsing Kit," and Vic couldn't disagree. Privately, he groused that at least Van Helsing got a cool coat. Hargrove knew about the kit, but Vic and Ross kept it quiet around the rest of the department.

Vic's hand went to the St. George medallion on a silver chain around his neck and the protective amulets Simon had given him. He kept a mojo bag and salt in the pocket of his jacket, as well as a handkerchief woven with spells that was a gift from Teag. Vic hoped that they would be sufficient to ward off the evil that remained in Sheldon's house.

When Vic called, Simon sounded eager to deal with the house.

"I need to pull some things together, so give me about half an hour. Please, Vic, promise me you won't go there without me."

"I promise."

True to his word, Simon joined them at the police station sooner than expected. "Pete's handling the store. How can I help?"

"Before we head to the house, I want to show you something we found in the same place as those letters. I have a feeling it might be important." Vic directed Simon to the runed box. "What do you make of it? When I opened it and saw sigils, I closed it right away and didn't touch it again."

"Smart move." Simon held a hand over the box, and frowned, concentrating. "Magic has been channeled through it, but it's inert now." He used a pencil to lift the lid, and turned on his phone's light to get a better look inside. "I've got a theory...not sure how to tell for sure. I think that this box was part of the spell Sheldon used to either steal Irving's magic or bind his ghost. If that's the case, then the cards are definitely a link to Irving."

"Is it still dangerous?" Vic eyed the box as if it were a snake.

"I don't think so, but better safe than sorry. Once we banish the ghosts permanently, then any resonance clinging to the box will be gone," Simon told him. "We need to find the rest of the cards. They're still likely to be magically charged."

"That's part of the whole 'field trip' back to the house," Vic replied. "Ready to go?"

"Definitely. I don't think we're ready to un-haunt the house yet, but if you can find the pieces you're looking for—and we're right about how Sheldon used them—we'll be a lot closer."

"What about Sheldon's ghost?" Vic asked.

"Another reason to finish this sooner rather than later." Simon climbed into the backseat of the car. "The more time that passes after his death, the stronger his spirit is likely to get. Two bad ghosts are enough—I'd hate to deal with three."

"How many cards did it take to kill Sheldon?" Vic slung the duffel into the trunk and slammed the lid before he got into the passenger seat.

"Twenty. Technically he died from asphyxiation." Ross sat behind the wheel and held up the photo on his phone that he had taken of the front and back of the cards. "The cards have a distinctive pattern on the back—probably custom-made."

"So there should be cards of a matching deck somewhere at Sheldon's house. Makes sense for it to be a custom deck—that would make a tighter connection between it and Irving. Probably held some special meaning to him that gave Sheldon more magical leverage," Vic replied.

"Keep an eye out for anything about the doomed wedding while we're poking around," Simon added. "Pictures, invitation, anything. That might be part of what's trapping the ghosts."

"Good thought. God, for all his success, Sheldon fucked up everything else, didn't he?" Ross mused. "Screwed over his business partners, never found a long-time love despite all his romances, and stole the magic that made him famous."

"I hope he enjoyed fame while it lasted, because the ride to the bottom came pretty hard," Vic said.

They pulled up to Sheldon's house and looked around warily, making sure nothing had been disturbed since their previous visit. The place appeared deceptively harmless, but Vic wondered if it sent a shiver down anyone else's spine. From Ross's expression of discomfort, he suspected that the house had enough bad energy to give anyone the willies. Vic couldn't read Simon's expression, and he figured his fiancé was channeling his gifts to sense the ghosts.

After donning gloves and booties, Ross let them in with the key and locked the door behind them. The house felt silent and abandoned.

"A watch, a partial deck of cards, and wedding stuff," Ross muttered. "Needle in a haystack."

Simon frowned, moving in a slow circle in the living room. "Maybe not. The watch and cards would have been essential to keeping Irving bound and Bowden trapped. Sheldon wouldn't have packed them up with old memorabilia or second-hand equipment. He would have wanted them where he could reassure himself that they were safe."

"Makes sense," Vic agreed.

"The wedding stuff might have been a twisted sort of trophy," Vic went on, working off a hunch. "It's when things went really wrong between him and Irving, the start of his 'quest' to triumph in their competition."

Ross gave him a look. "If you weren't a cop, I'd worry about you. You think like a killer."

"I'll take that as a compliment."

The same strange scent he had smelled during the last visits caught Vic's attention as they moved from room to room. This time, he realized what it was. "That's sage with some rosemary."

"I don't think Sheldon was a cook. I bet he was burning the stuff by the handful for protection," Simon replied.

"Didn't do him much good," Ross observed.

Vic shrugged. "Maybe it did for a while—until it didn't."

After walking through the house again, Vic felt certain that the items they needed were somewhere within Sheldon's easy reach.

"I doubt Sheldon spent much time in the rooms that were chock full of magician crap," Vic said. "My bet is on the kitchen, master bedroom, or in the office near his desk."

"Want to split up?" Ross asked although he didn't sound in favor of the idea.

"I don't think that's wise," Simon objected.

Vic's gut gave him a strong "no." "We don't know what traps or protections Sheldon might have set. We might accidentally trigger something we didn't notice the first time we were here. I think it's safer to stick together."

"And since we haven't dealt with the ghost in the bedroom, let's make it quick," Simon urged.

He put the duffel with their "special" tools on the hallway floor. Vic kept his gun holstered and opted for salt and an iron knife, better for fighting off angry ghosts. Ross did the same, and Vic noticed that his partner had remembered to wear the protective silver amulet Simon had given to both of them on a recent case. Simon carried a length of iron rebar like a sword, and a canister of salt bulged in his jacket pocket.

"Where first?" Ross glanced around as if expecting to see someone.

He feels it too. Like we're being watched. Is it Irving or Sheldon—or a spirit we haven't run into yet?

"You look for the cards and the watch," Simon told them. "I'm going to see if the other ghosts will talk to me."

Vic and Ross had plenty of experience searching for evidence. They divided the kitchen and went to work, checking inside and beneath drawers, looking behind objects in cupboards, and going through the freezer. Simon guarded the doorway.

"Sheila's grandpa had Alzheimer's before he died, and when we helped her mom clean out his house, we had to look in the strangest places in case he hid valuables," Ross said as he tackled the sparsely-filled pantry. "Never thought that experience would come in handy."

Vic doubted they would find the cards in the kitchen. From what the neighbors had reported, Sheldon didn't allow anyone into the house, and his occult protections probably kept strangers away. Hiding something in the kitchen was more likely if the owner feared a random break-in. Vic's hunch was that Sheldon wanted the crucial items where he could check them often to reassure himself they were secure.

"I've got a big, fat nothing," Ross said when he finished his designated half of the room.

Vic straightened after searching the oven. "Me, too. But we had to rule it out."

"I even rattled all the cans. My aunt had a fake soup can for hiding jewelry. I thought it was cool when I was a kid."

Vic chuckled. "I grew up in a house full of cops and retired police dogs. They had more of a 'fuck around and find out' approach to home security."

The feeling of being watched made the hair rise on the back of Vic's neck, but he didn't catch sight of any ghosts.

"Any luck?" he asked Simon when they all returned to the living room.

Simon nodded. "The women's ghosts said they hid when Irving attacked Sheldon, but they again confirmed he's the killer. They only care about making sure Bowden's ghost stays trapped in the bedroom, and they don't know where Sheldon kept the watch or the other cards. I can't sense Sheldon or Irving—for now. Bowden's furious, but still trapped. Don't take longer than you have to—we don't want to be here if those ghosts come home."

They went to the master bedroom next. Simon stayed in the doorway where he could keep them from being ambushed if vengeful ghosts attacked.

Even with the lights on, the room seemed dark. Boxes and stacks filled the corners. A long dresser and chest of drawers took up most of one wall, while the others held bookshelves stuffed with paperbacks. Sheldon hadn't bothered to make his bed on the last day of his life. A nightstand with an alarm clock, lamp, and book propped open to save the place covered the top.

"I'll do the dresser and chest," Ross volunteered. "I don't want to go digging around in the guy's nightstand. Don't need to find his porn or his toys. Some things can't be unseen."

"Thanks for that visual," Vic muttered. He'd been thinking the same. The book Sheldon had been reading was an old thriller. He checked to make sure nothing was hidden between the pages, then examined the lamp and clock and finally the drawer. The contents were surprisingly tame, rounding out Vic's impression of Sheldon as an extremely lonely man in his final years of seclusion.

Vic moved on to the closet, checking inside clothing and searching pockets.

"I didn't find any watches, let alone cards. And the only photos this guy seems to have kept were of himself in the glory days." Ross's annoyance was clear.

"Does it seem darker in here than it should be?" Vic voiced the concern he'd had since they entered the house. "The blinds are open, the lights are on, but everything's dim."

"Maybe the house doesn't face the right direction to catch the sun." Ross's tone suggested he didn't fully believe his comment.

"It's not your imagination," Simon warned. "The house is haunted, and the spirits don't like being disturbed. Hurry."

Vic's right hand gripped his amulet, and his left touched the mojo bag in his jacket pocket, reassuring himself of their protection.

"That leaves the office." Vic itched to leave. Every moment they stayed ratcheted up his tension, the feeling that something was going to happen.

"Let's do it so we can get out of this freaky place," Ross agreed.

"I know you looked for cursed things the last time, but what about all those stage props?" Vic asked Simon, giving one of the gaudily painted vanishing cabinets the side eye.

"Most of them are harmless," Simon replied, still scanning for danger. "Cassidy's touch magic would go nuts in here. She says that things absorb tainted energy the way cigarette smoke sticks to clothes. That's probably what your subconscious is picking up on."

Simon's head jerked as if following movement.

"See something?" Vic asked, on edge.

"Caught another glimpse of Sheldon's pissed off former partner. He's not a strong enough ghost to be dangerous. I'm guessing he chose to hang around to punish Sheldon with his presence."

Vic carried the duffel to the next room and set it near the desk, pulling out the lead box in anticipation of finding what they sought.

Sheldon's office felt small because of the imposing desk and other furniture. His desktop held a computer, office supplies, and an old landline phone. The desk blotter calendar was surprisingly doodle-free, without appointments or other notes.

Ross headed for the filing cabinets, picking the locks in minutes. "What the hell did a magician need to file?"

Vic jimmied the locks on the desk. The large center drawer held a gun, an unusually sharp letter opener that looked like a dagger, and a scramble of paperclips, rubber bands, and ballpoint pens. He tapped on the drawer to make sure it didn't have a hidden compartment.

"The first drawer files appear to be notes about magic tricks, other magicians, stage plans for shows, playbills, and programs from his appearances," Ross reported.

"The center drawer has weapons and office supplies—perfectly normal." Vic's voice dripped with sarcasm.

Ross started on the second file drawer while Vic opened the desk's side drawers

"We need to take some of these files back with us," Ross said. "They're about people on those lists I made—I recognize the names. People Sheldon thought were rivals or enemies. Some of them died under very unusual circumstances."

Vic looked up. "You think Sheldon used magic to off them?"

"I think it's possible," Ross replied. "Maybe stealing Irving's magic went to his head. Or maybe he figured if Irving used magic to get away with murder, so could he." Ross shoved files into collection bags in the duffel.

Vic opened another drawer. "Bingo." Vic stared at a man's gold Rolex watch and a partial deck of cards with patterned backs that matched what Ross found in the evidence locker.

The temperature dropped. Vic's hackles rose.

Ross grabbed the salt and iron knife from the bag. "He's here, isn't he?"

Simon's grim expression told Vic more than he wanted to know. "One of the stronger spirits is just beyond my range. I can't tell whether it's Sheldon or Irving. Better wrap up."

Vic used the iron tongs to place the watch in the lead box, avoiding skin contact since they didn't know what type of magic Sheldon had used. A cold wind stirred, sending loose papers fluttering. Vic picked up the stack of cards with the tongs and felt invisible hands shove him backward, sending him sprawling.

The hazy outline of a man loomed over Vic.

"Hey, asshole!" Simon swung the rebar through the ghost's image, making it break up like static. Ross followed up with a handful of salt.

Vic scrambled to his feet, put the cards into the lead box, slammed the lid shut, and shoved the protective box into the bag. "Let's go."

The heavy wooden desk suddenly shifted, screeching across the floor as something shoved it at Vic, making him jump aside to avoid being pinned.

"Get out of here—now!" Simon yelled.

Boxes trembled. Dust blew into the air, making Vic's eyes sting. Ross grabbed his arm, and together they stumbled toward the door. One of the heavy filing cabinets fell over. Papers flew, swirling in a vortex. Vic knew gut deep that he dared not get caught.

Unseen hands tried to rip the duffel from Vic's shoulder, nearly yanking him off his feet. Ross threw salt again, forcing the ghost to let go and winning them a moment's reprieve to get a few feet closer to the door. Vic suspected their amulets and protective charms had bought them time.

Simon swept the rebar down through where the ghost had been, followed by more salt.

They ran for the door.

"Go—I'll make sure he doesn't surprise us." Simon let them pass.

"Not leaving you to deal with him alone." Vic grabbed Simon's wrist and pulled him toward the outside.

"I'm going with you, but I might need to buy us a few more minutes dispelling the ghost. Get in the car. I'll be right behind you."

Summoning his full abilities as a psychic medium gave Simon an entirely different presence Vic had only glimpsed before when life and death were on the line.

He was damn hot when he was so fucking formidable.

Survive first, sex later.

Vic and Ross ran for the car and got in. They could hear Simon raise his voice in the chant, and a loud crash punctuated the final exclamation.

Simon slammed the front door and sprinted toward them, throwing himself into the backseat. In the rearview mirror, the house looked deceptively quiet. Ross pushed the speed limit as they left the home behind them.

"I dispelled the ghost, which is like giving it a shove back to the other side. He'll be back," Simon told them. "I wasn't prepared for a full banishment."

"Was that Irving's ghost?" Vic hoped his heart rate would drop back to normal.

Simon shook his head. "I'm pretty sure that was Sheldon. I don't think anyone should go inside without me. Too dangerous."

Vic met his gaze in the mirror. Simon seemed too calm to have been surprised by the situation.

"You had a vision that we were in trouble, didn't you? Before I even called you. " Vic was already sure of the answer.

Simon nodded. "Yeah. I couldn't get the house out of my mind, and then I had a vision of you in danger. I was planning to drive straight to the house when you called."

"I'm glad you went with us," Vic answered. "But now we've got three angry ghosts instead of two. With all that going on inside, how do we keep the house from going up like a powder keg?"

8

SIMON

"You don't have any appointments this morning," Pete confirmed.

"Good. Just to be safe, let's close until lunch," Simon told him. "You can take the morning off or go upstairs until I give the all-clear." A small, heavily-warded apartment over the shop served as a sometime safe house when Simon feared one of their cases might pose a threat.

"Hell, no. You need someone to watch your back." Pete's stubborn expression made it clear he wouldn't change his mind.

"I don't know how the ghosts I'm summoning are going to respond," Simon cautioned. "They have every reason to be furious if our theory's right. I don't want you to get hurt."

"Vic would have my ass if I let you do this without backup," Pete countered. "If I have to choose between a pissed-off Vic or angry ghosts, I'll take the ghosts."

"Okay, you win. Get the shop ready and make a salt circle for yourself. Be sure you've got the rebar in case you need it. I'll set out the items for the séance. Keep your phone handy."

"I'm on it." Pete headed to get what he needed.

Last night after the ruckus at Sheldon's house, Simon had gone back to the police station with Ross and Vic. They had studied the files Ross retrieved from the filing cabinets, which helped them flesh out the list of people whose suspicious deaths could have been caused by magic.

Simon had made a copy of that list and done some digging of his own over breakfast. He hadn't slept well, worried that they might have overlooked some important tidbit that would help them rein in the vengeful ghosts and put the case to rest before someone else got hurt.

"Whose ghosts are you calling—in case you get knocked out and I have to explain to Vic?" Pete asked.

Simon gave a bleak chuckle. "Between the files Ross took yesterday, and what I found online when I cross-checked dates, I think that first Irving and then Sheldon used magic to target their enemies. I can't prove it yet, but I think Sheldon was afraid that Irving was building up to attacking him, so he found a way to steal Irving's magic first."

"Sounds complicated," Pete mused.

Simon nodded. "Sheldon stole Irving's magic and later killed him, binding his ghost to help Sheldon use the stolen magic. Sheldon had a list of people he wanted revenge on and used magic to target them. Then Irving's spirit got loose and knocked off a few people he'd missed before he died before he returned and killed Sheldon."

"And the deaths looked like accidents, so the police didn't realize the link," Pete supplied.

"Most cops aren't looking for a supernatural connection." Simon's rueful tone reflected his own initial difficulty gaining Vic's trust. "Plus, if Irving's ghost could possess people, he'd have the perfect way to hide the real cause of death."

Only a handful of the people from the files Ross took had died under strange circumstances. Simon chose those most likely to have been murdered by magic—Ted Wainright, Carl Johnson, Bobby Connor, Addison Hutch, and Patrick Radcliff—to reach with a séance.

Pete readied a salt circle large enough for a chair and supplies and settled in with his phone clearly outlined in the pocket of his jeans and a length of rebar across his lap.

"You've got all your charms and the mojo bag?" Simon reminded him.

"Right here." Pete sounded far cheerier than the situation warranted, holding up some of the protections.

Simon double-checked his own protective amulets, verified that the salt circle Pete put down around his chair was solid, and settled in at his chair behind the séance table to gather his focus.

He closed his eyes, took several deep breaths, and grounded himself by silently repeating several mantras that helped him push away worry and fill himself with positive energy.

When he opened his eyes and called to his gift, he could see the shop as it was and the world of spirits.

"Ted Wainright. If you remain in the shadows and have not moved on, I summon you."

Simon waited and resisted the urge to drum his fingers on the table. Ghosts who stayed close to the mortal world usually responded quickly when called unless guilt or shame made them hide.

Wainright's ghost matched the photograph in Sheldon's file. He looked like a character out of Vegas in the seventies, an older man with a pot belly sporting a bellbottom suit and wide-collar shirt open to mid-chest.

"Who are you, and what the hell do you want?"

"You were Nathan Irving's manager."

"I was a lot of people's manager. What's it to you?"

"Did you skim off the top of all your clients' earnings like you did with Irving?" Simon cut to the chase.

"Bit late to worry now, ain't it?"

Simon noted that Wainright had not denied the charge. He had a smug expression as if he enjoyed putting one over on everyone.

"What caused the car wreck that killed you?"

Wainright's smug smile slipped. *"How do you know about that?"*

It was Simon's turn to smirk. "Goes with being psychic."

Wainright actually looked spooked. *"I was driving, and out of the blue the AC went full blast—started to ice up my windshield. My foot floored the gas, and my hands wouldn't turn the steering wheel. Started going a hundred miles an hour. Missed a curve, hit a building. Bada-bing. Dead."*

"I think you've left something out. Try again?" Simon pressed.

Wainright's ghost squirmed. *"You mean how I could hear Nathan Irving laughing in my head the whole time while I tried to get my body to listen to me? People always said he was a witch. Guess they were right."*

Simon didn't sense a threat from the spirit. It lacked the ability to do harm in its spirit form, so he didn't waste energy on a banishing.

Carl Johnson's ghost had the same smug entitlement, a banker who had foreclosed on the house Irving had grown up with, which had led to a series of tragedies for the family.

"I was taking a bath in my locked apartment, and it got cold like a meat locker. Next thing I know, I hear Nathan Irving in my head telling me I'm going to pay for my sins, and then my body sank to the bottom of the tub, and I couldn't move. I don't know how the little asshole did it, but he goddamn drowned me."

Bobby Connor's spirit seemed sad and resigned. *"Irving, Sheldon, and Bowden hated each other. Irving resented Sheldon's success with the crowds and with the ladies. Sheldon saw Irving as a rival. Bowden was a creep and a pervert who didn't like that Sheldon stuck up for the people he bullied, especially the women. When Irving's daughter married Sheldon's nephew and they both ended up dead, that just fueled the fire. It didn't help that the woman Irving had a crush on—Katrina Dawson—hated him and shacked up with Sheldon, or that Bowden harassed her."*

"Why did Irving's ghost come after you?"

"I was the head booking agent for the biggest live entertainment company on the Strand. Irving could put on a good show, but he didn't have the glitz and glamor Sheldon did, and he'd get drunk and surly with the backstage crew. He was more trouble than he was worth, so I stopped booking him."

"This was after Sheldon had the Ocean Paradise gig sewn up?"

"Yeah. Irving was an asshole, and everyone in the business knew it. Word got around, and he wasn't getting hired by the big venues anymore. He was back to lounge lizard territory and playing graduation parties and bar mitzvahs."

"He blamed you?"

"I guess so since he took over my body and threw me off my balcony."

Simon heard similar stories from the next two ghosts, Addison Hutch and Patrick Radcliff. Hutch was a lawyer who had cheated Sheldon, while Radcliff had been an accountant who embezzled thousands from Sheldon's accounts. Simon felt certain that Timothy Sheldon had used his stolen magic to get revenge.

He sensed his energy waning and sent the ghosts away before he dismissed the protections he had raised and re-centered himself.

"You done, boss?" Pete asked.

"Yeah, they're gone. You can get out of the circle." Pete brought Simon a bottle of water and a candy bar.

"Did you get what you needed?"

Simon nodded, and recounted what he'd learned from the ghosts who had answered his call. "Irving's ghost—once he broke free from Sheldon—definitely possessed three of them. Sheldon used his stolen magic a little differently—he pushed one guy down the stairs and shoved the other in front of a bus."

"Yikes. You got any ideas of how to get rid of killer ghosts?"

Simon paused to finish his drink and candy. The sugar and caffeine only went so far to replenish him. "Yeah—but we're going to need backup. I have to make some calls."

"I can sweep up the salt and open the store if you need time in the office," Pete offered.

"Thanks. And Pete—make sure you and Mikki wear the amulets I gave you all the time until this is over. Sheldon's ghost hasn't powered up yet, and Bowden is still trapped, but Irving's in the wind —and he's dangerous as fuck."

"Gotcha. D'you mind if we stay in the apartment upstairs until this is over?"

"I was hoping you'd ask. I think that's safest."

Simon's thoughts went back to Sheldon's very haunted house. *Getting rid of the ghosts is only part of the issue. There could be all kinds of stuff in there that shouldn't turn up at a garage sale. We might be able to prevent a supernatural murder or two by making sure Sheldon's collections don't fall into the wrong hands.*

He pulled out his phone and hit Cassidy's number on speed dial. She picked up right away.

"Hi, Simon! How are the wedding plans coming?"

"Lately they seem to be taking turns between stressing me out or giving Vic hives, but so far everything's worked out. Actually, I'm calling about that case I mentioned with the house full of haunted stuff."

"How can I help?"

"We've got a house full of magician's props, some of which are definitely supernaturally sketchy," he told her. "Once we un-haunt the place, all that stuff ought to be gone over before any of it gets sold. Is there a chance you could put in a bid to just buy the contents 'as is'?" he asked.

"Believe it or not, that's happened more than once, where someone bequeathed a house full of haunted stuff to Trifles and Folly because they didn't know what to do with it," she said, surprising him. "If you get the contact information to me, I can see what can be arranged."

"Thank you." Simon felt a weight lift. "That solves a huge potential problem."

"No matter how creepy you think the stuff is, I guarantee you we've seen worse." Cassidy laughed. "Check that off your list."

"I'll send you the information."

"That's what cousins are for," Cassidy replied. "In the meantime, I'll brush up on magic paraphernalia. Send pictures!"

He ended the call, surprised at how relieved he felt.

His relief faded when an unknown ringtone sounded. He looked at the number and realized it was Gideon Kent, the filmmaker.

"Simon? Jeremy was attacked by a ghost. I'm afraid I'm going to be next. We need your help."

"What happened?" Simon's relief after the conversation with Cassidy shifted quickly to cold dread. Only one ghost was likely to be attacking people, and Simon wasn't quite ready for that showdown.

"Can you come to my house? We'll tell you everything. Jeremy's hiding here. It's safer than his place, but I don't know if my protections are strong enough if the ghost tries again."

"Certainly. I'll hurry," Simon told him. "I'm going to see if I can get some talented friends to help. Stay indoors, make a circle of salt and iron, and don't leave it until I call you to let me in. Do you need groceries or medical supplies?"

Simon made a list of the food and first-aid items Gideon asked for, and promised to bring them with him. He ended that call and immediately dialed again, hitting Gabriella's number on speed dial.

"We've got a situation," Simon said when she picked up. "I was going to call you and Miss Eppie to strategize how to deal with a murderous ghost, but he's upped the ante on me and he's going to kill two more people if we don't figure out what to do."

"Eppie and I have been working on a few things that might help," Gabriella replied.

Simon wasn't entirely sure what her magic entailed, but she had an uncanny way of "guessing" what would be needed.

"Can you meet me at the address I'm going to text you? I'm heading there now. Short notice, but—"

"Nonsense," Gabriella said. "I will be there, and I'll bring Eppie if I can."

"Thank you. I intended to do some planning for the big showdown, but I thought we might have more time."

"Go do what you can, and I'll meet you. And Simon—be cautious. The situation is not 'normal,' even by our standards."

"I will. I promise." *Because killer ghosts will be the least of my worries if Vic finds out I've gotten hurt.*

Simon stopped at the store to get the things on Gideon's list and threw in a few frozen pizzas, basic groceries, and canisters of salt. He brought amulets, mojo bags, and charms for good measure.

Simon drove to the address Gideon had given him, remembering that the squirrely filmmaker had told him about the elaborate wardings he had created for his home, fearing retaliation from the Ocean Paradise's ghosts.

That didn't really prepare him for the reality of the small house and yard. An iron fence surrounded the plot. Inside, statues of the

Virgin Mary, crosses, crucifixes, bells, and prayer flags filled the yard.

Simon: *I'm here.* Simon texted, unwilling to tamper with any of the protections without knowing what Gideon had devised.

The front door opened, and Gideon skittered out. He held a bedsheet over his head that moved stiffly in the breeze.

"Hurry up." He lifted the sheet so it covered them both. "I soaked the sheet in salt water. Figured it can't hurt."

Simon had to run to keep up. As soon as they got inside, Gideon slammed the door and refreshed the line of salt at the bottom.

"Here's the stuff you wanted, along with some extra protective items and enough food to get you through a couple of days." Simon set the bags on the kitchen table.

Gideon looked haggard, with dark circles under his eyes. "Thank you. You took a risk coming here."

"Where's Jeremy?"

"In here." Gideon led Simon into the living room, where Jeremy lay on the couch, a black eye and bruising on his throat and face evidence of a fight.

"What happened?" Simon asked, and Gideon motioned for him to take a seat in one of the armchairs. The filmmaker went back to the kitchen and returned with a pitcher of iced tea and three glasses.

"After I saw you at the library, I read your books, and then I went looking online for how to fend off ghosts." Jeremy managed to sit up. "Good thing or I'd probably be dead. I'd felt like someone was watching me, and I got creeped out by seeing movement when nothing was around."

He took a sip of his iced tea. "Then, last night, something attacked me in the stairwell to my apartment."

"Some*thing*?" Simon echoed.

Jeremy nodded. "I felt hands on me, but I couldn't see anyone. Since I'd read up on fighting ghosts, I bought a cast iron spoon rest and carried it with me, along with some salt. I managed to swing the spoon rest where the ghost must have been, and then I threw salt.

That let me get to my apartment, where I'd already put down salt along all the doors, vents, and windows."

"How did you get here?" Given the bruises on Jeremy's throat, he'd survived a close call.

"I called a priest who's a friend of mine. I asked him to bless my apartment and bring all the cast iron he could find," Jeremy replied. "He said when he gave the blessing in the hallway, it felt as if 'darkness departed.' I'd already called Gideon and packed up, so I got my priest friend and his car full of cast iron to drive me over here until we could figure out what to do."

Simon chuckled. "That's brilliant. Good thing you were careful —we think the ghost that attacked you has killed before."

Jeremy and Gideon shared a frightened look.

"Do you know who it was?" Gideon asked.

"My money is on Nathan Irving. Remember him?"

Both men nodded.

"The guy everyone said was a witch. He was a stage magician back in the day who played some of the big hotels on the Strand, then sort of faded away," Jeremy spoke up.

"He's turned into a vengeful ghost—long story—and gotten an energy boost from all the publicity around the Ocean Paradise's anniversary," Simon told them. "My colleagues and I are working on the situation, but it's complicated. If you can stay here for a couple of days, I think you'll both be safest. I brought some things to make the house even more secure, and I'm meeting some friends who might be able to help with your wardings."

"We weren't looking to be ghostbusters." Gideon sounded scared and miserable. "We're historians. History isn't supposed to fight back."

"I shouldn't comment on an active police investigation except to say that there's a reason they called me in to consult. Once we handle the situation, you should be safe."

Simon helped Gideon put the groceries away and went over how to use the charms and hex bags he had brought.

"Leave the mail in the box, and avoid ordering deliveries for the drivers' safety," Simon told him. His phone buzzed, letting him know Gabriella and Eppie had arrived.

"I've got some friends with special abilities outside—they'll do what they can to increase your protections. Sit tight, and I'll call you when it's safe."

Gideon and Jeremy thanked Simon profusely. He turned down using the salt-soaked sheet in case Gideon needed it in an emergency, but he paused when he stepped over the salt line to check for angry ghosts.

He couldn't sense Irving's spirit and let out a sigh of relief. That didn't mean the ghost wouldn't attempt to get through the wardings, but at least for now, he wasn't looming nearby.

Gabriella and Miss Eppie waited for him just outside the iron fence. He could feel the stir of energy, which told him they'd been busy.

"Lordy, it's been a while since I've seen a place done up like this," Miss Eppie said. "They got it mostly right too. I added some goofer dust and graveyard dirt and washed all along the front of the fence with a mix of Four Thieves vinegar and red brick dust."

Simon had used those protections on the bungalow and the shop in the past and knew that the Hoodoo magic worked.

"Figured you also gave away your extra mojo bag and jack-balls, so I brought you more." Miss Eppie handed off a sack to Simon.

"I added my magic to the wardings to reinforce them and shore them up," Gabriella said. "For now, your friends should be safe if they stay inside."

"Thank you," Simon told them. "Do you have time to get coffee and strategize? We're headed for a reckoning on this situation, and I'd sure feel better with you backing us up."

They headed to Le Miz, got their drinks, and took a table in the back room where they could talk privately. Decorations remained from the space's previous tenant, including a life-size pirate figure with a parrot on its shoulder and a treasure chest. Simon had long ago warded the shop as a favor to Tracey.

Gabriella and Miss Eppie listened intently as Simon caught

POINT BLANK | 133

them up on new developments in the case and what they had learned about Irving, Sheldon, and Bowden's ghosts.

"We can help you banish and trap the ghosts and then pass them along to your cousin's necromancer friend," Gabriella said when Simon finished his update. "They're evil spirits and not demons, so while you can say the rite of exorcism along with a banishment and sap their energy, it's not going to expel a ghost the way it would a demon."

"Do we need to bring in a priest as well? The one who's doing our wedding ceremony is an exorcist."

Miss Eppie chuckled. "I'm going to skip all the jokes that come to mind because this is a serious situation."

Gabriella just shook her head. "If you have time to bring someone all the way from Charleston, it wouldn't hurt. You may not have that much warning. It sounds like Irving's ghost is getting more unstable—not a surprise after having his magic stolen, being murdered, and then being enslaved for years. If he was an angry man when he was alive, it's much worse now. You'd better take care of this quick."

Simon nodded, having come to the same conclusion. "I'll call Vic and see how soon we can get back into the house. I'll let you know so you can join us."

"Just tell us when you need us, and we'll be there." Miss Eppie reached across the table and took his hand. "We've got your back."

Miss Eppie and Gabriella went back to their shops, and Simon nursed his now-cold coffee, needing some time to decompress. He was about to pull out of the lot when his phone rang. With his mind still on the situation with Gideon and Jeremy and his conversation with Gabriella and Miss Eppie, he answered the call instantly without checking the ID.

"Sebastian, thank you for taking my call. I'm sure you're terribly busy these days." Gloria, Simon's mother, managed to combine Simon's hated first name with an implied accusation of ignoring her.

"I *am* busy—and you know I prefer Simon."

"Still going on about that? Sebastian is a beautiful name."

"I'm just going into a meeting. Why did you call?" Simon had made up his mind long ago that he was done with his mother's passive-aggressive games.

"Surely they won't mind if you have a call from your mother," Gloria coaxed.

"What do you need?" Simon did his best not to let it sound like his teeth were gritted.

"Always so busy. I hadn't heard from you, and I wondered how things were going, whether you had any interesting plans."

She knows about the wedding. And she's toying with me.

"I'm working on a triple murder case with the police as their official psychic." Simon didn't feel at all guilty for making it clear others valued the talents she had always found unseemly. "I don't have time for anything else."

"That sort of thing is so sordid," Gloria said. "Not like when you were at the university."

"Was there anything else? I have to go." He knew from experience and therapy that an argument couldn't be won. She'd just pull him deeper into the web of justifications and accusations.

Keep it short and simple. Don't give her anything she can use.

"You never come to Columbia anymore," she pouted.

"I have a life, a business, and a partner where I am."

"You mean the policeman."

"Homicide detective. And his name is Vic."

She sniffed. "I never wanted you to settle. Jacen is still single. There's still a chance—"

"I didn't 'settle.' Vic and I love each other. This conversation is over."

"Jacen never tried to cut you off from your family."

"Vic didn't cut me off. I left on my own. Meeting's starting. Gotta go." Simon ended the call and dropped back in his seat.

He realized he was shaking and that his stomach had tightened in a knot. Simon forced himself through breathing exercises until he felt like he had regained control.

I hate that she can do that to me after all this time.

But I managed the conversation, he reminded himself. *I didn't let her pull me into an argument, and I didn't justify myself. I was civil, but I maintained my boundaries.*

While Simon was proud of how far he had come taking charge of the relationship with his mother, it galled him that hearing from her still upset him so much.

She's fishing for information about the wedding. I've got to come up with a plan. There's no way I'm going to let her ruin the most important day of my life.

His phone rang again, and Simon recognized Vic's ringtone, his favorite Springsteen song.

"Just checking in. I'm going to look at some more rental houses during my lunch break. You doing okay?" Vic asked.

"I got a call from Gloria. I stupidly picked up before I realized it was her, and now she's got me scrambled," Simon admitted.

"Breathe, babe. You're not stupid—certainly not for answering the phone. Scrambling people is what she does best, and she's had decades of practice. Don't beat yourself up over it. Of course she can push your buttons—she's your mother."

"I keep thinking I'll handle her better 'next time,' and then—"

"And you do…better and better. Don't do her work for her by making yourself miserable," Vic coaxed. "Come solve a murder with Ross and me instead. We've got donuts."

Simon smiled, despite himself. "Well, that makes all the difference." He gave Vic a recap of Irving's attack on Jeremy, his call to Cassidy about Sheldon's magic props, the situation at Gideon's house, and his strategy session with Gabriella and Miss Eppie.

"We're running out of time," Simon fretted. "How fast can we go back to the house?"

"I'll find out and let you know. Just remember, I love you. No matter what happens, always," Vic assured him.

"Love you too." He ended the call and blew out a deep breath.

I'm not going to let her spoil my day—or our wedding. And right now, there's a murder investigation we need to wrap up so Vic and I can have a nice, long, peaceful honeymoon.

Fuck the mind games. I'm done playing around.

9

VIC

"There's enough room for everyone, but I'm not sure the kitchens will be okay." Vic fretted as he walked his mom and aunt through the beach rental house on a video call. He thought this one might be the closest to hitting the mark.

"It looks lovely," Bernie said.

"Everything in that kitchen is newer than what's in my house," Aunt Lucia added. "There's a full-size refrigerator, a stove, and an oven. It's all good."

"Are you sure?" Vic had seen four rental houses and dismissed the others for location, size, or lack of a truly functional kitchen. He didn't have time to keep looking and was starting to get desperate. "The beach view isn't great."

"Vic, we're coming to see you and Simon get married. We can walk down to the beach if we want to see the ocean," his mom assured him.

"And I couldn't get the houses next to each other. There's one house in between."

"Closer than we live to each other in Pittsburgh." Aunt Lucia dismissed his concern.

"It looks lovely," Bernie assured him. "You've got a wedding to plan. Chalk this up to a win and move on. You're still working, aren't you?" She used the tone Vic knew from childhood that meant she already knew the answer, and he had better not fudge the facts.

"We're finishing up a case—should be done in the next day or so," he added quickly, crossing his fingers that would be true. "Then Simon and I can relax and enjoy our honeymoon."

"You've only got a few days left before the rehearsal dinner, and your brothers have been talking to Ross about taking you out on the town for your bachelor party," his mom said as if he needed reminding.

Vic groaned, wondering what his brothers and Ross would concoct. "Please remind everyone that I still have to show my face in town as a representative of law enforcement, so nothing too wild and crazy."

"I'm sure they'll use good judgment," Bernie said.

Aunt Lucia snorted. "Sure they will."

"Not helping," Vic groaned. He wasn't too worried—after all, his brothers and Ross were all cops, and an arrest looked bad on the resume. At the same time, they were all experts in just how far one could go without actually breaking the law. While Vic trusted Ross to watch out for his dignity, he had no such assurance about his older brothers. The D'Amato boys cared about each other, and that ruled out malice, but it still left a lot of room for pranks.

"How's Simon doing?" Bernie changed the subject.

Vic sighed. "He's stressed about the case, like me. A few last-minute catering changes didn't help, although I think everything worked out okay. But the biggest thing is, he's worried his mom will show up and cause a scene. There's a good reason they're estranged."

"I'm sorry to hear that," Bernie said.

"I know our family can be loud and a little much at times, but seeing the issues Simon's had with his mom, I'm so grateful you are all exactly the way you are," Vic confessed.

"You make sure to tell Simon that I'm his mom now too," Bernie said. "Even if he doesn't change his name, he's an official D'Amato."

Her immediate, stalwart defense warmed Vic's heart. "I'll make sure he knows, Mom. Thank you."

"Pfft. That's what family's for," Bernie said, and Aunt Lucia murmured her assent. "Now go put the deposit on the beach houses before someone grabs them out from under you. We'll see you real soon. Don't work too hard."

"I'll be careful," Vic replied, knowing what his mom really meant.

"Humph. You'd better be. Love you—and Simon too."

"Love you." Vic ended the call.

He returned to the front porch, where the leasing agent waited for him. "We'll take it. It passed muster with the head honchos—my mom and aunt."

She laughed. "I know how that goes. Let's get everything signed, and then you can get on with the rest of your wedding plans. The big day's almost here, you know!"

As happy as Vic was about marrying Simon, he knew he'd be ecstatic when the ceremony and fuss were over. He finished up with the leasing agent and then checked the time.

"Crap. I'm late for my fitting. I've got the keys—do I need anything else?"

"I'll email you the paperwork. Go—I'll close up."

Vic jogged to his motorcycle, glad he had asked for a longer lunch hour. Ross met him at the clothing store, looking as harried as Vic felt.

"Let's hope this time the suits fit," Ross said. "Otherwise, I'm tempted to wear a Hawaiian shirt and board shorts."

"You and me both."

An hour later, Vic breathed a sigh of relief when they left the shop with suits that fit perfectly.

"Well, that's two good things," Vic said. "We're doomed for the rest of the day."

Ross snickered. "There's that optimistic streak of yours again."

Vic batted his shoulder. "I just don't want to get used to it. We've still got too many loose ends to tie up."

"Are all the arrangements confirmed for the photo shoot tomorrow? The Showalter Sculpture Gardens is going to be a great back-drop. Although it seems like it would have been easier to do all the photos at once, instead of you and me at one time and Simon and Tracey at another," Ross replied.

"Did you do wedding pictures with Sheila before the ceremony? Were you allowed to see her in the dress?"

"Hell, no."

"I rest my case." Vic didn't mind letting Simon have a few wedding superstitions. Given his fiancé's knowledge of occult lore, he wondered if there might not be some deeper reason behind the custom, but he wasn't going to ask.

They hung their suits in the back seat of Ross's car and headed to the station with Vic following on his bike. Simon had insisted that Ross put protective charms in his pool vehicle as well as his personal car, and Vic had done the same for his motorcycle and their office. While they couldn't ward the whole building or fully protect such a public space, Vic figured it was better than nothing and might put Irving's vengeful spirit on notice that his attacks wouldn't go unpunished.

"D'Amato, Hamilton—a word." Captain Hargrove motioned them into his office and shut the door.

Vic's mind spun trying to think what they might have done to incur the captain's ire.

"You feeling guilty about something, Vic? Want to share with the class?" Hargrove asked with a raised eyebrow.

"No, sir. Nothing at all."

"I bet." Hargrove motioned for them to sit. "This isn't official police business. I think I've managed to pull off Operation Deflect and Serve."

Vic looked up. That was the sarcastic name they'd given to their secret project to keep Simon's mom from crashing their wedding. "What's up?"

Hargrove's grin showed teeth. "I pulled in a few favors up in Columbia. An old friend of mine—Phil, my first partner on my first assignment—now runs a charity that takes care of injured K-9 officers and finds them forever homes. Turns out Simon's mom gave them a donation that was sizable for the organization but probably pocket change for her."

Hargrove's eyes glinted. "Phil invited Gloria Kincaide to a nice dinner at a restaurant. He had a friend who owed him a favor, and got a couple of friends in the mayor's office, to join them to 'honor' her and present her with a proclamation from the mayor of Columbia and a plaque. The only out-of-pocket is the engraving on the plaque, and since she really is a donor, that's legit. They'll make sure she gets her picture in the paper, too. Coincidentally, it happens to be on the same day and time as your wedding," he added with a smirk.

"Cap, I'm forever in your debt," Vic said. "You don't know how stressed Simon has been about that."

"And when Simon's stressed, Vic's stressed." Ross gave Vic the side eye.

"Don't tell Simon just yet," Hargrove cautioned. "We want to make sure Gloria takes the bait. He planned the timing so she can't get from Columbia to Myrtle Beach to interfere."

Vic felt stress he didn't realize he was carrying melt away. "Seriously—that's the best wedding present we could get. I've been afraid that Simon was right about his mom wanting to cause a ruckus, and while that wouldn't ultimately stop anything, it sure would bring down the mood and the memory. Thank you so much."

"Just in case, you might want to hire extra security for the parking lot and give them his mother's picture," Hargrove suggested.

"Good idea. I think this diversion will work, but Gloria's persistent," Vic replied.

"I don't have patience for people like that," Hargrove replied. "You and Simon deserve better. I'll keep you posted—but I think we'll know by tonight."

Hargrove listened intently as Vic caught him up on the new developments Simon had shared and the urgency around dealing with the magicians' ghosts. He laid out their theory that Sheldon had killed Irving, and then Irving's ghost had murdered Sheldon, and that both men had been responsible for other unsolved deaths.

"You have my approval to do what you need to do when everything you need is in place," Hargrove said. "Keep me posted—and good luck."

Vic repeated his thanks, and then he and Ross went back to the conference room where they had been reviewing the Timothy Sheldon evidence.

"Simon wants to wrap up the banishment tomorrow so Irving, Sheldon, and Bowden are put to rest," Vic told Ross. "That still leaves us a couple of days before the wedding to tie up the paperwork."

"We've technically solved the original case—Sheldon's murder," Ross replied. "I imagine Hargrove will want us to officially chalk it up to an elaborate suicide made to look like one last sensational magic trick."

Vic grimaced, unhappy with the pretense but knowing 'death by magic from a malicious ghost' wouldn't fly. "Probably so. But we've got to get rid of Irving and Bowden—and Sheldon, too—so they can't hurt anyone else, even if that wasn't part of the case. They're a clear and present danger we can't just allow to run loose."

"Oh, I agree completely." Ross held up a hand to forestall argument. "And we've made our case to Hargrove. I'll be as relieved as you are when we wrap this one up. I'm wondering what's going to happen to all the weird stuff in Sheldon's house when we're all done."

"Simon's been working on that. Cassidy said she'll find a way to take care of it. I imagine Trifles and Folly will make the high bid at auction and buy the contents. Then they can go through the items and make sure to pull out anything that might be haunted or cursed. They can sell off the rest to collectors."

"And the bad stuff?" Ross asked.

"According to Simon, one of Cassidy's allies runs a rather strange organization that works like bomb disposal for supernatural items. They'll make sure the pieces are destroyed or trapped somewhere they can never hurt anyone ever again."

"This is the same cousin Cassidy who's bringing the necromancer and the vampire to the wedding?"

"Uh-huh. I've met both of them. They're chill. And Father Anne, the priest who's doing the ceremony, is also a whiz with exorcisms."

"Handy. I've been to a couple of weddings that probably could have used her help," Ross noted.

Simon knocked at the doorway, bearing a bag with sub sandwiches, as promised. They all moved to the end of the table and cleared away files so they could eat.

"Everything go okay so far today?" Simon squeezed Vic's shoulder in greeting.

"Don't jinx us," Vic warned. "But, yes. Fingers crossed we can keep on a streak. Sounds like we've had it easier than you have. Thanks for bringing food."

"Go ahead and eat—I already did. But I haven't forgotten that you promised me donuts."

Vic laughed. "They're on the side table by the coffee. Help yourself."

"Anything new at the shop?" Vic opened up his club sandwich and positioned napkins to catch any stray shredded lettuce or Italian dressing.

"I didn't have appointments, so I did a séance for five of the people on Ross's list," Simon reported.

"I bet that was interesting." Ross put a napkin over his tie so he didn't lose any marinara sauce from his meatball sandwich.

"You have no idea." Simon shook his head.

"You didn't have to channel any of them, did you?" Vic immediately worried and checked Simon over for signs of injury.

"I'm fine," Simon reassured him. "Just mentally tired. But I did get some useful information. Irving and Bowden both hated and resented Sheldon, but they loathed each other even more."

"Interesting," Vic mused. "Why?"

"Irving resented that Sheldon booked prime appearances he coveted," Simon continued. "Irving had a bad temper, and the big places stopped hiring him. Sheldon saw Irving as a threat, and hated Bowden for how he treated people. Bowden was a creeper and a pervert. To further tangle things, Irving and Sheldon blamed each other for the wedding deaths. Oh, and there was a whole love triangle thing where Irving had the hots for a woman who ended up as one of Sheldon's girlfriends and who got harassed by Bowden."

"Wow—soap operas have nothing on ghosts' gossip," Vic remarked.

"I'm no longer surprised that Irving and Bowden haven't moved on. They're so consumed by their rage they're stuck on this plain of existence even without Sheldon interfering."

"So what's the plan?" Ross wiped away the last bit of red sauce and crumbled up the sandwich wrapper.

"If we can access the house tomorrow, I think we can wrap this up before the wedding and head off any more attacks by Irving," Simon replied. "When Cassidy and Sorren come in for the ceremony, they can check out the house for themselves and pull some strings to be sure to win the auction. Ghosts gone, problem items neutralized, end of story."

Vic knew it was never that easy, but he admired the logic of Simon's strategy. "Are you calling in backup?"

"I've already talked to Gabriella and Miss Eppie, and they're willing to help trap the vengeful spirits who aren't going to leave on their own. We can call Father Anne if we think it's necessary. Then Cassidy can pass the trapped ghosts on to Donnelly, who can get rid of them permanently," Simon replied.

Simon looked to each of them in turn with a warning glance. "You need to both make sure you're wearing all the warding amulets and protective medallions you've got, as well as carrying your mojo bags. Irving and Bowden aren't likely to go easy, and now that Sheldon's ghost has shown up again, it's going to be a wild ride."

That night at dinner, Vic noticed that Simon mostly pushed his food around on his plate. "What's on your mind? You're not eating."

Simon looked down at his plate as if suddenly aware of what he'd been doing. "Sorry. Just preoccupied."

"It's Hunan beef, one of your favorites," Vic prompted. "We

have a big day tomorrow, and you'll be dealing with powerful ghosts. You need a couple of good meals in you—that sort of thing takes a toll."

Vic knew that while he didn't truly understand everything about his lover's talents, he could see when the energy drain left him tired and out of sorts.

"You're right. Thanks for reminding me. I'm just too nervous to be hungry."

"Talk to me." Vic reached out to take Simon's left hand. "What's bothering you? And don't say 'everything.'"

Simon managed a weak smile. "I'm a little nervous about the photo shoot tomorrow morning."

"Which one? The shoot with you and Tracey, or the one with Ross and me?"

"Both."

Vic smiled. "It will all go okay; I know that. We have a good photographer, the weather is going to be gorgeous, and the location will give us great shots."

"I want everything about the wedding to be perfect, and I'm not a huge fan of having my picture taken." Simon twisted his napkin, nearly shredding the paper.

"It's okay if things aren't completely perfect," Vic reassured Simon. "We're not perfect, either. We're capturing a moment. I have complete faith in you."

Simon let out a long breath. "I'm glad we got the catering and the suit alterations and the beach houses squared away. The venue is confirmed, and they're coordinating the flowers and cake, so it's all good. I'm excited to become your husband." He returned Vic's hand squeeze. "But I'm still worried about what my mother might do."

Vic struggled not to reveal their plan, but he didn't want to promise safety and then have something go wrong. "I have a feeling she's going to steer clear," he said, making eye contact.

"You're not secretly working with Cassidy to send vampires, are you?"

"Nope."

"Werewolves?"

Vic smiled and shook his head. "Tempting, but no. And if she does show up, we've got more than enough muscle to deal with her and give her a police escort out of town."

Simon leaned over to kiss Vic. "Thank you for putting up with my panics."

"Any time. We're going to have a good day with the people who love us, and we'll end up married. That's all that matters." Vic returned the kiss with quiet fervor.

"Just stay close tonight. I need you to ground me."

"Anything you need—always," Vic promised.

10

SIMON

"Relax." Chris, the wedding photographer seemed boundlessly patient.

"I'm sorry. There's just a lot going on," Simon apologized.

"No worries," Chris assured him. "Everyone has jitters when the big day is coming up. Try to focus on how beautiful this day is and the lovely garden. No rain to worry about. Just let go and have fun."

"Yeah, what he said," Tracey teased, elbowing Simon. As his "best person," Tracey was in some of the shots with Simon, even though most were reflective and fun poses of him alone. He wondered how well Ross and Vic had done in their shoot earlier.

"Just let the love shine through," Chris advised. "We'll see it in your eyes."

They moved from beneath the big live oak trees with their Spanish moss to the sculpture garden, to the koi pond. Sometimes Chris made suggestions of poses or moods, and at other times he followed unobtrusively, snapping unguarded moments.

Tracey joked with Simon, knowing from their long friendship how to jolly him out of a mood and get him to stop thinking so hard. Her good humor helped to pull him out of his worries.

Which is why she's my best friend.

"And that's a wrap," Chris announced, surprising Simon that the time had gone by so quickly. "I'll have proofs to you early next week. You can pick which ones you want to print, or you can get digital copies or a mix. I'll send you all the information. And I'll see you at the wedding."

Tracey, Chris, and Simon walked back toward the main office, chatting about everything and nothing. Simon tried to focus on the warmth of the sunlight on his skin, the feel of the breeze, and the beauty of the garden. None of those things erased the background tension knowing that the confrontation with three vengeful ghosts loomed.

They waved goodbye to Chris and headed to the garden's cafe. Tracey picked a salad and a lemonade, while Simon got a ham sandwich and a Coke.

"You looked good," Tracey told him as they settled at a small table where they could see a bank of flowers. "Chris does great work —I think you'll like the photos."

"I hope so. I'm sure Vic's will be fine. I just never like how I look in pictures."

"Are you doubting my word?" Tracey teased. "Take the compliment and accept it. Don't make it complicated."

"I know, I know." Simon used the pretense of eating his sandwich to hide from the conversation, a tactic that only lasted a few moments.

"Is everything else set?" Tracey asked, having polished off her salad in record time.

"Caterer, officiant, venue, DJ, cake—check. All the official paperwork is done. We've got the rings and the honeymoon plane tickets and hotel arrangements. Vic's family will start coming into town tomorrow," Simon told her. "Then we'll do the rehearsal and be ready for the big day."

"Didn't you forget something?" Tracey needled. "The bachelor party! Shayna and I have been planning this for months. We are going to have so much fun!"

Simon looked at her skeptically. "Try not to get us arrested or put on the no-fly list. I need to get on a plane for the honeymoon."

"We will stop having fun just shy of federal intervention." Tracey crossed her heart.

"Not helping."

"Oh, come on. Don't be such a grumpy butt," Tracey cajoled.

Simon knew he could overthink situations, and from their very first meeting, Tracey had excelled at getting him to lighten up.

"I'm worried about this afternoon," Simon admitted. "We've got a plan and powerful helpers, but there's always a chance that something could go wrong."

"You've got this. You are both good at what you do. Just keep your mind on what you're doing. It's going to be okay."

Simon hadn't shared the full story with Tracey since technically Sheldon's murder was still under investigation. She knew they were dealing with restless spirits, but he hadn't told her just how dangerous Irving, Sheldon, and Bowden could be. Still, he appreciated her encouragement.

"I just don't want to be cocky or underestimate the situation," he said. "And I keep waiting for the other shoe to fall with Mom. I really don't want her to show up and spoil the day."

Tracey put a hand on his arm. "I understand why you're worried. I wouldn't want someone crashing my special day to cause a ruckus. But you said Vic hired extra security and will be giving them her picture so they could stop her before she gets in from the parking lot. That makes sense—even if getting rent-a-cops is kinda funny for a reception full of police and witches. You're still going to introduce me to your vampire friend, right?"

Simon smiled. Tracey was like the sister he never had. "Of course. Just don't try to get him to flash his fangs. That's not polite. I think he'd prefer to pass as human."

"I will be the soul of discretion." Tracey had a glint in her eye that made Simon a little nervous.

Once they finished lunch, Simon drove Tracey back to Le Miz.

"Get ready for a great bachelor party!" Tracey winked when she climbed out of the car.

"My reputation is in your hands."

Simon returned to the blue bungalow and showered since they

had walked all over the garden for the photographs. He tried to let the warm water sluice away his tension and apprehension over the upcoming afternoon at Sheldon's house.

Once he changed into casual clothing, Simon sat on the couch and closed his eyes, meditating before it was time to go to the magician's house.

Simon's phone rang with Vic's ringtone. "Hello?"

"Vic's not quite himself right now." It was Vic's voice, but everything about it felt wrong. A chill went down Simon's spine, and his heartbeat sped up with fear.

"Vic?"

"Nathan Irving, at your service. Vic's taking a little nap." Vic's familiar voice sounded haughty and cold.

"Leave Vic alone," Simon growled. To Simon's knowledge, Irving had killed everyone he'd possessed.

"That can be arranged…for a price," Irving said through Vic. "You've been causing trouble, poking around. I'm willing to make a deal. My freedom for your boyfriend. Come to Sheldon's house. No tricks, or Vic will be a ghost too."

The call ended, leaving Simon in shock. He jumped when the phone rang again, with Ross's tone this time. His hand shook as he answered.

"Ross, what—?"

"Simon. Something's gone wrong," Ross said, breathless. "Vic and I were going through the files on the victims we think Irving's ghost killed, and then all of a sudden it got really cold in the room, and Vic fainted. When I went to help him up, he clocked me on the jaw and left. I don't know—"

"Irving's ghost is possessing him," Simon said tightly, trying to hold his emotions in check. "Do you know if Vic had any of his protective items with him?"

"It looked like the chain broke on the medallions he always wears—they were lying on the floor. And he left his jacket behind, so anything in the pockets didn't do him any good," Ross replied. "I'm still freaked about finding out ghosts can possess people. I thought it was only demons who could do that."

Simon answered. "Most ghosts can't. Irving's exceptionally strong, fueled by rage, and very disciplined. Plus he could do real magic. I thought you and Vic were protected. I was wrong."

"Don't blame yourself—Irving outfoxed the amulets. I've made sure I have all of mine," Ross assured him. "What are we going to do?"

"Vic—Irving—called me right before you did. Wants me to come to the Sheldon house to make a deal. We let him go, and he gives back Vic, unharmed." Simon felt cold rationality overtake his initial shock.

"You can't let him go. Irving will keep killing his enemies if he goes free." Ross's tone made it clear he recognized the stakes.

"I know. And he'll kill Vic if we don't. So we work the plan, just a little sooner than we expected," Simon replied.

"I need to stop by the precinct for something, and then I have to go to the house and hope I'm in time," he told Ross. "You bring Miss Eppie and Gabriella to the house. We do what we originally intended—but I'll make Irving think we're playing it his way." Simon found himself crossing his fingers.

"What if Irving senses their magic? You know he's likely to double-cross you," Ross warned.

"We don't have a choice. Vic will hate it if more people die because we saved him. But I'm not willing to let him die. And we've run out of time."

Simon picked up what he needed at headquarters and drove to the Sheldon house, trying not to envision doomsday scenarios.

He nervously fingered the watch on his left wrist. It was made for a man with larger bones, and the weight was unfamiliar. He'd had to do some fast talking to borrow it. Simon pushed down his fear for Vic's safety. Irving was desperate, and he had little to lose. Simon hoped he had read the situation right, or Vic wouldn't make it to their wedding.

He pulled up to the Sheldon house and took a few deep breaths. His stomach was knotted with tension, and he suspected the strain on Vic would be even worse. Irving's assault was likely to have been swift and violent, like a kidnapping.

Hang on, Vic, Simon thought.

Simon walked up to the door, already feeling a shift in the house's energy with Irving's ghost in charge, making it even more oppressive than usual. The front door swung open like in a bad horror movie. Simon accepted the unspoken invitation and walked inside.

The door slammed behind him, and Simon did his best not to startle.

"I thought you might not show, and I'd have to prove my point." Vic stood across the room, but everything about his stance and voice was wrong. His eyes were cold, he looked like he was spoiling for a fight, and the sardonic tone was all Irving.

That, and the kitchen cleaver Irving made Vic hold to his own throat.

"Put down the knife." Simon forced himself to hold eye contact. "No one needs to get hurt. You wanted a deal. I'm here to make one."

A tremor shuddered through Vic's form, and Simon wondered if his fiancé was fighting the possession.

"Just like that?" Irving mocked with Vic's voice.

Simon nodded. "Why not? The cops can't arrest a ghost. They'll close Sheldon's case and move on. Unless you're still working your way through a kill list?"

The laugh was chilling. "Maybe. Maybe not. Either way, I've got no use for the afterlife and no desire to go there."

In the background, Simon sensed the other ghosts in the house. Bowden's trapped spirit pounded furiously on the walls of his prison, shouting curses and insults only Simon and the other revenants could hear. The women's spirits who had remained to keep watch on Bowden hung back, unsure and afraid. Simon sensed a presence that might be Sheldon's ghost, but it, too, stayed just out of reach.

"Then let's do this. Let go of Vic without harming him, and I won't try to stop you from leaving." Simon gripped his left wrist with his right hand, letting his sleeves hide the watch and the way his fingers were ready at the clasp.

"I could just kill you and hedge my bet." The glint of cruel humor in Vic's eyes was all Irving. Hearing the threat coming from Vic made Simon's stomach curdle, even though he knew the ghost was talking.

"You might be able to. But I'm not the only medium in the Lowcountry. Once word got out, they'd be gunning for you." Simon tried to keep his voice even and hide his emotions. "My cousin knows a powerful necromancer who could crumple up your ghost, shred your consciousness, and slam dunk what's left in hell. So you might not want to go that route."

That seemed to rattle Irving.

He's gotten away with his murders for so long he forgot that he's not untouchable.

The blade trembled, raising a thin line of blood on Vic's throat. For a fraction of a second, Simon swore he saw Vic's panicked gaze looking out from those dark eyes before Irving was in control once more.

"It's been delicious having a body again," Irving taunted. "I can see why you like him. He's strong and pretty…and packing heat," he added with a leer. "I could just keep him for a while. We could get up to a lot of fun together."

"For a week, maybe less." Simon forced himself to sound coldly clinical as if the life of his husband-to-be didn't hang in the balance. "Possession burns through both the ghost's energy and the vessel's. Demons can do it because they're immortal. You're already dead. As a ghost, you'll eventually fade into a faint echo. That could take decades or centuries. But possessing a body will burn you up. You'll both be gone in days."

Simon hadn't been lying about the damage prolonged possession would cause. The longer it went on, the more likely Vic would be badly hurt.

He had just watched a documentary about hostage negotiators, and now Simon struggled to recall their methods. *Getting him to monologue works in our favor. Irving's got a huge ego. Letting him air his grievances buys us time for the cavalry to get into position.*

"Sheldon had it coming," Irving said through Vic. "Don't feel bad for him. I enjoyed every minute it took to shove those cards down his throat. The guy used his so-called friends for everything they could do for him without returning favors. Slept with any woman who'd take him. Got away with everything because he was 'charming.' Never cared who got hurt." His voice dripped with contempt.

"Including your daughter and Katrina Dawson?" Simon gambled on hitting a nerve bringing up the doomed bride and the woman Irving had been obsessed with, Sheldon seduced, and Bowden abused. Irving's unrequited crush had added fuel to the spiral of retribution and murder.

"Don't you say her name! Don't you say it!" Irving's hold on the cleaver was white-knuckled, and it scraped against Vic's flesh, raising fresh blood.

Simon held up his hands, palms out. "Easy. Easy." He started breathing again when Irving's hold lightened enough to not press the blade into Vic's neck. "Sheldon did you a good turn by killing Bowden, didn't he? Bowden hurt Katrina and got away with it— officially, anyhow."

"Bowden was a thief and an abuser. He wouldn't listen when Katrina told him to go away, tried to take what he wanted anyhow. I was going to kill him, but I hadn't figured out how, yet. Doesn't make Sheldon a hero. Sheldon murdered me, stole my magic, and took my girl. He deserved what he got."

"That's why you killed Sheldon?" Simon wanted confirmation, even though the official record might say differently.

"Yeah—and I'd do it again. Go ahead and tell the cops. Nothing they can do to me. Killed some of the other bastards from back then once I knew what I could do—like Sheldon's good-for-nothing-nephew. My daughter would be alive if she hadn't gotten tangled up with him. I'm not sorry for what I've done. No one else would stop them. They didn't believe in my magic. Didn't like my act. Wouldn't give me a chance. Who's laughing now?"

The irony of being just as dead as the victims of his vengeance seemed to elude Irving.

Simon saw a glimpse of panic in Vic's eyes again.

"We made a deal. I'm here to keep it. The cops won't stay away forever, so are you going to hold up your end of the bargain?" Simon knew he was playing with fire pushing Irving, but he didn't know what would happen if Vic gained the upper hand and tried to evict the ghost on his own or if Irving thought up some new reason to hold on.

Simon felt another spirit skirting the edge of his awareness and was certain it was Sheldon, dead long enough now to figure out how to manifest. *Of course he wouldn't want to miss a slugfest with Irving.*

"Timothy Sheldon—if that's you, help me stop Irving and protect his hostage," Simon sent silently, hoping the ghost was listening and remained sane enough to take direction.

"This guy's too much of a Boy Scout for me anyhow," Irving said. "He'd feel too guilty to enjoy the ride. You can have him back."

The cleaver hand lowered.

"Except I don't like the names he's been calling me." Irving shifted his grip on the cleaver to hold the point toward Vic's belly. "He shouldn't say those things."

"Don't!" Simon shouted, seeing Sheldon's ghost draw closer.

Timothy Sheldon's ghost grabbed Vic's wrist before Irving could plunge the blade into Vic's stomach. Then Sheldon knocked the knife out of Vic's grip and pushed his own spirit through Vic's body, trying to shove Irving out.

At the same time, Simon reached to touch Irving's ghost and pulled with all his might. He saw the instant Irving's revenant was thrown clear of Vic, who slumped to the floor. Sheldon floated above them. Simon clicked the clasp on the watch he wore—Bowden's Rolex—and let it fall to the floor, where he ground it beneath his heel.

The energy shift felt like a thunderclap as the barrier trapping Bowden shattered. Bowden's spirit wrenched free of its prison and flew screaming into the room. Ice-cold hands tossed Simon to one side.

Bowden's spirit howled in rage. It attacked Irving and Sheldon's ghosts with the full strength of his fury.

"Now!" Simon yelled.

The door behind him burst open. Gabriella and Miss Eppie's voices rose above the furor of the ghosts' battle, chanting their spells in Spanish and Gullah. Ross stood behind them, gun drawn, ready.

Simon wanted to rush to Vic, but he still had a part to play. He put himself between the warring ghosts and Vic's too-still body and began the banishment ritual, sending the angry spirits toward where Gabriella and Miss Eppie held out a black, mirror-lined "coffin box" that could trap the revenants until a priest or necromancer could force them into the afterlife.

At their feet were the tools of their magic: two burning pillar candles—one white and one black, sigils chalked on the porch floor and sprinkled with graveyard dirt, a shallow silver bowl atop a cloth woven and embroidered with runes, what remained of Irving's playing cards, and the rest of the women's photos.

Green flames rose from the silver bowl as Gabriella dropped the cards one by one into the fire along with the photo of the ill-fated newlyweds.

Simon's skin prickled with the energy Miss Eppie and Gabriella raised, as well as his own psychic ability. The hair on the back of his neck rose from the dark energy of the three ghosts.

"Nathan Irving—you have abused your gifts and used magic to murder. I banish and abjure you. I cast you out and bind you to negation," Simon shouted above the roar of the battling spirits.

Miss Eppie waited with an open coffin box. She shouted something Simon didn't catch, and Irving's ghost screamed as the mirror-lined black box dragged him toward it.

"Bill Bowden, release the energy that holds you here." Gabriella's voice rang out as she tossed the women's photographs into the fire. "Leave this place and never return. Renounce the ties that hold your victims to this world, and be gone."

Gabriella and Miss Eppie shouted in unison, and Bowden's shriek echoed in Simon's head, so piercing he thought his ears would bleed. Bowden's ghost swirled like a cyclone of blood-red mist, drawn inexorably toward the mirrored box.

"Timothy Sheldon—you stole magic, used it to kill, and imprisoned other souls. I banish you from among the living. Release what binds you here and go into what awaits you," Miss Eppie ordered.

Magic pulled the angry spirits toward the coffin box, stripping off strands of mist until the mirrored prison contained the last of their essences, and Miss Eppie slammed the lid shut.

"Vic!" Simon ran to where Vic lay and knelt beside his fiancé. "Are you hurt?"

Vic didn't rouse, and Simon's heart rose to his throat. "Vic!" He drew a finger over the shallow cut on Vic's throat. It came away bloody, but the marks weren't deep enough to do real harm.

Vic groaned, and Simon helped him to sit, resting against him. "How do you feel?" Simon pressed, still frantic for his safety.

"I'm okay." Vic's voice was firm but quiet. He looked too pale, and a cut bled on his forehead in addition to the marks on his neck. "Just shook."

Simon pressed a kiss to his temple. "You scared me."

"Yeah, well I was pretty freaked out myself," Vic replied. He reached for Simon's hand. "What about you?"

"I'm fine, just got thrown around a little."

"Sheldon saved me," Vic said quietly, sounding rattled. "It felt like he and Irving were playing tug of war with my body."

"Are all three ghosts gone for good?" Simon looked up at Gabriella and then glanced at Miss Eppie, who had gathered the coffin box into a spelled bag.

"Yes," Gabriella replied. "Coffin boxes are strong magic. And since the ghosts attacked in unison, they are trapped together for eternity—or until your necromancer and priest friends send them elsewhere. When your cousin's people come to take care of the house, we'll pass the box to them. They can make sure Irving, Sheldon, and Bowden never bother anyone again."

"Supernatural supermax," Vic snarked. "I didn't know it was a thing."

"What about the other ghosts?" Ross asked.

Simon concentrated despite the pounding headache that had started behind his eyes. He shook his head. "Gone. All of them. When we got rid of Bowden, the women's spirits no longer needed to keep watch. Sheldon's old partner was avenged. The ghosts moved on. I hope they find peace."

Ross and Simon helped Vic to his feet. He and Simon both staggered, but they leaned on one another to hold their weight. Gabriella and Miss Eppie extinguished the candles, released the wardings, and thanked the elements before packing up their ritual materials.

"Thank you," Simon told both women. "You were magnificent. You saved our butts."

"The way I see it, we didn't have a choice if we were going to dance at your wedding—and I intend to have a fine time," Miss Eppie replied with a broad smile.

"Now we can celebrate without unfinished business," Gabriella chimed in. "And I'm laying claim to a second piece of cake."

Ross started to laugh. Simon and Vic looked at him as if he'd lost his mind.

"What?" Simon asked, amused and intrigued.

"Us," Ross replied, still chuckling. "We look a sight, all bruised up. It's a good thing we got most of the pictures taken already because at the moment, they'd be more like mug shots."

Simon helped Vic into his Toyota. He paused to call Gideon and let him know that he and Jeremy were safe to leave the warded house and that the dangerous ghosts were contained. Ross followed them back to the bungalow and waited until they were safely inside before driving off.

Vic protested that he was fine, but the fact that he allowed Simon to steady him on the way to the couch told the real story.

"Rest. At the very least, you've had a shock to the system." Simon disappeared into the bedroom and came back with pillows and a blanket. "I'll get you some ibuprofen because I'm certain you're going to have a headache—if you don't already."

A text message pinged on Simon's phone.

Ross: *I'll drop off dinner, Advil, and ice so you don't have to worry about anything. Hope you both feel better soon.*

Simon's gaze fell to the cuts on Vic's throat. *It could have been so much worse.*

He didn't realize he had started shaking until Vic took his hand. "Hey, Simon, look at me. I'm alive and so are you. Don't play the 'what if' game."

Simon gave a curt nod, struggling with his fears. "I'll be right back with the pills." He made a break for the bathroom and shut the door, then leaned on the sink and hung his head, trying to steady his breathing.

I almost lost him.

His mind replayed the moment Irving's ghost shifted its grip on the cleaver, intending to gut Vic as he released the body. Only in Simon's imagination, the blade stuck hilt-deep, and Vic collapsed in a pool of blood as Irving's ghost ripped free, filling the house with gloating laughter.

Simon fell to his knees and retched into the toilet, shaking with full-body chills.

"Simon?" Vic's voice sounded muffled through the door.

"I'm coming," Simon called over his shoulder. He got to his feet, flushed away the evidence, and washed his face, brushing his teeth for good measure. Then he remembered to grab the ibuprofen and the first aid kit and returned to the living room.

"You don't look so hot yourself." Vic gave him a worried glance.

"Aftermath," Simon admitted. He got a glass of water from the kitchen and held out a couple of tablets for Vic, then settled beside him on the couch.

"Let me clean up your neck." He used an alcohol wipe to disinfect before spreading antibiotic salve and covering it with a gauze square.

"That's not going to look great in the wedding photos."

"This is just to keep the ointment off the couch and the sheets. By the time it's absorbed, the cuts should already be scabbed over."

Even though Simon knew the marks had been barely scratches, he couldn't tear his gaze away from the bandage.

Vic took his hand. "Hey—my eyes are up here," he joked.

Simon managed a wan smile and glanced up, knowing Vic could read the crazy whipsaw of emotions in his eyes.

"I don't know how you can do it, letting ghosts in like that," Vic said quietly. "I must have touched something in the evidence box that had a strong connection, because the next thing I knew I was on my back on the floor and it felt like my brain got hit with a battering ram. That's when I realized I couldn't move or speak. For a second, I thought I'd had a stroke—and then Irving started talking inside my head."

Vic looked away, but he kept a death grip on Simon's hand. "He made me hit Ross. I'm not sure how we got to Sheldon's house. All the while, Irving was gloating about the murders he'd gotten away with, and how he was going to make you watch while he killed me and then killed you and Ross. And I couldn't shake him loose."

Tears started at the corners of Vic's eyes, and his voice sounded wrecked. "I fought. I screamed and struggled, and I couldn't get away. Then you showed up, and he had the cleaver, and I thought this was it. That we weren't going to get our wedding."

Simon smoothed the tears away and gave a reassuring smile. "As for how I channel spirits—it's not like what happened to you. I invite the ghosts in, they don't try to take over, and they leave when they're supposed to. What Irving did was violation." He knew Vic could hear the angry rumble in his voice.

"It scared the shit out of me when he called, and I knew it wasn't really you talking," Simon went on. "There were so many ways Irving could have hurt you, and I knew he was a sadistic son of a bitch. I had to trust Ross and Miss Eppie and Gabriella to do their part, but all I wanted was to rip that fucker out of your head and send him straight to hell."

"Tell them 'thank you' for me." Vic stroked his thumb over the back of Simon's hand. "You were totally badass."

"Pretty sure all of us were pretty bad mofos," Simon answered with a weak laugh. "I'm just glad we're safe and it's behind us."

"I know Captain Hargrove will have to fudge the case notes a bit, but how many cold cases did we close along with Sheldon's murder?"

"Bowden and Irving's deaths and all of Irving and Sheldon's victims," Simon replied. "So at least eight, maybe more? That's a pretty good score. I think we've earned our vacation."

Simon's text message chime let him know that Ross had dropped off the delivery. He was already gone by the time Simon got to the door, but Simon texted him their thanks and added Vic's heartfelt apology for busting him in the jaw.

Ross: *No teeth lost, so I'm counting it as a win. Take care of each other. I plan to get the maximum sympathy coddling from Sheila that I can over this.*

Simon put the ice in the freezer so he could make cold packs for their bruises after supper. Dinner was from their favorite Mexican place—a family-sized sharable batch of carne asada with rice, beans, guacamole, chips, queso, and flan for dessert. He made plates for both of them and set up tray tables next to the couch.

"I hope the photographer can retouch the photos from the ceremony, or we're going to look like we lost a cage fight," Vic said. Simon was pleased to see that after everything, Vic dug into his food with gusto.

"We could go low-tech and have the photographer dab on concealer," Simon replied after he swallowed his mouthful of rice and beans. "He can probably retouch the pictures and get rid of all the marks. Or we can see if one of our witchy friends can zap the bruises away."

"None of those options will offend my masculinity," Vic joked. "I want to remember our wedding, not Nathan-fucking-Irving's ghost, when I look at those photos for the next fifty years."

"Only fifty?" Simon teased. "You planning to ditch me in our eighties for some cute twink?"

"Sixty? Forget the twinks—you're stuck with me forever," Vic countered.

Simon bent to kiss him, and the heat of Vic's lips wasn't just from the hot sauce.

"Sounds like a plan to me," Simon murmured.

After they finished eating, Simon took the plates to the kitchen. He had pulled a couple of beers from the fridge and stuck popcorn in the microwave when his phone rang.

He recognized his mother's ringtone and froze for a moment. *I am so not in the mood to deal with this. But I guess I need to get it over with.*

"Mom." He knew he sounded curt, but after the day they'd lived through, Simon couldn't bring himself to care.

"Sebastian. I'm afraid I have some bad news for you," Gloria recounted in her typically dramatic fashion. "I had hoped to drop in on you this weekend, but that's not going to be possible. So sorry, some other time. The fantastic news is that I'm being honored as a donor and K-9 Corp champion by one of my charities. They're hosting a dinner, and people from the mayor's office will be there. There might even be a proclamation in my honor," she added with a sly, self-congratulatory lilt in her voice.

"That's great—about the honor," Simon managed, feeling relief flow through his whole body. "I'm sure it'll make the papers and the evening news."

"Oh, count on that," Gloria replied. "The charity is working with the mayor's office to make sure it's front page. They're hoping it will inspire more donations. Such a worthy cause."

"Absolutely."

"I knew you'd understand. Just wanted to let you know. Got to run." She ended the call.

Conflicting feelings cascaded through Simon. Relief that Gloria wouldn't ruin their special day. Curiosity over how the event had popped up perfectly to conflict with their wedding—and the suspicion that Vic might have had something to do with it. And in a dark corner he didn't want to examine, a child's hurt that once again he wasn't—and never would be—her priority.

Simon didn't try to unsnarl the tangle of emotions as he carried the beers and popcorn to the living room and sat next to Vic.

"Your mom?"

"Yeah. She's suddenly getting a high-profile honor from one of her charities, so she won't crash our wedding." He gave Vic the side eye. "You don't happen to know anything about that, do you?"

Vic grinned. "Thank Hargrove. I'm sure he'll still give us a fondue pot or something, but averting that disaster is the best wedding gift he could give us."

"He has my total gratitude." Simon lifted his beer bottle in a toast. "To us." Vic echoed the words, and they clinked the longnecks together.

Simon found a movie on streaming they hadn't seen, and they shifted to lie down together with Simon as the big spoon and the popcorn in easy reach for both of them. When the onscreen action lagged and their beers were empty, Vic set the popcorn aside and turned to face Simon. They kissed slow and easy, nestled against each other, hands roving in gentle confirmation of being safe and whole.

Sometimes after a near-death experience, the lovemaking was fast and hard, proof of life, fucking away the remaining fear and tension. Tonight, Simon didn't care if their touches escalated to more, content to have Vic alive and well in his arms. After what Vic had gone through, he doubted his lover was in the mood for anything athletic. Sleepy kisses seemed like the perfect validation.

"You good just like this?" Vic asked in a low rumble.

"Yep, this is perfect. A little abstinence makes the wedding night that much better," Simon teased.

"Hmm…hadn't thought of that. After how things went today, this is all I've got," Vic admitted in between kisses.

"Which is pretty damn fine." Simon kissed him back. "I love you —just like this."

11

VIC

"So, little brother, are you ready for a big night out tonight?" Micky, Vic's oldest brother Michael, asked, two days before the wedding. Vic and Simon had picked that day for their separate bachelor parties.

"Bring it," Vic replied. "I can't wait to see what you've cooked up. Just remember that if I can't function at the wedding, Simon will send ghosts to haunt your room."

Micky smirked. "Oh, you'll be able to 'function' all right," he promised. "And it would be awkward to end up in jail. That's all I'm going to tell you. It wouldn't do to spoil the surprise."

"Make sure he has a good time," Simon told him. "I have a feeling we are both going to have a night to remember."

Those words rang in Vic's mind a few hours later amid the din of clanging video games and the flashing lights of Myrtle Beach's newest mega-arcade bar.

"Come on," Leo shouted to be heard over the noise. "It's our time for the go-karts."

He practically dragged Vic toward where the rest of their party queued for their turn to ride.

"How much more fun do we need to have?" Vic asked as Leo hauled him across the arcade.

"All the fun you can stand, and then we go back to the suite and play poker," Leo replied. "It's your last night as a free man."

Vic knew his very-married brother was joking and flipped him off. "Do you want me to quote you the next time I talk to Ellie?"

Leo's eyes widened. "You want to get me killed?"

"That's what I figured," Vic snarked.

They raced the go-karts with as much brotherly ruthlessness as when they had played best two out of three games of blacklight bowling or pitted their skills against each other in the escape rooms. As they lapped each other, vying for position to shave seconds off their time around the track, they shouted joking insults and made rude gestures like when they were kids.

Vic laughed as they tried to one-up each other on pinball scores and the basketball game and compared their times escaping the mirror maze. Laser tag with a bunch of cops proved interesting. Ross kept up with them and accepted their teasing good-naturedly as a badge of belonging.

None of them overindulged, but hiring a super-stretch limo to take them to the hotel freed everyone to drink throughout the evening.

"The party isn't over, bro." Micky slapped Vic on the back just a bit too hard, making Vic gasp. "I hope you brought your lucky socks 'cause that's the only way you'll ever win at poker."

"In your dreams," Vic rejoined. "I could use some extra cash for the honeymoon."

"Big talk. You'll have a chance to show us what you've got," Micky said. "See if you've upped your game. Otherwise it's like taking candy from a baby…brother."

"Yeah, yeah. We'll see. Just wait."

As much as Vic had come to love his new life in Myrtle Beach, he missed his family in Pittsburgh. They often talked online and constantly swapped texts and emails, but nothing compared to the non-stop repartee that flowed effortlessly when they were together.

"Your poor mother," Ross joked. "The lot of you must have driven her to distraction growing up."

"You're not wrong," Vic replied as they left the arcade and piled into the limo. "Although Mom always got the final word—even with Dad. When she raises her voice, watch out. It's like God speaking from the clouds with one last chance before you get zapped with lightning. We all knew how far we could push things—and when to stop."

The short ride to the hotel provided ample opportunity for the brothers to top each other's stories from growing up, including fond memories of the times they put one over on their parents. Ross just shook his head and chuckled.

The hotel suite offered two rooms with double beds, a large sitting area with couches, and a wet bar. From the bottles of good scotch and the six-foot sub sandwich and a heaping charcuterie board on the counter, it was clear that Ross and his brothers had taken care of all the details.

Ross pushed a sports drink into Vic's hand. "Drink. I'm in charge of keeping you hydrated."

Vic accepted the bottle and guzzled it. He had been pacing himself, drinking enough alcohol throughout the evening to maintain a pleasant buzz but mindful to not give himself a hangover.

"You never said what your friends did for your bachelor party." Vic set the empty bottle aside, and one of his brothers pressed a glass of scotch into his hand to take its place.

Ross shrugged. "The kind of thing you do when you're right out of college and in your early twenties. Casino, then strip club, and a couple of lap dances. I was…underwhelmed."

"Thank you for not trying to relive the moment," Vic replied. "I hate casinos, and the only lap dances I want are from Simon."

"TMI, dude!" Ross protested with a laugh. "And I didn't have to be the wet blanket. I get the impression your sisters-in-law had already handed down some 'guidelines.'"

"Oh, I wouldn't be at all surprised. D'Amato women are fierce." Vic turned back to where his brothers had set up a green felt-covered poker table top and spread out the chips and cards. "Are we going to play, or what?"

"Sure are," Micky replied. "Grab a seat, and let us take your money."

"Dream on," Vic snarked.

The next few hours passed in a pleasant blur of food, scotch, and hands of cards. The later it got, the more the smack-talking reverted to what Vic remembered when they were in middle and high school.

Micky, knew how to needle the others to get a reaction, but he was also the first to cut things off before they got heated. Vic had always thought that Leo, the next oldest, could have done stand-up if he hadn't been a cop, and he frequently had the others laughing hard. Anthony seemed quiet until he spoke up with a perfect zinger. The youngest, Paul, still beat-boxed sound effects to get a laugh.

"I can't imagine what your house must have been like when you were growing up," Ross remarked between games.

"Pure chaos," Micky said as he shuffled the deck.

"Except that with Dad and our uncles all being cops, we couldn't get away with much," Leo added.

"We lived in one of those neighborhoods where everyone knew everyone, and the mothers and nonnas looked out for all the kids—and had no trouble coming after you with a wooden spoon if they thought you needed it," Paul put in as Micky dealt the cards.

"Not to mention the nuns," Anthony recalled. "They instilled guilt like a kill switch for when no one was around to keep you in line."

"Did I tell you that Mom and our aunts were all nurses? So there was no hiding being hung over, stoned, or hurt from stupid stunts," Vic told Ross. "It's really no surprise we turned out like this."

"Card sharps?" Ross asked, raising an eyebrow at the chips stacked on the table.

"Cops," Anthony said with a sigh. "It's the family business."

"Except that little brother went all *X-Files* on us," Leo joked. "Have you found Jimmy Hoffa yet?"

Vic flipped him off. "That's Atlantic City, not Myrtle Beach. We do more magic than mobsters here."

"Simon can't turn you into a chicken if he gets mad at you, can he?" Anthony asked. "'Cause I'd pay money to see that."

Vic slugged him in the shoulder. "Simon's a psychic and a medium, not a witch. So, no chicken—or toad."

"You've always been a toad," Paul countered with a grin. "I just wondered if he could give you an upgrade."

They wrapped up the game in the wee hours of the morning, when they had polished off the food, finished the scotch, and run through their betting allowances. Anthony was the night's winner, followed by Vic, prompting good-natured grumbling and gloating, none of it with any heat.

Vic and Ross each claimed a double bed on the basis of being the wedding party. Vic's brothers crashed in chairs, on the couch, or the floor, ready to grab a few hours before check-out.

"Evening weddings are a good reason to invite a vampire," Vic said as he tumbled into bed, fully clothed.

"I've never read that in an advice column, but I'll take your word for it." Ross switched off the light.

"Like you'd read an advice column."

"First time for everything," Ross replied.

"Set an alarm," Vic directed. "I've set two on my phone, but just in case. Need to get cleaned up. If I oversleep, Simon might get one of his friends to turn me into a toad."

"Doubtful. But I'll set an alarm anyhow."

12

SIMON

"Do you trust me?" Tracey teased.

"Usually, yes," Simon replied. "But on this bachelor party stuff...maybe."

"It'll be fun."

"Just don't make me raise bail," Simon warned. "That would be embarrassing."

Tracey pantomimed marking an X across her chest. "Cross my heart—no bail, no jail. Now hurry—everyone else is waiting."

Simon found Pete and Shayna, Tracey's girlfriend, waiting by Tracey's Subaru. Shayna handed out Mardi Gras beads to all of them, and Simon got an award ribbon pin that read "Groom."

"Get in," Tracey told them. "We're tourists on the town tonight."

She parked in the lot for Olympus, one of Myrtle Beach's many over-the-top mini-golf sites. The Strand was famous for intricately decorated putt-putt locations of everything from volcanos to pirate ships to jungles filled with dinosaurs.

Olympus was Simon's favorite, built on the levels of a former parking garage, with murals of the Greek gods and eighteen challenging themed holes. Tracey went to get clubs and balls for all of them and returned with a red daiquiri slushy for Simon.

"I'm the designated driver, so the rest of you can have all the fun," Tracey told him. "Drink up!"

Simon enjoyed playing mini-golf, although even without alcohol, he knew he wouldn't have the low score. They laughed their way through the silly tableaus and took selfies against the murals.

"I can't believe your ball went over the wall and into the lake," Tracey teased Pete on the walk back to their parking spot.

"Guess I just don't know my own strength." Pete took the joke in stride.

They piled into Tracey's car. "On to the next adventure!" she announced.

Simon couldn't hide his surprise when she parked at FunLand, a compact amusement park just a block from the beach. "I walk past here all the time, but I don't think I've ever gone in," he admitted.

"Time to change that." Tracey grabbed his wrist and nearly dragged him to the ticket booth, where they each got bands for unlimited rides.

"You've lived here how long and never actually visited FunLand?" Tracey said as they queued up for the vintage wooden coaster. "This will be a night to remember."

The coaster wasn't as large or as fast as some Simon had ridden, but it still provided plenty of thrills, and he whooped and hollered with the rest of them as the car sped down the first hill.

"I haven't been on a rollercoaster since I was fifteen," Simon admitted as they got off the ride, legs a little wobbly. "That was fun."

"Just wait, there's more," Tracey promised with a mischievous smile. "But first, cotton candy."

They walked the midway pulling wisps of spun sugar from their treats. The carnival lights blazed, and music carried above the roar of the ocean on the salt air. When they finished their snack, Tracey led the way onto the bobsled ride that sent its cars slaloming on a circle filled with drops and dips.

"How did you like it?" Pete asked.

"My stomach feels like the ride is still going," Simon told him, feeling a pleasant vertigo.

Tracey pressed a cold Coke into his hand. "Drink this. It'll settle your stomach. We aren't done yet!"

Despite its small size, FunLand had more rides for adults than Simon expected. They rode swings that rose high above the park for a view of the ocean and the lights of the town. On another ride, their seats plummeted from the top of a tall tower and rushed toward the ground like a runaway elevator. He begged off riding the log flume, not wanting to get soaked, but let himself be talked into a turn on the wild-mouse-style steel coaster and a giant pirate ship that threatened to swing them completely upside-down.

When they had done everything once, Simon and the others bought funnel cakes and savored the chance to settle their nerves sitting on park benches eating and watching the crowd.

"If you're feeling adventurous, there's the bungee jump." Tracey pointed to twin neon-lit towers. As Simon watched, someone stepped onto the platform and was strapped into a harness, launched skyward, only to drop like a rock, and then bounced for what seemed like forever until they were removed from the rig and escorted away.

"No way in hell. Nope. Not doing it in this life or the next."

"I've done it," Pete said. "Once was enough for me. It's true what they say about your life flashing in front of your eyes— although I was in high school, and it didn't take long to see the highlights!"

After the funnel cake, they got soft-serve ice cream cones dipped in chocolate and covered with sprinkles and then strolled the board-walk to the next stop—the Skywheel, located not far from Simon's shop.

"Gotta finish the cones first, but you'll love the view from the top," Tracey told Simon.

He eyed the massive Ferris wheel with hesitation, but saw that the cars were enclosed and looked far more sturdy than the rides he had experienced as a kid.

"All right," he agreed. "My life is in your hands."

"You're gonna love it." Tracey practically skipped to the entrance ramp with Shayna right behind her.

"You feeling okay?" Pete asked as they followed at a more measured pace.

"I'm good. Real good." Simon felt surprised that it was true. "After the past couple of days, I didn't know if I could shake off everything that happened and get in the right headspace for the wedding, but this is helping a lot."

Simon and Pete shared one of the Skywheel cars, leaving Tracey and Shayna some privacy in their pod. The wheel was much smoother on the ascent than Simon expected, used to the jerk and rocking of the older, less well-maintained versions of the ride he'd encountered at county fairs. Although the wheel also went much higher, the enclosed cab made falling seem unlikely, which allowed Simon to enjoy the view.

"Wow—this would be pretty in the daytime to look out over the ocean, but at night with all the lights, it's really something." Simon had seen the beach and the city from the high balconies of hotels, but the Skywheel provided a singular experience as their car rose and descended.

After the crazy thrills at FunLand, Simon relaxed with the Skywheel's smooth ride and beautiful views. He wondered how Vic's night was going with Ross and his brothers. As much as Simon appreciated his friends planning a special night for him, and despite enjoying everything they had done, he missed having Vic along.

"What's Mikki up to while you're at my wild bachelor party?" Simon asked. Mikki and Pete had been dating for a while, but Simon still wasn't sure how serious they were.

"He's with a bunch of friends watching the big game," Pete replied. "He just told me 'don't wreck the car, and don't puke on the floor.' I think I can exceed those low expectations."

When the ride ended, they walked back down the boardwalk, the strains of music and conversation from the bars behind them and the pounding surf to their left. Simon felt peaceful and contented, enjoying the moment and feeling loved.

"The night's still young," Tracey said when they reached her car. "We have just begun to party."

She parked and led Simon to Roger's, one of the Grand Strand's most popular gay-friendly bars, famous for its karaoke. The bartenders and bouncers all wore sexy pirate costumes, the counter looked like the prow of a ship, and a foul-mouthed mechanical parrot perched behind the bar randomly spoke up with bad advice.

Roger's was famous for its tiki drinks, a favorite with tourists who enjoyed the "show" that went with ordering one of the special cocktails, including blinking lights, comments from the parrot, and the servers all joining in a rousing chorus of "yo-ho, blow the man down" as the drinks were delivered.

Simon thought of Roger's as the adults-only alcoholic version of Tracey's coffee shop, so it didn't surprise him that she included it on his bachelor tour.

"We've got a table reserved in the back," Tracey yelled over the pounding music. "And we're just in time for karaoke hour."

They settled into their table where they could watch the stage and the dance floor. Tracey returned with a pitcher of mojitos for everyone else and a Coke for herself. "Start thinking about what you want to sing." Tracey handed out a list of song titles as the DJ set up on stage.

Simon's eyes widened. "You don't—"

She lifted her chin defiantly. "Oh, I do too, Sebastian Simon Kincaide. Huh? Thought I forgot your whole name, didn't you? I want at least one song with you. We are gonna rock the house tonight!"

Despite Simon's reservations, he got caught up in the excitement as they debated what to sing. He wasn't exactly shy, but performing onstage had never been his thing. Small groups like his ghost tours were fine, but he had never longed to be a rock star.

"Drink up." Tracey presented him with a mojito and a glass of ice water. "Down the hatch. You don't have to be drunk to rule at karaoke, but it certainly helps!"

When they had chosen their songs, Tracey got in line to submit their choices, along with a generous tip.

"You're really going to do this?" Pete asked, like a kid on a dare.

"Sure. Who needs dignity?" Simon replied. "Half these folks are only in town for a week, and the others won't remember most of what happens tomorrow morning. Singing off-key definitely isn't the most scandalous thing to ever happen here."

Tracey and Shayna covered "I Love Rock And Roll" to thunderous applause and whistles. After a few others took their turns, Pete did a credible rendition of "Friends in Low Places," and blushed at the positive response.

"We're up next," Tracey told Simon when a number flashed on the reader board. "Don't worry—Pete promised to get video to show Vic."

Simon recognized a few faces in the crowd. He and Vic weren't much for the club scene, but they had visited the bar before and knew several other gay couples who owned shops along the waterfront. He hoped he looked more confident than he felt when Tracey pulled him on stage.

"Give it up for Simon—he's getting married day after tomorrow!" Tracey yelled to the crowd, who whooped and hollered as the familiar opening strains of "Sweet Caroline"—possibly the easiest Karaoke song ever—filled the club.

Maybe it was the mojitos, or Tracey's unbridled enthusiasm, or the way the crowd chimed in on the "bum-bum-bum" between the lines, but Simon found himself swept away on the good vibes. Even Pete's prominently raised cell phone and the specter of video proof didn't bother Simon. He belted out the words, although he'd always considered his singing voice to be mediocre at best, cheered on by Tracey's broad smile and the encouragement of the crowd.

"You did great!" Tracey told him with a slap on the back as they returned to their seats. A fresh pitcher of mojitos and another of ice water had come while they were on stage, as well as a large tray of Buffalo wings, a basket of fried pickles, a bucket of fried mushrooms, and a plate of nachos.

"Vic is going to love that video," Simon told Pete as they scarfed down the food.

"You know what they say—pictures or it didn't happen," Pete replied.

"We're not done yet!" Tracey announced. They trooped out of Roger's and Tracey took them all to the next stop.

Aloha Cowboy's neon sign featured a Hawaiian shirt and a bright red lei. There was nothing subtle about the Grand Strand's foremost gay strip club, a haven for locals and tourists to the perennial annoyance of the town's less open-minded residents.

Simon groaned but let himself be herded past the leather-clad bouncer and into the club's bright lights and pulsing energy. Blue neon waves highlighted the bar, named "The Wet Spot."

A disco ball sent a dazzling pattern across the dance floor. The upbeat tunes drew a crowd who wanted to move to the beat. Tracey got Simon out for a couple of faster songs, letting enthusiasm make up for any lack of skill.

"Vic and I usually wait for the slow dances," Simon told her, breathless, when they returned to the table. "I haven't danced like that since college."

"Sounds like you're long overdue," Tracey replied, giving Simon a break while she and Shayna took to the floor. Pete waved them off.

"I'm comfortably numb right now and not super well-coordinated even when I'm stone-cold sober," Pete told them. "I'll just sit right here and be the party photographer."

They left the dance club after midnight. Tracey drove them back to the blue bungalow, where they all planned to crash since Vic was spending the night with his party.

Tracey popped open the trunk, and as the others lugged their overnight bags, she carried in a drink cooler. "Pre-made hurricanes," she announced. Pete went back for another trip, returning this time with firewood and a bag of groceries.

"We're going to make a fire in your firepit, cook s'mores, and drink hurricanes," Tracey said. Before long, flames danced merrily and warmed the night chill. Tracey set out the cooler, some red drink cups, and the makings for s'mores. Simon fetched the metal hot dog sticks they used for cookouts, and everyone pulled up Adirondack chairs around the fire.

"Thank you," Simon told them as he tried not to burn his marshmallows. "This was a fantastic evening."

"You're welcome." Tracey licked a mix of melted chocolate, marshmallow goo, and graham cracker crumbs from her lips. She had tied back her beaded braids earlier to keep them in place on the thrill rides, but they hung long and loose now around her shoulders. Shayna fed her a perfectly toasted marshmallow, and Simon wondered if his friends thought he and Vic looked equally cute together.

If so, he never intended to share that secret since "cute" was anathema to Vic—or so he claimed. Secretly, Simon suspected his soon-to-be-husband didn't mind nearly as much as he pretended.

After they had put a dent in the hurricanes and feasted on s'mores, they doused the fire, cleaned up the picnic table, and headed inside. The contentment of a sugar-and-alcohol rush along with the company of good friends made him blissfully exhausted.

"I know the ceremony isn't for another day, but you'll want time to pull your wits together, eat, and do any last-minute stuff," Tracey told him. "I'll get breakfast in the morning. Your job is to get some sleep and look pretty."

"I'm so stuffed I don't want to think about eating. Good night—and thanks again for everything," Simon told her.

"Yeah, yeah. Good night, sleep tight, don't let the palmetto bugs bite."

"I thought that was 'don't let the bed bugs bite.' That's what my grandmother used to say."

She arched an eyebrow. "You tell it your way, and I'll tell it mine."

Tracey and Shayna took the guest room while Pete made himself comfortable on the couch. Simon headed to the master bedroom, still awake enough to go through his usual routine. As he slipped beneath the covers, he caught a whiff of Vic's scent and pulled his partner's pillow closer, burying his face in it, missing him.

It's a good thing I'm exhausted, or I'd never be able to sleep.

Sweet dreams, Vic. Not much longer now, and we'll be married.

Tracey and the others cleared out after a breakfast of bacon, Krispy Kreme donuts, and coffee. Ross dropped Vic off shortly afterward. Vic paused long enough to scarf down a couple of donuts and guzzle a cup of coffee before he pulled Simon into a kiss.

"If you want me coherent, I need more sleep," he told Simon in a whiskey-roughened growl. "Bed. Now."

"Exactly what I was thinking," Simon agreed. They fell asleep almost immediately.

The day passed quickly with last minute preparations and errands. For dinner, they went to their favorite seafood place in nearby Murrell's Inlet where they could watch the sun go down over the water. They took their time with an appetizer of fried calamari and hush puppies, followed by the house specialty seafood platter stacked high with clams, oysters, shrimp, and fresh fish.

"After how much has been going on, it's nice to get a chance to catch our breath," Vic said.

Simon could tell that all the craziness on top of wedding preparations had worn on Vic. *Even good stress is still stress.*

"I'm glad we had a chance to relax a little." Simon took Vic's hand across the table. "I feel like a ball in a pinball machine."

"Let's go home, open a bottle of wine, and de-stress the old-fashioned way." Vic gave a look that made his intentions plain.

"Sounds good," Simon agreed. "There's a lot going on tomorrow—and that's before we even get to the ceremony. I could use an easy night tonight."

Vic smirked. "Sometimes *hard* is better than easy."

"I like the way you think."

Hours passed in what felt like minutes as the alarms startled them into wakefulness the next morning.

"Wake up, sleepyhead. We don't want to be late for our own wedding," Simon teased.

Vic's eyes blinked open, and the sleepy warmth of his gaze made Simon's heartbeat race.

"We have an evening wedding." Vic closed his eyes again. "We should rest up."

Simon poked him in the shoulder. "Are you forgetting something? Like the box of homemade, chocolate-filled cornetti your mom and aunts dropped off? Then we have an all-day spa pass, thanks to Tracey, Shayna, Pete, and Mikki."

"Hot rock couples ninety-minute massage with aromatic oils, sea salt soak, and afternoon tea," Simon continued. "And after that, you and I have a stylist appointment for hair, manicure, and maybe a little touch-up to cover the bruises—with complimentary appetizers and champagne as part of the wedding package."

"And afternoon practice sex, so we're ready for the wedding night?" Vic rolled over to meet Simon's gaze with a wicked grin.

"We've been 'practicing' for a while now—don't think we'll forget that fast," Simon teased indulgently. "Besides, that would kind of undo all the other spiffing up."

"How about we exchange blow jobs before the ceremony—for luck?"

Simon wasn't completely certain Vic was kidding, and much as his cock twitched at the idea, he shook his head. "Save it for after. All that pent-up desire will make it even better when we're alone."

"We have to meet with Father Anne to sign the marriage license before the service, and the photographer will probably want to snap a couple of candid shots too."

Vic gave an exaggerated sigh. "Fine." He sat up, adorably rumpled, looked around their bedroom, and his gaze rested on their suitcases. "Are we all packed? Did we forget anything?"

"We're packed, and if we forget anything, we'll make do or buy what we need," Simon told him. "I've got the hotel reservation in Charleston—in a not-haunted B&B—for tomorrow night and the next night as well as the airline tickets, passports, and hotel information for London and the castle." They had agreed to a post-wedding brunch the day after the ceremony at the beach house since they weren't having a rehearsal dinner. That also gave them a chance to open gifts and spend a little more time with their guests and Vic's family.

"I can't believe Ross, Hargrove, and the guys at the station went together on those travel passes for us." Vic reached out to take Simon's hand. "That's a pretty awesome present." Ross had let them know in advance that Vic's co-workers had gone together to get them passes for UK museums as well as London public transit and train transport throughout Britain.

Once they left London, they were planning to stay at a real castle that had become a hotel—one they had visited before and enjoyed so much they wanted to return. That first trip had turned into solving a ghostly mystery. The earl appreciated their help and offered them a steep discount on their honeymoon return in thanks.

"I vote for telling any ghosts, fae, and supernatural creatures that we are officially off the clock." Vic stood and stretched, giving Simon a delicious glimpse of his belly and happy trail.

"I just want to sightsee, eat awesome food, and have steamy sex with my husband." Simon leaned in for a kiss.

"How come sex comes third?"

Simon rolled his eyes fondly. "Because we're in our thirties, and it takes longer between rounds than it used to."

"Hmm." Vic pretended to consider that answer. "Did you pack any 'toys'?"

"Do you really want to explain them to the TSA people with the X-rays?"

"Good point."

"You'll be happy to know I packed the maximum number of ounces of lube we can take on a plane," Simon joked. "We can buy more once we get to London."

Vic kissed him again. "I like how you think."

Simon's phone buzzed, and he checked the text message. "Just Kara from the Train Depot confirming that everything is going well for the set-up." He laughed. "I think she's convinced we're 'high maintenance.'"

Vic shrugged. "I've been called worse. I'll be happy if the ceremony goes smoothly."

Simon pulled him in for another kiss, long and slow. "It would be nice if it all went perfectly, but it doesn't matter because no matter what, we'll be married."

They showered together, stroking each other off. Even though they had the spa and stylist ahead of them, Simon took his time washing Vic's hair and massaging his scalp. Vic did the same in return, making sure to gently tug at Simon's long hair like when they made love.

Simon traced the *serch bythol* tattoo on Vic's hip that matched his own and roamed his hands over Vic's other tattoos that covered his shoulder and upper arm. "Been a while since I licked all of your tats. I'll put that on my to-do list." Vic's shiver made Simon smile.

Simon's fingertips ghosted over Vic's skin, lingering where the bullet wounds had been. *I could have lost him.*

Vic placed his palm over Simon's scar where he'd been shot point blank. "Hey. Don't get stuck in 'what ifs.' We're here and alive. We're getting married today. Leave the past in the past."

Simon pressed a kiss to his lips. "You always know the right thing to say."

Vic kissed him back. "Much as I enjoy seeing you naked, we should probably get dressed and eat breakfast—again. We're due at the spa before too long."

"If nothing else, we won't forget the rings." Simon looked down at the blessed silver band on his right hand that matched Vic's. They were engraved on the inside with protective sigils as well as the *serch bythol.*

Vic took Simon's hand and rotated the ring on his finger. "I'm looking forward to putting this where it belongs."

Simon hung their suits in the backseat of the car and put their suitcases by the door, packed and ready so they didn't have to worry about doing that tonight. They were coming home to the bungalow after the ceremony, and heading out to Charleston after brunch the next day. Ross and Pete had promised to check on the bungalow while they were gone. "I think that's everything," Vic said.

The spa wasn't far. Simon had driven past it many times but had never considered a visit. He'd had massages a few times when he was with the university in Columbia, but not since he'd come to Myrtle Beach. Other than the ones they gave each other, Simon doubted Vic had ever had a massage that wasn't physical therapy for an injury.

"Looks like a swanky place. We might be outclassed," Vic quipped when they parked.

"I'm quite sure they have a 'no weapons' policy, so you'll probably feel naked even though we leave some clothes on."

They checked into the spa and changed into comfortable robes, leaving everything except their boxer briefs in the dressing room. The scent of lavender and orange perfumed the air, and quiet instrumental music created a sense of peace. Carafes of water flavored with fruit or cucumber slices were everywhere, a reminder to stay hydrated throughout the day.

"We just lie on the tables, and they work us over?" Vic eyed the massage room skeptically.

"It's like what we do at home—without the happy ending," Simon told him. "Very soothing. Even when they find a place where you're knotted up, the soreness feels better after we have a good salt soak and spend time in the sauna and the cool bath."

Simon looked forward to the massage and hoped Vic could get comfortable enough to enjoy it too. He was pleased when Vic seemed to relax and go with the flow, and at one point, Simon wondered if his partner had fallen asleep.

"Drink." Simon's masseuse pressed a glass of water into his hand, as Vic's person did the same. "You'll feel better later if you have plenty of water today."

The sauna felt wonderful, loosening up any tightness that remained after the massage, and the salt soak was surprisingly different than just floating in the ocean. A cool bath felt refreshing, waking them back up just in time for the afternoon tea.

"Wow—that went fast," Vic said as they sat at the table. He looked at the tiered plate holding small sandwiches and little cakes. "This reminds me of what we had at the castle."

Simon grinned. He had wondered if he could get his tough cop fiancé to relax and enjoy the afternoon tea shop treats, but Vic fell in love with the tasty tidbits and became a fan.

When they finished, it was only a short drive to Well Groomed Man, where Simon had booked them the wedding package.

Vic eyed the shop suspiciously. "Kinda fancy for a barbershop."

Simon laughed. "I know you like to keep it simple. And they won't do anything you don't want. I swear your fade is safe."

Vic reached out and tousled Simon's long chestnut hair. "Don't cut any off. I like it just the way it is." He gave a gentle tug for emphasis that went right to Simon's cock.

"I promise. They're just going to spiff us up so we look our best. A little more pampering and some champagne," Simon told him. "And I let them know we got roughed up on official police business, so they didn't think we'd been pounding on each other."

Vic grimaced. "Probably a good idea. I'd hate to get arrested when all the cops in town are waiting for us to get married." He swept his arm forward and gave a shallow bow. "I'm with you, so lead the way."

The salon had the dark green and wood accents of a billiard room at a classy club. The air smelled of cedar, orange, and a hint of cherry tobacco. Vic smiled at the classic rock soundtrack and looked more at ease when he saw that the styling chairs were customized leather recliners.

They followed the receptionist to a private room in the back with two styling stations and a sideboard with champagne punch and a spread of meats, cheeses, pickles, and olives. Simon and Vic nibbled and had a glass of punch as they talked with the operators, then settled in to have their hair washed and styled, their hands massaged and manicured, and their bruises covered with a light dab of concealer.

"You clean up well," Simon teased when they were done, enjoying a last flute of punch and finishing the snack tray.

"I was going to say the same about you." Vic gave Simon an unabashed once-over that made him blush.

Vic leaned in so only Simon could hear. "I'm having all sorts of lustful thoughts, in case you're wondering. Are you sure we couldn't work in a quickie?" He gave a wicked grin.

"Wish we could because you look good enough to eat," Simon joked in a low, quiet voice that made Vic's pupils dilate. "But I'd rather not be crusty for the ceremony, so hold that thought."

"One more stop." Simon held out his hand to Vic. "You ready for this?"

Vic squeezed his hand. "Been ready for a while. Let's do it."

The sun was setting as they headed inside the Train Depot, an event venue created from a remodeled railroad station. Simon and Vic had fallen in love with its historic feel, unique look, and lack of ghosts.

Kara met them at the door. "Happy wedding day!" She ushered them in and stood to one side so they could take in the decorations.

Clear twinkle lights and swagged, sheer white curtains cascaded down the walls setting off the exposed beams. Round tables with white linens had gold seashell boxes at each place setting that held pastel Jordan almonds and saltwater taffy. Glass centerpieces with sand, shells, and fairy lights gave off a warm glow.

At the far end of the long room was a white gazebo where they would exchange vows, set off with more lights and bunched sheers. A dance floor separated that from the tables, buffet line, and bar. After the ceremony, their DJ would take up residence in the gazebo.

"It's beautiful," Simon told her, and Vic nodded, looking momentarily overcome. Simon gave his hand a squeeze.

"I'm so glad you're happy with everything—I think the design came together nicely," Kara said with a broad grin. "We want you back for all the milestone anniversary celebrations."

Their guest list was limited to family and close friends, as well as Vic's colleagues from the homicide team. Given the distance, Vic's entire extended family hadn't made the trip, so that meant only his aunts, uncles, and closest first cousins would be present. Their list topped out at eighty, far less than the venue could hold, but that meant room to stand and talk as well as plenty of space to dance.

"The boutonnieres for you and your honor attendants are in the back—they look lovely," Kara went on as they followed her toward the front. "They also brought the corsages for your mother and sister," she said with a nod to Vic, "and your aunt," she added, looking to Simon.

"You've made my life so much simpler by not having a huge number of attendants! You wouldn't believe the crowd we have to get up front for some ceremonies. Plus flower girls, ring bearers, and dogs." She grinned. "I'm happy to give them what they want, but it can be a bit of a circus."

Simon and Vic had chosen simple boutonnieres with orange ranunculus backed by greens and a bit of white baby's breath. Ross and Tracey's were done with orange carnations, while the wrist nosegays had orange roses.

Kara walked them over to the long table against the wall. Stainless steel buffet warmers lined the table with the wedding cake and bar at the far end. "We'll have everything out on the table before your ceremony but covered so no one is tempted to snack early. That way we don't have to be clanging around while the guests are here or holding things up after you're done with the vows. The bartender won't come out until the food is ready. A short ceremony certainly helps move things along!"

"We figure people will eat dinner before they come since the ceremony starts at eight," Simon told her, leaving out that they were holding the event after dark so Sorren could attend. "Then they can snack, drink, and socialize even if they don't want to dance."

The heavy hors d'oeuvres included shrimp cocktail, a charcuterie spread, crab puffs, a platter of crudites and sliced fruit, quiches, spanakopita, and a chocolate fountain. For dessert, Simon and Vic had chosen a multi-tiered vanilla wedding cake with blue fondant icing at the bottom that faded to white on each layer, decorated with marzipan sea shells and starfish. An open bar for beer and wine would last for two hours after the ceremony.

"Speaking of dancing, the DJ has already set up the sound system and checked it," Kara told them. "And he's got the playlists set for before the ceremony while everyone's coming in and then for your procession and recession—and the dancing afterward. His table is on the gazebo under a black drape, so once the officiant leaves, he can get the party started in minutes."

Simon looked around for Father Anne and the photographer. "Is our priest here?"

Kara nodded. "She's in the back office, expecting you. And the photographer should arrive shortly so he can snap some pictures of the venue and a few candids before the ceremony. I think everything is ready."

"Tracey and Ross should be here soon," Simon told her. "We need them to witness signing the marriage license."

"I'll send them back. Congratulations!"

Simon's heart soared, and his stomach swooped at her words. From the slightly stunned look on Vic's face, he figured his fiancé felt the same heady mix of excitement and nervousness.

The Reverend Anne Burgett—known to her flock at St. Hildegard's Episcopal Church in Charleston as Father Anne—got up from her seat at the table in the Depot's office to greet them with warm hugs. The long sleeves of her clerical robes hid the colorful tattoo sleeve of St. Expeditus, patron saint of monster hunters and the namesake of the fellowship of priests who fought supernatural threats. Since this was a wedding and not an exorcism or hunt, she had traded her usual Doc Martens for black flats, but her pompadour still made her easy to spot in a crowd.

"Father Anne—thank you again for coming to do our ceremony," Simon said when they finally stepped back from the hug.

"I'm honored. Thank you for including me," she replied with a big grin. Simon had not worked with Father Anne as often as his cousin Cassidy had, but they had still come through several harrowing situations together.

"And before you wonder about it—Miss Eppie and Gabriella have already been here. I helped them with wardings and the usual protections," Father Anne added.

"I thought I smelled sage and vervain," Simon replied.

She nodded. "I think we've got enough supernatural 'firepower' in this crowd to protect against nearly anything, but there's no point taking chances, especially since we'll have 'civilians' among us."

Simon knew she meant people like Vic's family who didn't know the full story about paranormal threats.

"And for anything that's not spooky, we've got more than a dozen cops," Vic added. "I'm hoping we can get through this without needing to start a private war."

She led them to the table, where a document lay with two pens. "This is your marriage license. Signing it in front of witnesses means you're married in a civil sense. Trading vows is ceremonial, but this is what gets you tax benefits."

A knock at the door made them look up as Tracey and Ross joined them. Tracey wore a navy blue pantsuit with a satin tuxedo collar, while Ross wore a suit that matched Vic's.

"Happy wedding day, best wishes, congratulations, and all that," Tracey greeted them, giving Simon and Vic big hugs.

Ross slapped them on the back. "There's no turning back now," he said with a broad grin.

Tracey and Ross witnessed the signature, and Father Anne tucked the document into her messenger bag to file with the Register of Deeds. She looked up with a smile. "If you have your rings and any notes for your vows, that's it for now. I'll be waiting for you when it's time."

Simon let out a long breath and managed a shaky smile for Vic. "Guess we ought to get dressed. The photographer's going to want us next."

"I know we've been running around all day, but this is still low-key compared to the High Mass weddings my brothers had," Vic said. "Those were quite a production—with the entire D'Amato clan in attendance." Since a Catholic wedding hadn't been an option for them, Simon and Vic had chosen their own course.

Chris, the photographer, was waiting for them in the hallway. "Once you've changed, we'll get some candid 'day of' photos and a few of the four of you together before it gets crazy. The video camera is set up to record the vows, and I'll be in position to get great shots of the ceremony without blocking anyone's view. In the meantime, I'll snap some photos of the venue before people get here. See you out there!"

"We'll get the boutonnieres and wait for you by the gazebo."
Ross left the room with Tracey.

Simon and Vic went to the car to retrieve their suits and a small
bag for their casual clothing. They went back inside to their dressing
room and changed quickly.

When Vic went to do his tie, Simon reached out and stopped his
hand. "Let me." He stepped behind Vic so he could do a perfect
bow tie. Simon met Vic's eyes in the large mirror, a moment of
silent intimacy.

"My turn." Vic's voice was a low rumble. He did the same for
Simon, leaning in so Simon felt Vic's breath against the nape of his
neck.

"You've been practicing." Simon was surprised that simply tying
a tie could be so erotic.

As if Vic could read his mind, he slid his fingers across the
smooth silk of Simon's tie. "Wanted to do this right for you."

Simon turned to him and rested his hands on Vic's hip. "You
couldn't do this wrong. I love you, and we're going to be husbands.
This is the happiest day of my life."

Vic kissed him slow and tender. "I love you too. And I have to
keep pinching myself to believe this is real. I wasn't sure this would
ever happen for me—and you made it come true."

Simon leaned back reluctantly. "We'd better get out there before
they send a search party."

Vic laughed. "Ross would be afraid to interrupt, but my brother
Micky would barge right in if we were late. He's shameless—and
terrifying."

The next half hour flew by. Simon felt certain all he would
remember was the strobe of Chris's flash.

Finally, Kara found them. "Guests are starting to arrive. You'll
want to go back to the office until I come for you once everyone's
seated and we're ready to begin. Good luck!"

Before he knew it, Kara returned. "It's time! All you have to do
is walk out the doors and up the steps onto the gazebo. Father Anne
is waiting for you. Congratulations!"

Vic took Simon's hand. Tracey and Ross fell into step behind them. If Vic noticed that Simon's hand was sweaty and shaking, he didn't let on.

Kara was waiting to open the doors for them and signal the music change for their brief processional. They had chosen a pre-ceremony playlist made up of instrumental versions of their favorite songs. As the doors opened, "Stand By Me" began. Simon and Vic exchanged a grin and walked at a dignified pace the few feet to the raised covered dais. The music ended when they stood in front of Father Anne.

"Honored guests, we are here today to witness the marriage of Simon Kincaide and Vic D'Amato. Your presence blesses this union and shows your love for these men. Please send your thoughts of love and joy as we join them in matrimony," Father Anne announced.

Simon and Vic stood facing Father Anne, with Tracey and Ross behind them and slightly to the side. He tried to avoid looking straight into the video camera poised over the priest's shoulder, although the blinking red light caught his attention.

"Simon Kincaide—speak your truth," Father Anne said.

Simon cleared his throat, suddenly nervous. He met Vic's dark eyes, and the love he saw there sustained him. "Vic D'Amato, I love you with all my heart. You are my soulmate and my partner in every way. I trust you with my life. Thank you for making me the happiest man in the world. I will stay by your side through the good and the bad, happiness and sorrow, all the days of our lives."

He felt his throat tighten, but he'd managed to get through the hard part. "With this ring, we are wed." He took Vic's right hand and removed the ring, transferring it to his left.

"Vic D'Amato—speak your truth."

Vic blinked a couple of times, and Simon saw tears in his lover's eyes. "Simon Kincaide, you taught me to believe again—in love, in the good of this world, and in things beyond. I love you with every fiber of my being, my whole heart, and my soul. We are true mates. You have saved my life more than once, and I trust you to always have my back. Thank you for loving me. I will walk the long road ahead with you, come what may, every step of our lives."

Vic swallowed a couple of times before he could get the words out. "With this ring, we are wed." Simon could feel Vic's hand shake as he moved the ring from one hand to the other.

Father Anne motioned for them to turn to face the audience. "By virtue of the power vested in me by the state of South Carolina, I pronounced you married. You may kiss the groom!"

Simon and Vic leaned in for their kiss as camera flashes lit up the room. Vic slipped the tip of his tongue teasingly across Simon's lips, a promise of things to come. When they drew back, grinning wide, the whole room clapped, and the music changed to "This Life," just the first of many Springsteen songs that super-fan Vic had included in the playlist.

When they reached the dance floor, the music switched again to Train's "Marry Me." Vic put his hands on Simon's hips, and Simon wrapped his arms around Vic's shoulders, pulling him close as they swayed to the song, overcome by emotion.

After the first verse, other guests began to join them, first Tracey and Shayna, then Ross and Sheila, and soon more.

After that, the DJ served up an eclectic mix of the varied songs Simon liked as well as several more tunes by Springsteen and the Michael Stanley Band for Vic. The younger guests headed for the dance floor as the tempo picked up while the others drifted toward the appetizers and bar.

"Don't look now, but your mother is having an in-depth discussion with a vampire," Simon murmured to Vic, who turned to see his mom chatting with Sorren.

"Your aunt is deep in conversation with a necromancer," Vic replied, with a nod toward where Archibald Donnelly sat with Simon's Aunt Karen. "And neither of them will ever have a clue about why that's so unusual."

"It's good to keep the weirdness in the family," Simon joked. "And in case you wondered, Dante made it too." He had noticed the ghost in the very back of the room right after he and Vic made their vows. Dante wasn't visible to anyone except the mediums in the crowd, but it touched Simon that his ancestor had made the effort to share their special night.

"Welcome to the family," Carmen D'Amato boomed before enfolding Simon in a bear hug once he and Vic left the dance floor. Vic's mom, Bernie, followed suit as soon as Carmen released him.

"You're part of the crazy D'Amato clan now—no turning back," Micky, Vic's oldest brother, said as his siblings crowded around them to tease Vic and congratulate Simon.

"I'm perfectly happy with that," Simon assured them.

"Nice ceremony, good music," Leo complimented.

"Love the shrimp cocktail and the chocolate fondue," Lisa, Vic's younger sister, told them. "Tony and Paul didn't want to risk missing out on the food, so they'll stop by to see you later. Priorities!" she said with a laugh.

After that, Simon's Aunt Karen and Uncle Jay made sure to give hugs and congratulate them. "I'm glad you're happy in the blue bungalow."

"You made all this possible by giving me a place to live when I moved here," Simon told them. "It's been the perfect home for us."

Cassidy Kincaide and her boyfriend Kell Winston found their way over. Cassidy had plates of food for Simon and Vic. "Eat. You haven't made it to the table yet, and the shrimp is popular."

"Thank you," Simon said with a sigh of relief. "I'm starving."

Kell handed them each a glass of wine. "You probably could use a belt of something stronger, but I figured this might take the edge off."

"Beautiful wedding," Teag Logan chimed in, with his fiancé Anthony Benton close behind. "Giving us all kinds of ideas." He elbowed Anthony.

"We still haven't figured out a venue yet," Anthony admitted. "Yours is beautiful—and different."

"You'll find something just as perfect," Simon told them. "Charleston has a lot of choices."

Simon and Vic nibbled as they made the rounds, stopping to talk with all their guests and thank them for the wedding gifts. Tracey and Ross brought them more wine, switching to soda as the night wore on.

"Congratulations and best wishes." Donnelly and Sorren

greeted them. "Your guests are good conversationalists. It's been more than a lifetime since I attended a wedding, although it appears there'll be another soon." Sorren glanced toward where Teag and Anthony were dancing.

"It's good for the soul," Donnelly said. "And I should know."

Gabriella and Miss Eppie found them at the chocolate fountain, where Vic finally got the strawberries and marshmallows he had been eyeing all night.

"Congratulations," Gabriella said.

"Best wishes," Miss Eppie added.

"Thank you for cleansing and warding the space," Simon told them. "And for your gifts. We're grateful for the protection."

"Happy to be part of your special day," Gabriella said. "Now I need to ask, when are you going to cut the cake?"

Simon laughed and led Vic toward the table. "It's almost too pretty to cut," he told Vic as they took a moment to admire the confection.

"We want cake!" Micky called and ducked behind Leo.

Gabriella didn't say anything, but she raised an eyebrow to remind Simon of his promise of an extra slice.

"I think we'd better do this before we have a riot," Vic replied.

Chris snapped a picture of them holding the knife and another as they shared the first slice. A server came to cut the rest of the pieces, and the two grooms stepped back out of the way.

"Nice ceremony." Captain Hargrove came up behind them with a plate of shrimp. "Great spread. And good job on the Timothy Sheldon situation—you also managed to wrap up a slew of cold cases. Show offs."

"Just clearing the deck so we can have a peaceful honeymoon," Vic replied, but Simon could see his husband was pleased with the praise.

"We'll try to carry on with the two of you gone for a while," Hargrove snarked. "Just stay out of trouble—like that's possible."

"We'll do our very best," Simon told him, although he doubted that was likely.

Michelle, Pete, and Mikki caught up with them carrying slices of cake.

"Great party," Pete said, and Mikki nodded, mouth full of dessert.

"Beautiful wedding." Michelle licked the icing from her lips. She was one of Simon's psychic students, the group he called his "Skeleton Crew," and had been with him the longest, one of the few still in town. The others had been unable to attend, but Simon was glad Michelle had made it.

"Thank you. It's been wonderful to have everyone together."

They chatted for a while, then drifted toward the dwindling buffet. Simon and Vic made the rounds again, thanking everyone for attending, accepting hugs and well wishes.

As people began to say goodbye and head out, Ross and Tracey found Simon and Vic.

"We wanted to let you know that we didn't do anything juvenile to your car," Tracey told them with a hint of mischief in her eyes.

"We absolutely didn't string cans behind it or wrap it in toilet paper or pick the lock and hide all your underwear," Ross said with a suspiciously cherubic grin that confirmed his guilt.

Simon and Vic exchanged a look. "Uh-oh," Simon groaned. "Is this an annoying prank or an embarrassing prank?"

"Like is the radio going to blare and all the blinkers and wipers go off, or did you cover the seats with itching powder?" Vic asked suspiciously.

"None of the above." Tracey bounced on the balls of her feet. "Let's just say it's the gifts that keep on giving."

"Are we going to need shots?" Simon wasn't expecting anything malicious, but he was cautiously curious.

Tracey rolled her eyes. "Of course not—unless you do something really wrong."

Ross bumped her shoulder. "Let them figure it out for themselves. Don't spoil the surprise."

With that mysterious comment, Ross and Tracey repeated their well wishes and then found their partners and headed out with the rest of the crowd.

"Are you boys driving back to the bungalow tonight?" Vic's dad asked as they walked to the door.

"I switched to soda hours ago, so I'm fine to drive," Simon replied, aware he now had a cop for a father-in-law as well as a husband.

"I wasn't doubting that," Carmen said. "Just want to make sure you get on your way smoothly."

"Our reservations in Charleston aren't until tomorrow night. The flight to London doesn't go out until late the next day, and it's an overnight, so we have time to recover," Vic told them. The aunts, uncles, cousins, and siblings surrounded them, and Simon felt loved and a little overwhelmed.

"We'll see you tomorrow for breakfast," Bernie told them. "It'll be ready by nine."

Simon and Vic lingered near the door to say goodbye until the last guest had left. As the servers began to clean up, Kara joined them.

"I'd say that went smoothly," she told them. "Congratulations. Chris packed up the cameras a while ago, but he said to tell you he'll be in touch."

"Do we need to worry about leftovers?" Simon nodded toward the buffet.

Kara laughed. "Nope. Your guests ate everything. There's cake left, which I'll freeze for you, and you can pick it up when you get back. Now get out of here—you've got a honeymoon waiting for you."

Vic took Simon's hand as they walked to the car. "That was... perfect," he said, and the open honesty of his smile warmed Simon deep inside.

"Yes, it was. And whatever dark magic you and Ross and Hargrove did to keep my mother away? Thank you."

"It worked, didn't it?" Vic laughed.

"It was the perfect sting," Simon replied. "And the best wedding present you could have given me."

"Speaking of presents...we still don't know what Ross and Tracey did to your car."

They approached the Toyota warily, but nothing seemed amiss. Despite the late hour, the parking lot lights were almost bright as day, definitely enough to reveal any embarrassing messages painted on the windows or other pranks.

Simon unlocked the doors, and they found a red bag with pink hearts printed on it sitting on the passenger seat. It bulged in suspicious ways, and Simon could have sworn he had seen that heart logo before.

"Oh, my God." Vic snatched the bag from the seat and opened the drawstring. He turned it for Simon to see, and Simon couldn't help breaking into a fit of giggles.

"It's full of toys," Vic said. "I'm not even sure what some of these are for. Are there instructions? And how did my very straight work partner know what to buy?"

"No clue. I can't imagine my very not-straight best friend giving him ideas," Simon said when he could find his voice again. "Tracey's definitely not into dick. And that's a literal bag full of dicks."

"And lots of other things." Vic wiped tears of laughter from his eyes. "We are going to have a lot of fun...but we are absolutely not taking these through TSA."

EPILOGUE

VIC

"I don't think I've seen this much food in my life," Simon told Vic as they walked into the beach house his family had rented for their post-wedding brunch. Since their very simple ceremony hadn't required a full rehearsal, Vic's mother insisted that the brunch take the place of a rehearsal dinner.

"Sure you have. It's not much different than when you came home with me for Christmas." Vic nibbled a cannoli.

"How are you still eating after all the food last night?" Simon put a hand over his stomach.

"It's a D'Amato family skill. You've got to learn to pace yourself," Vic answered. "That's why we usually do an all-day buffet at the holidays. That way you can eat for hours and never feel stuffed."

"I'm getting indigestion just thinking about eating that much," Simon confessed. "Although the food is so good, I'd die happy."

Vic bumped shoulders with him. "That's what they mean by 'food coma.' It's totally true. Something to aspire to."

"Are you finding enough to eat? Can I get you something else?" Bernie bustled into the kitchen of the beach house. "There are a few more trays in the fridge if you don't see what you want."

"Everything is so good," Simon told her. "Thank you for all of this."

"Oh, honey. It's just what we do." Bernie flashed a broad smile. "I know they say that food isn't love, but I think whoever said that just didn't have the right food. Good times or bad times, food and family make it better."

She stepped up to Simon and enfolded him in a hug. "I am so glad to have a new son. You're a D'Amato now."

Simon hugged her back, then Vic accepted his hug in turn. Bernie patted him on the shoulder. "Go. Eat. There's more of the fried ravioli that you like. It's not every day I get to feed you."

Vic kissed her forehead. "You know my weakness."

"Well, they're pretty awesome ravioli, if I do say so myself," Bernie said. "I need to make sure your brothers haven't cleaned us out of all the food on the platters in the other room. Go mingle," she told them, with a gesture that meant "scoot" before heading back to the dining room.

Vic took Simon's hand and pulled him in for a gentle kiss. "She likes you. They all do. Good thing. I like you too."

"Just so happens that I like you as well," Simon whispered between kisses.

"We should go back to the party," Vic murmured.

"I like our party of two." Simon had a glint in his eyes.

"And we have our whole honeymoon for that." Vic took Simon's hand and tugged him to follow. "Come on. I'm sure there are a few cousins you haven't met."

Vic enjoyed introducing Simon to relatives from Pittsburgh. They were all intrigued with his abilities as a psychic and a medium and plied him with questions that Simon answered patiently, even if Vic knew the replies skipped some of the more disturbing aspects.

Simon and Vic were leaving for their honeymoon that afternoon, but they had given themselves time to enjoy Charleston before their flight left so they could take their time here. Vic's dad, Carmen, and his oldest brother Micky set two chairs in the middle of the living room while his mom and aunts surrounded Simon and

Vic with the gifts that had been brought to the wedding or mailed ahead of time.

Vic and Simon took turns reading the cards and unwrapping boxes. "A fondue maker from Michelle." Simon held up the gadget so the others could see.

"A poker set with an 'S&V' monogram and a bottle of good scotch from Micky," Vic said, and his brother beamed.

"Don't drink it all in one night," Micky teased. Bernie took the gifts and walked around the circle so all the guests could see before setting the items on a side table.

"And look—a set of monogrammed rocks glasses from Leo and Ellie." Vic glanced at his second-oldest brother and his wife.

"Need to have something to drink the scotch in," Leo replied with a shrug.

"Hey—more monograms! It's a bar and grill set marked 'S&V.' Thanks, Paul," Vic said to his youngest brother.

"Mine isn't monogrammed!" Lisa, Vic's sister, spoke up as everyone laughed. Simon and Vic tore away the paper to reveal an Italian ceramic serving bowl decorated with a traditional geometric pattern and a charcuterie tray made of patterned, hammered aluminum from a craft shop well-known in the Pittsburgh area.

"They're beautiful." Simon examined the pieces closely.

"Mine aren't monogrammed, either," Anthony chimed in. Vic unwrapped a new multi-player video game for their favorite gaming system and an RPG tabletop game he and Simon had put on their wish list. "I figured you've got to get out of bed sometime," Anthony added with a grin.

Vic balled up the wrapping paper and threw it at his brother's head as Simon blushed and cleared his throat.

"Just so you know, Tracey, Shayna, Pete, and Mikki gave us a spa day certificate," Simon added before they moved to the next gift.

"And my team from work went together on passes and tickets for our trip," Vic added.

Simon's aunt and uncle gifted them a retro orange Fiestaware chip and dip platter and bowl that perfectly matched the bungalow's "mid-century modern" vibe. Vic's cousins went together on a year's wine club subscription and a set of monogrammed goblets. Their out-of-state ghost hunting friends who had been unable to attend sent generous gift cards.

"This one's from my cousin Cassidy," Simon told them as he unwrapped one of the packages Cassidy had brought to the wedding. He caught his breath, and Vic's eyes widened when Simon opened the box to reveal vintage Kugel blown glass Christmas ornaments of seashells and marine creatures, all in vibrant colors.

"Cassidy runs an antique shop in Charleston," Simon explained. "I told her about the retro aluminum Christmas tree we 'inherited' from my aunt and uncle. These will look perfect."

"I think there's something else in the box," Vic whispered, nudging Simon.

Simon picked up the small box, and Vic guessed from the look in his eyes that Simon felt a spirit nearby.

"Dante says it's from him and Colt, that he made it on a long-ago voyage," Simon whispered to Vic.

Everyone murmured as Simon took out a beautiful piece of scrimshaw. Simon's eyes teared up. "This was made by Dante, an ancestor of mine who was a privateer," he told them.

Vic's parents and Micky looked up sharply, remembering how Dante had helped save Simon and Vic from a killer.

"*That* Dante?" Micky asked.

Simon nodded. "Yes. He likes to…hang out with us." Vic knew that explaining the ghost issue was difficult for people who weren't used to such things.

The next gift was exquisitely wrapped and ribboned. "From Sorren," Vic read the tag and exchanged a look with Simon. They both seemed to share the same question—*What does a nearly six-hundred-year-old vampire give as a wedding gift?*

Simon withdrew a silver chalice inscribed with sigils and runes as well as the first letters of their names intertwined. "For protection," he said, and Vic suspected that Simon picked up on arcane energies from the antique.

Teag Logan's gift was a small, framed tapestry. A nod from Simon confirmed to Vic that it was imbued with magical protections that the Weaver witch had woven into the cloth. Gabriella's box held handcrafted candles marked "peace, health, and protection."

Vic knew Simon's friend would have used her botanica and *bruja* knowledge to create and personalize the candles, giving them more mojo than mere decorations. Miss Eppie sent a small, abstract, rectangular piece of art that Vic guessed incorporated root work spells and ingredients.

"Hang this on the inside of your house, over the front door," Vic read from the accompanying card. "This will bring happiness, harmony, and protection."

Father Anne, the priest who officiated their wedding, sent a ceramic talisman in the shape of St. Expeditus's ritual symbol, another protective gift.

"Your friends seem concerned for your safety," Aunt Lucia commented. "Should we worry?"

"Nonna Maria had saints' candles, crucifixes, and icons on every flat surface," Carmen spoke up, and Vic knew his dad was deflecting attention from the supernatural dangers of their work. "She said novenas and prayed the rosary for every cop in the family. It's the same sort of thing, but not Catholic," he said, which seemed to satisfy Lucia's curiosity.

"Well, your aunts and uncles might not be quite as 'spiritual,'" Lucia said, "but we thought we'd help you keep body and soul together." She passed an envelope to them decorated in the red, white, and green of the flag of Italy. "It's a year's subscription to Pennsylvania Macaroni's themed boxes. Plenty of good, authentic, Italian food all year long—you won't go hungry!"

Vic had taken Simon to the famous imported food store in Pittsburgh's Strip District, boasting an impressive array of Old World comfort foods.

"Thank you," Vic said. "Now I might have to learn to cook more than spaghetti."

Bernie and Carmen exchanged a smile and look, and Carmen brought over a large, heavy box, which he put in front of Vic and Simon, along with two smaller boxes and another envelope.

"Go on, open it," Vic's mom urged.

202 | MORGAN BRICE

Simon and Vic tore away the paper from the big box to reveal a stand mixer. The smaller boxes held pasta-making attachments and a set of ravioli molds, while the envelope had a gift certificate for online cooking classes.

"Just remember—in our house, food is love." Bernie stepped up to give both men a kiss on the cheek. "You are very loved."

"Ross and Pete said they'd put the gifts in the bungalow," Carmen told them. "That way, you don't have to worry about anything except getting your honeymoon started."

"Thank you all so much." Vic choked up at the clear evidence of how much his family and their friends loved them. Simon took his hand and echoed his thanks.

"Just helping you celebrate your special day," Bernie said, but Vic could see happy tears in his mother's eyes.

Aunt Lucia stood and clapped her hands to get their attention. "Now that's done, who wants more food?"

As the day went on, more of their friends drifted in to add their well-wishes. Cassidy and some of her Charleston friends stopped by late in the morning before heading back. Simon's aunt and uncle made sure to wish them well. Tracey, Ross, Pete, and the rest of their local gang put in an appearance closer to lunch, giving Simon and Vic more time with his family.

By early afternoon, after a surprising amount of the food had been consumed, guests trickled home. It took a while to say goodbye to their friends and Vic's aunts, uncles, cousins, and siblings since everyone had a bit of advice or well-wishes to add along with lots of hugging, kissing, and backslapping.

"Enjoy your trip and travel safely." Bernie gave them each a squeeze and a kiss when they finally made it to the door. "Take lots of pictures so you can show us at Christmas."

"Have a good time," Carmen said, adding a bear hug for emphasis. "Make some great memories."

"Thank you and the family so much for the brunch and making

the trip, and everything," Vic said, overwhelmed with the feeling of being loved and supported.

"Of course. We love you and Simon—that's what families are for," Bernie assured them. "Now go on your honeymoon and let go of all your worries."

Their room was ready by the time they got to Charleston.

"You booked us the honeymoon suite." Vic looked around with a smile.

"It's our honeymoon. Seemed logical." Simon carried their overnight bags from the car and set them on a luggage stand next to the king-sized bed.

The bed and breakfast was in the historic district, painted in soft pastel blue like the homes on Rainbow Row. While the house itself was centuries old, the furnishings were comfortable reproductions suited to modern tastes. Their large suite had a sitting area and a bathroom fitted with a large clawfoot tub.

Vic pulled Simon into his arms once they shut the door behind them. "That was one hell of a wedding." He drew Simon in for a kiss.

"Was it what you hoped it would be?" Simon asked, breathless, when they came up for air.

"All that and more." Vic held up their entwined left hands so that their rings glinted in the lamplight. "We're really married."

"Yes, we are."

"Did you have anything in mind?" Vic's voice was a low purr.

"I had some ideas. Let's make good use of that big soaking tub."

"Didn't you get enough spa time already?" Vic teased. They had dressed casually and made themselves as comfortable as possible for the drive.

"You don't want to soak naked with me? The suite even comes with a selection of bath bombs, and there's a bottle of champagne. I thought we could share…and make the rest up as we go along."

Simon's voice had gone deeper than usual, and Vic saw desire in his eyes.

"You're wearing too many clothes." Vic stepped forward and unbuttoned Simon's shirt, pressing a kiss to his chest each time more skin was revealed. Vic slid the shirt from Simon's shoulders, letting his hands caress as they moved.

"Let me." Simon returned the favor, undressing Vic with clear intent, never breaking eye contact. "You know, it would have been very sexy to have a pagan wedding. Skyclad under the full moon, handfasting with a blessed cord, and then making love to seal the vow."

Vic laughed. "My mother accepted not having a High Mass, but I think dancing naked around a sacred oak and public sex would have pushed her tolerance past the limit."

"We could do our own version sometime if you want. Just for us."

"I thought you were Episcopalian? Not that I mind…"

"I've always liked the imagery," Simon confessed.

"I'm open to the idea…but maybe at a time when there aren't mosquitos."

Vic's hand fell to Simon's belt. In seconds they were both naked, and Vic pulled them close, skin to skin. Their stiff cocks rubbed together with delicious friction.

"Tub." Vic took Simon by the wrist with a low groan. He ran a hot bath and tossed a bath bomb of sandalwood and cedar into the tub that was clearly built for two.

As the tub filled, Vic climbed in and held out a hand for Simon to join him. When Simon moved to sit facing him, Vic shook his head. "Uh-uh. Come here." He spread his knees to make room for Simon between his thighs.

"Give me a minute." Simon bent over to give Vic a good view of the green butt plug in his ass, then stepped away for a moment before returning. "I needed to do something first."

"Was that one of—?"

Simon settled between Vic's legs, back to chest. "No. I didn't try one from our bag of dicks. I bought this a while ago, figuring we might want to move things along after a busy day."

"You have no idea how hot that is," Vic breathed, knowing Simon could feel his stiff cock against his ass.

Simon wriggled against him. "Oh, I think I do."

Vic pulled Simon against him, running his hands up and down his chest. He traced circles around his nipples, stroking and tugging until they were hard nubs. Simon groaned and let his head fall back onto Vic's shoulder.

Vic's hands slipped down Simon's skin, following his happy trail down to the base of wiry, manscaped pubes and his very stiff cock.

"It'll be my turn to use that toy next time."

"When we get back. I'm looking forward to prepping you the old-fashioned way, with my fingers up your tight ass," Simon answered, sounding dazed as Vic stroked him. "But after the day we've had, I won't last long if you keep doing that, so you'd better fill me up."

"Thought you'd never ask." Vic used some of the waterproof lube he had brought with them to slick his cock. The water sloshed as they repositioned so that Simon straddled Vic's lap. Vic put his hands on Simon's hips and maneuvered him into position, spreading his ass cheeks, and Simon rose and then let himself down on Vic's hard prick.

Vic felt Simon's tight heat encase him inch by inch, and he groaned in appreciation, steadying Simon but not hurrying him no matter how much he wanted to be as far inside as he could get. Finally Simon settled fully, with Vic balls deep inside him.

"Move," Vic urged.

Simon started a slow rhythm, making Vic glad they hadn't filled the tub any further or they'd be sloshing water out onto the floor.

Vic knew because of everything that had happened over the past few days, coupled with pent-up demand, they wouldn't last long. "Come for me, Simon. We've got our honeymoon and the rest of our lives to take it slow."

"Want to see how long I can edge you later." Simon's breathless voice was a big turn-on.

"Maybe we make it a competition," Vic teased. "But not now. I'm not going to last. Ride me, Simon. Get me off."

Vic reached around to encase Simon's hard cock with his slicked hand, jacking him in unison with Simon's undulating movement. Vic could feel his orgasm rising, and he matched Simon's pace, wanting them to climax as nearly together as possible.

"I'm—" Simon gasped and shot over Vic's fist a second before Vic's hips bucked up into him, chasing his release.

"That was…" Vic managed when they had worked through the aftershocks.

"Yeah."

The water had cooled. Simon shifted, and Vic's cock slipped free. They untangled themselves, and Simon stood.

Vic laughed.

"What? I'm a grower, not a shower. You already knew that," Simon said, mock-annoyed.

"You…sparkle!" Vic said when he could find his voice. "Dude—the bath bomb had *glitter*."

Simon looked down at himself and then at Vic and burst out laughing. "We'll be fabulous together," he said, stepping out and helping Vic to his feet. "But hey—we have soft skin and smell good. Take it as a win."

Vic sighed. "You know we'll never get rid of it all. We'll still be finding sparkles when we're old and wrinkled."

"Fine with me." Simon leaned in for a kiss. "We're marked for life."

"I like the sound of that." Vic returned the kiss. "Now and forever."

AFTERWORD

The Ocean Paradise Hotel is loosely inspired by a real place—the Ocean Forest Hotel that opened in 1930 in Myrtle Beach. It was grand, palatial, and doomed. The Ocean Forest was the centerpiece of an entrepreneur's vision to create an upscale vacation destination complete with golf courses and a country club. In its heyday, the Ocean Forest attracted A-list bands and celebrities.

The owner hoped to compete with Miami Beach, but the stock market Crash of 1929 ruined him financially. Plans for anything beyond what had already been built were abandoned. The hotel passed through several hands and struggled for several more decades but was never profitable enough to survive. In 1974, like many other huge resorts of its era, the Ocean Forest was imploded to make room for condominiums.

The Ocean Forest beach house was moved to Springmaid Beach, where it houses the local art museum. The lighthouse that had been on top of the hotel tower was sold to Family Kingdom Park and appears in pictures of the waterpark. Hotel furnishings were likely sold off, but few pieces of memorabilia seem to remain beyond vintage postcards.

I have a weakness for huge, elaborate, haunted hotels, and I've written several into various books, nearly all of which were based on real places. The over-the-top hotels of the late Victorian era and Roaring Twenties, for me, hold tragic noir glamor. They represent an opulent, unsuspecting world on the brink of massive, fundamental change—two world wars and global financial collapse—after which nothing was ever the same.

The Train Depot is also a real place, but everything about Simon and Vic's ceremony there and any services offered are completely from my imagination.

ACKNOWLEDGMENTS

Thank you so much to my editor, Jean Rabe, to my husband and writing partner, Larry N. Martin for all his behind-the-scenes hard work, to my beta readers, and to my wonderful cover artist Natania Barron. Thanks also to the Shadow Alliance and the Worlds of Morgan Brice reader street teams for their support and encouragement, plus my promotional crew and the ever-growing legion of ARC readers who help spread the word!

I couldn't do it without you! And, of course, thanks and love to my "convention gang" of fellow authors for making road trips and virtual cons fun.

ABOUT THE AUTHOR

Morgan Brice is the romance pen name of bestselling author Gail Z. Martin. Morgan writes urban fantasy male/male paranormal romance, with plenty of action, adventure, and supernatural thrills to go with the happily ever after.

Gail writes epic fantasy and urban fantasy, and together with co-author hubby Larry N. Martin, steampunk and comedic horror, all of which have less romance and more explosions.

On the rare occasions Morgan isn't writing, she's either reading, cooking, or spoiling a very pampered dog.

Watch for additional new series from Morgan Brice and more books in the Witchbane, Badlands, Treasure Trail, Kings of the Mountain, Sharps & Springfield, and Fox Hollow universes coming soon!

Where to find me, and how to stay in touch

Join my Worlds of Morgan Brice Facebook Group and get in on all the behind-the-scenes fun! My free reader group is the first to see cover reveals, learn tidbits about works-in-progress, have fun with exclusive contests and giveaways, find out about in-person get-togethers, and more! It's also where I find my beta readers, ARC readers, and launch team! Come join the party! https://www.Facebook.com/groups/WorldsOfMorganBrice

Find me on the web at https://morganbrice.com. Sign up for my newsletter and never miss a new release! http://eepurl.com/dy_8oL. You can also find me on Twitter: @MorganBriceBook, on Pinterest (for Morgan and Gail): pinterest.com/Gzmartin, on Instagram as MorganBriceAuthor, on YouTube at https://www.youtube.com/c/GailZMartinAuthor/ on Bookbub https://www.bookbub.com/authors/morgan-brice and now on TikTok @MorganBriceAuthor

Check out the ongoing, online convention ConTinual www.facebook.com/groups/ConTinual

Support Indie Authors

When you support independent authors, you help influence what kind of books you'll see and what types of stories will be available because the authors themselves decide what to write, not a big publishing conglomerate. Independent authors are local creators supporting their families with the books they produce. Thank you for supporting independent authors and small press fiction!

ALSO BY MORGAN BRICE

Badlands Series

Badlands

Restless Nights, a Badlands Short Story

Lucky Town, a Badlands Novella

The Rising

Cover Me, a Badlands Short Story

Loose Ends

Night, a Badlands Short Story

Leap of Faith, A Badlands/Witchbane Novella

No Surrender

Point Blank

Fox Hollow Zodiac Series

Huntsman

Again

Fox Hollow Universe

Romp

Nutty for You

Imaginary Lover

Haven

Gruff

Kings of the Mountain series

Kings of the Mountain

The Christmas Spirit, a Kings of the Mountain Short Story

Sins of the Fathers

Sharps & Springfield Series

Peacemaker

Treasure Trail Series

Treasure Trail

Blink

Treasure Trail Universe

Light My Way Home, a Treasure Trail Novella

Witchbane Series

Witchbane

Burn, a Witchbane Novella

Dark Rivers

Flame and Ash

Unholy

The Devil You Know

The Christmas Crunch, a Witchbane Short Story

Sandwiched, Witchbane Short Story

Made in the USA
Thornton, CO
07/17/23 20:14:01

c4939cfb-3aea-4004-ad8c-fe16307ad343R01